DROP
DEAD *sexy*

Cara,

Happy reading!

Love ya hard!

Katie
Ashley

DROP DEAD *sexy*

KATIE ASHLEY

Drop Dead Sexy
Copyright © 2016 by Katie Ashley Productions

ISBN-13:9781530575169

ISBN-10:1530575168

Cover Model: Colby Lefebvre
Photography: Scott Hoover

Cover Design by
Lettia Hasser | RBA Designs

Formatting by
Indie Pixel Studio | www.indiepixelstudio.com

PROLOGUE

Call me kinky, but I've always wanted a man to tie me up. Of course, in my fantasy the guy would have looked less like an extra from *Deliverance* and a hell of a lot more like Chris Hemsworth. I would also be bound by silk scarves, not the itchy rope that was wound extremely tight around my wrists and ankles. Most of all, I wouldn't be on a floor that was covered in sawdust and God knows what else. Instead, I would either be in the comfort of my own bedroom or in a five-star hotel suite. And most important of all, I would have given my consent to be tied-up, not been taken against my will by Bubba or Cletus or whatever the hell his mountain man/redneck name was. He hadn't been big on introductions before he shoved a sawed off shotgun in my face, which was just another aspect that so wasn't part of my fantasy.

Sadly, it's been my experience that *nothing* in my life

resembles my fantasies, and more often than not, they're something out of my nightmares instead. If you had to put my love life into a genre, it would probably be horror. By the same token, I'm not even sure that the master of scary shit, Stephen King, could adequately express it on paper.

Since I had some time on my hands, I couldn't help pondering how things had gone so far off the rails. A month ago, everything in my life made sense. To most people, I'm sure it looked boring as hell, if not strangely odd. After all, I was an unmarried, thirty-year-old mortician who ran the most successful family owned funeral home in the North Georgia Mountains. I also had the extreme privilege of being the first female coroner for my county, not to mention the youngest.

Regardless of my professional accomplishments, I wore the figurative "S" scarlet letter for being single. A spinster. That fact was a fate worse than death to my mother. At least once a day, she would peer curiously at me and shake her head of perfectly coiffed brown hair. "I don't understand how a beautiful girl like you can still be single?"

I could put forth a vast array of arguments such as the fact we lived in a small, Southern town where we were related to a vast number of the citizens. I could have argued that there was nothing wrong with me, but instead, the fault lay with the pool of unmarried men I had access to. Well, you know, the ones I wasn't related to—although that hadn't stopped a second cousin from propositioning me once, but that's another story. I could have further argued that men never seemed to warm to the fact I worked with dead people. Talk about a surefire conversation killer…pun intended.

Really, it all boiled down to the fact I was just completely and totally unlucky when it came to love.

They say when you're about to die that your life flashes before your eyes. In my case, it was my love life…or lack thereof. Instead of being bound and gagged in the ramshackle shack, my mind whisked me away to my teenage bedroom where I had been tangled in the sheets and the long legs of my high school boyfriend, Jesse. It had taken six months of courtship to get to this moment of pre-coital bliss. At seventeen, I was more than ready to give my virginity to the guy I loved.

With my parents away for the afternoon, we had the house all to ourselves. That is if you didn't consider Mr. Greyman who was in the freezer in the basement waiting to be embalmed when my dad got back home.

Jesse tore away from our intense lip-lock. "Ready?" he panted.

"Yes," I murmured somewhat apprehensively. Since I binge read my mom's historical romances, I knew the first time was going to hurt, and I might even bleed when Jesse put his "pulsing manhood" in me.

After ripping open the condom wrapper enthusiastically with his teeth, he slid on the flimsy looking piece of rubber. He covered my body with his before bringing his lips to mine.

Jesse spent a few more minutes kissing my breasts and stroking me between my legs. When it appeared he had deemed me ready for penetration, I felt the head of his penis butting against the entrance of my vagina. Or if I was talking historical romance lingo, his smooth shaft against the opening of my Venus mound.

"I'll go slow and try not to hurt you," Jesse said.

"Thank you," I squeaked. When he started *sliding* inside me, I pinched my eyes shut and sucked in a breath.

"Oh fuck," Jesse muttered or at least that's what I think he was trying to say. It came out more like, "Ohfwt."

And then something happened unlike anything I had ever read before. Instead of me crying out in the agony of my maidenhead being pierced by Jesse's sword, it was him screeching in pain. "Fwt, fwt, FWT!" he screamed.

When I opened my eyes, I also screamed. Jesse's lips were blown up three times their usual size to resemble something like the love-child of Mick Jagger and Steven Tyler hyped-up on collagen.

"Oh my God, what happened to your lips?"

Jesse once again screamed like a banshee. He jerked out of me and fumbled back on the bed. When he stared down at his crotch, his eyes widened in horror. As I sat up, he began clawing at his dick. "Jesse, stop! You're going to hurt yourself."

Ignoring me, his chest began to heave from his efforts. "Can't. Get. It. Off."

I grabbed the sheet and jerked it away from us. That's

when I saw something so horrifying it would haunt me for years. Something that years later after seeing pretty heinous shit in my coroner days, I will still remember it. It wasn't just Jesse's lips that had blown up. His penis had swelled to resemble an eggplant. The condom had stretched to the point I feared when it popped, the force of it flying off would hurt Jesse and maybe even me if I was in the trajectory of its path.

After staring wide-eyed and open-mouthed at it, I finally blurted, "Do you have a latex allergy?"

"No…I mean, I don't fwink so." He threw up a hand in frustration. "I dunno."

"You need help. Like serious medical help." My hand began fumbling on the nightstand for the phone. Once I had it, my trembling fingers began furiously dialing. Before I could bring the phone to my ear, Jesse knocked it out of my hand. "What are you doing?" I demanded.

He shook his head so wildly back and forth he looked like a cartoon character. "I can't let anyone see me like this!" he protested through his tears. Although it kind of sounded like, "I can't wet anyone see me wike dis."

"You need a doctor. That's just not going to go away with an ice pack," I argued while picking the phone up.

"911, what's your emergency?" a female's monotone voice questioned in my ear.

"Uh, yeah, my boyfriend is having an allergic reaction."

"Is this an insect or food allergy?"

"No. It's latex."

"I see. What areas of the body are affected?"

"His lips, and his…um, his…"

Jesse suddenly appeared to have changed his mind about getting help because he lunged over to scream into the phone. "My fwking dick is about to plode! Oh God, pwse, send someone! It's gonna take the Jaws of Wife to get wis condom off!"

There was a pause on the line. "Is this a joke?"

"Excuse me?"

"Look, we get at least two to three prank calls a day."

I huffed in outrage that she wasn't taking us seriously. "No. It's not a joke. My boyfriend and I were about to have sex, and right after he put on the condom, he started swelling. Well, I mean, it was swollen before, but then it got all out of control swollen."

"You're serious?"

If I could have reached through the phone to throttle the woman, I would have. "Yes, I'm very serious! Now would you please send someone to 251 Sullivan Street?"

"Okay, we're dispatching help. But if this is a prank—"

"What do I need to do to get you to believe me? Describe in detail how his penis looks like a purple eggplant hogtied in rubber?"

"Jesus," came the reply.

"Yeah, you ought to see it in real life. You'd be freakin' out just like I am!" When I met Jesse's pitiful gaze, I said, "I'm

sorry, but it's true."

At that moment, I heard an ambulance's wail in the distance. Without another word to the dispatcher, I hung up and threw the phone down. I then scrambled off the bed, so I could throw on some clothes. I didn't need any further embarrassment by the paramedics seeing me naked.

As Jesse writhed and moaned on the bed, I raced out of my bedroom and pounded down the stairs. I threw open the front door just as the ambulance and a police car screeched into the driveway.

"Never thought I'd be responding to a call here," a young paramedic said when he hopped out.

His older partner chuckled. "Yeah, you'll learn that the funeral home is a hotspot for calls. Something about dead people brings on the heart attacks and fainting spells where people hit their heads hard enough to cause concussions. And then there's always patching people up after fights."

"Fights? Damn," the young paramedic muttered.

After unloading the stretcher, they hurried up the front walk. I stepped out onto the porch to meet them. "He's upstairs," I said.

The older paramedic nodded. "Lead the way."

I hurried back into the house and started taking the stairs two at a time. When I reached the landing, I realized how eerily silent it was. Jesse's agonized moans were no longer filling the air. Forgetting the paramedics, I sprinted down the hall. I skidded to a stop inside the doorway. Jesse sat frozen on bed with the sheet lifted, staring down at his crotch.

"Jesse?" I tentatively asked.

He slowly lifted his gaze to meet mine. "T-he c-condom b-broke."

The paramedics came rattling into the room with the stretcher. When they looked at Jesse, he repeated, "The condom broke."

After exchanging a glance, the paramedics started over to the bed. "We're here to help, son," the older one said. His badge read *Bridgestone*. I vaguely remembered that I went to school with a Lyle Bridgestone. I wondered if he was his son. Inwardly I groaned because if it was, the story was going to spread like wildfire because Lyle always ran his mouth.

When Jesse's body language mimicked a feral animal about to attack, Bridgestone held up his hands. "I'm not going to hurt you, I promise."

The moment Bridgestone pulled down the sheet his eyes bulged. "Holy fucking shit!" His wild gaze flicked over to his partner. "The condom might've broke, but it's stuck around the head of the penis. Like rubber band stuck." He shook his head as if he were trying to shake himself out of his disbelief. "I'm going to need the scissors."

Jesse lunged at Brownstone. Grabbing the front of his uniform, he cried, "Don't cut my dick off!"

Brownstone patted Jesse's back. "I'm going to do

8

everything I can to save it. You have my word."

Before I could ask Jesse if he wanted me to hold his hand, one of the police officers who had just arrived wrapped an arm around my shoulder and started leading me out of the room. "Bless your heart. You've seen enough," he said when I started to protest.

He was right. I had already seen way too much. Of course, I would never be able to forget that eggplant penis or the scream of agonized pain that erupted from Jesse when they cut the remaining part of the condom off.

Needless to say, Jesse's and my relationship wasn't strong enough to survive Latexgate. Like Pearl Harbor, it seemed to be a day that would live in infamy not only for Jesse, but for every other male I knew. Not only was I the girl who had dead people in her house, but now I was the girl who caused dicks to blow up. You could forget trying to reason that I wasn't a Hogwarts graduate who had double toil and troubled a spell to inflict penis harm. It was so bad that I had to import a guy from out of town just to be able to attend my senior prom.

Fast-forward six years. I had made it out of my small town all the way to Athens to attend the University of Georgia. I ended up getting a degree in both Mortuary and Forensic science. After a few short-term relationships and some heavy-petting sessions, I was finally about to get back in the sex saddle. I'd met Eric Sanchez during one of my shadowing experiences at the morgue. He was a coroner's assistant, but more importantly, he was six feet of Latin lusciousness. Not to mention at thirty, he was an older, experienced man.

We only had a couple of dates before we were inseparable. Well, as inseparable as we could be considering I'd moved back home to work at my family's funeral home. After three months of steaming up my screen with phone sex, it was time to seal the deal.

That's how I came to find myself spread-eagled on the mattress with Eric's head buried between my legs. Clenching my eyes shut, my hips rose and fell manically as I rode out my second orgasm of the night. The first had come before we even got inside Eric's apartment. He'd pinned me to the front door, and within view of any nosy neighbors, he finger banged me to a mind-blowing orgasm.

Rising up, Eric swiped his mouth with the back of his hand before reaching over to grab a condom off the nightstand. Instantly my orgasmic high crashed and burned as I had a horrific flashback to the last time I tried to have sex.

When Eric started to open the condom wrapper, I grabbed his arm. "You don't have a latex allergy, do you?"

He gave me a funny look. "No."

"Are you sure?"

Eric chuckled. "Yeah, Liv, I'm sure. I mean, I wear latex gloves every day."

"Oh, that's right." I exhaled a relieved breath. "Thank God."

He cocked his dark brows at me. "Do I want to ask?"

"It's a story for another day."

He grinned—flashing his gleaming pearly whites at me. "Good. Because I'm really not in the mood to talk."

"What are you in the mood for?" I teasingly asked.

"To fuck you seven ways 'til Sunday."

I giggled. "How romantic."

Eric laughed. "I'll make love to you next time. This time I desperately need to fuck you."

His words caused my practically cob-web infested vagina to break out in a victory cheer.

After all, it had been six years since it had seen penetration of the penis kind. You can claim someone as legally dead at seven years, so my vagina was just a few months shy of being legally dead.

But that night it was gloriously reborn. Sex with Eric was everything I had dreamt it would be. I'd never imagined coming a third time, but I did thanks to Eric's sexual mastery. As I was coming down, Eric thrust into me one last time. With a groan, his body stiffened as he collapsed on top of me. My fingers ran up and down his back. "That was amazing," I murmured into his ear.

Eric didn't agree. Well, he didn't disagree either. He just kept lying there on top of me.

After a few more seconds passed, I cleared my throat. "Um, babe, would you mind rolling over. You're kinda heavy."

When he still didn't respond, I brought my arms to his

shoulders and shook him. "Eric?"

Okay, either he had sex-induced narcolepsy, or something was wrong. Like bad wrong. With all the strength I could muster, I pushed him off of me, which in turn pushed him out of me. He flopped over on the mattress like a fish out of water complete with the glassy eyes and wide, gaping mouth.

Bile and panic simultaneously rose in my throat. "No. Oh God no," I murmured.

I quickly rose up and slapped his face. Hard. "Eric, you better be teasing me!"

When he didn't respond, I grabbed his wrist to feel for a pulse. I couldn't find one. The tears clouding my eyes momentarily blinded me. I needed help. I scrambled off of Eric. My gaze frantically spun around the room as I tried to find my phone. Once I did, I called 911.

Unlike with Jesse, what happened following that call is mostly a blur. I remember the words Coronary Artery Anomalies. It was what the autopsy determined. After all, a healthy, thirty-year-old man's heart shouldn't give out. But Eric's had. Since the condition was worsened by exercise, he could have died during his morning jog. But no, he had to die on me. *Literally*.

He came, and then he went, which left me with a hell of a lot of fear and guilt. And it's that pathetically sad relationship history that has led me to this very moment. Well, I guess you could say it was more like my man-starved vagina had led me

to this moment, or better yet, led me to the man who got me involved in all this craziness.

Catcher fucking Mains—the man with ocean-blue, bedroom eyes, a body to die for, and a drop-dead sexy smile.

Craning my neck, I glared at him over my shoulder. If I managed to get out of this situation alive, I wasn't sure if I was going to kill him or screw him. It was a toss-up.

CHAPTER

1

After the minister spoke the final words of Mr. Garett Brown's eulogy, I made my way down the carpeted aisle. As the soft organ music piped in via the overhead speakers reached an emotional crescendo, I turned to face the mourners packed into the padded chapel pews. Appearing like a cross between a Miss America and an air traffic controller, I slowly lifted my arms to guide the crowd to rise from their seats. Once everyone was on their feet, I motioned for the family to begin exiting their pew.

As crazy as it might sound, there was a true art to presiding over a funeral. It was just one of the many things I had learned over the years from observing my late father and grandfather. As my grandfather had once said, "Run a funeral like a side show, and you'll be out of business." People were inevitably drawn to pomp and pageantry. Even though their loved one might have been a pauper, they wanted the same gallantry afforded to the funeral as a king or president's.

My grandfather had opened Sullivan's Funeral Home in 1955, and it had been a family operation ever since. Since I came from a large, extended family, everyone from aunts, uncles, and cousins pitched in from time to time. Growing up in a funeral home wasn't all death and sadness. I had a lot of happy, lively memories under this roof. I used to play hide and seek with my younger brother, Allen, where one of us would always end up wedged behind a casket to hide out. I'd spent hours laid out on the chapel's padded benches reading the newest *Babysitters Club* or *Sweet Valley High* books. My house had always been filled with people. I had learned at an early age to work a crowd, and my father had me helping out with viewings and services by the time I turned thirteen. "Livvie has the gift," he would say with pride sparkling in his brown eyes.

The memory of my father sent an ache through my chest. He had died five years ago after a very short battle with pancreatic cancer. Although I had experienced personal loss

with grandparents and other family members, it was my father's death that had brought true understanding and empathy for what other families were experiencing. It wasn't often that you got to meet your real life hero, but I had been blessed to have him for a father.

When the last of the "reserved" benches had emptied, I followed the crowd out the chapel door into the sunshine. After supervising the loading of the casket into the hearse, I turned to the deceased's wife. I forced a sympathetic smile to my face. While friends and family had wept unabashedly, Felicia Brown had remained an ice queen. Moreover, her grief had been pretty much extinct over the last few days, and in its place, she'd been one of the most demanding bitches I'd had to deal with in a long time. She wanted the VIP treatment despite having pulled all the cheapskate punches like wanting a low-end casket while she stood draped in diamonds.

"It's time for you to get into the car." I motioned to the black Lincoln sedan that we provided to escort the next of kin. Regardless of what had happened over the last few days, I afforded her the same warmth and kindness as I would to an actually bereaved family member. After all, in times like these a kind word was worth a million, even to an asshole. Of course, silently I was saying, "Bye, Felicia." in my head.

Felicia nodded in agreement and turned to the crowd behind her. "Jerry, why don't you ride with me?" she asked the tall, Silver Fox of a man who was standing next to her.

I motioned for Todd, one of our attendants, to open the back door of the car. The sound of a growl behind me caused me to jump out of my skin. Since I knew Motown, the neighborhood stray Pit Bull I'd adopted and often brought to work with me, was upstairs in the family quarters, I had to wonder what wild animal had come out of the woods. When I whirled around, I saw Felicia's oldest son, Gregg, wearing a venomous look. "Oh, that's just rich. It isn't enough you were fucking Jerry while my father was on life support, but now you want him to ride in the car with you on the way to bury him!"

As an incredulous hush fell over the mourners, I drew my shoulders back preparing myself for the potential verbal assault to come. After all, this wasn't my first time at the rodeo, so to speak. I was pretty much a pro at handling scenes like this. There were many times I'd witnessed the old adage that death brings out the worst in people. It brings out the claws that's for sure.

After she cast a glance over the crowd, Felicia fidgeted nervously with the collar of her designer suit. "Why, Gregg, I don't know what you're talking about."

Gregg rolled his eyes. "Like hell you don't. I don't guess you remember the other times either," he spat.

The impeccable reserve slowly slid from Felicia's face and was replaced by thinly veiled anger. "Don't you dare make a scene at your father's funeral!" she hissed back at Gregg. When she realized what she had done, she quickly recovered to give a weak smile to the other mourners.

"Me make a scene? You're the one acting like the grief-stricken wife when all you've ever done is be unfaithful," Gregg countered.

Sensing this was about to get even uglier, I tried stepping between them to diffuse the situation. "Why don't we proceed on to the cemetery?" I suggested. My gaze landed on the face of Felicia's younger son standing begrudgingly beside his brother. "Mark, why don't you ride with your mother?"

Gregg snorted contemptuously. "Sure, pick Mark. He was always Dad's favorite. Hell, he's everyone's favorite." A hateful gleam burned in his green eyes. "Well, I'm setting the record straight now. Mark's not even *my* father's son!"

Gasps of astonishment rippled through the crowd while Felicia's face turned pasty white. Raising her eyes to the shocked faces around her, she said, "I'm sorry everyone. Gregg's just so grief-stricken he doesn't know what he's saying."

"So upset my ass. I'm not too upset to know that Jim, our very own UPS man, is Mark's father," he countered.

The crowd turned with astonished eyes to the back of the crowd where Jim the UPS man stood. When he lowered his eyes to the pavement in defeat, it was all the confirmation anyone needed. The crowd turned their gaze back to Felicia and Gregg.

Suddenly Mark lunged at Gregg. "You bastard! How dare you?" He swung a fist into Gregg's face and then in his abdomen. Gregg collapsed onto the pavement, his nose pouring with blood.

Mark stood over him. "It's not enough that you had to screw my ex-wife to make me jealous, but now you have to embarrass me in front of all of these people."

I had just opened my mouth to once again plead with them to stop when Mr. Brown's best friend stepped forward. "You boys stop this right now. I can't believe you'd do this at your own father's funeral."

Mark reluctantly helped Gregg to his feet as they both stood to face their accuser. "Like you have any room to be talking, Ed," Gregg grumbled, as he held his head back to stop his bleeding nose.

Ed's face paled slightly as his hands went to fiddle with his tie. "I don't know what you're talking about."

Mark shook his head. "You honestly have the gall to come here when *everyone* knows that you were sleeping with my father," he countered.

At the accusation that not only was the deceased man's wife a notorious adulterer, his youngest son was not biologically his, but he was a bisexual, one woman in the crowd fainted and the rest were left in hushed astonishment.

All the color drained from Ed's face. "How did you know?".

Gregg looked at Mark before he spoke. "We knew something was up when you and dad went on all those fishing trips. *Alone.*"

Ed straightened his shoulders as he looked around at the wide-eyed, open-mouthed faces. "Fine. It's true. I loved Paul Brown for forty years, and he loved me. He certainly deserved better than his wife and sons making a scene at his funeral."

"Oh shut up, Ed," Gregg said.

Mr. Brown's middle son, Wes, stepped into the fray. "It's true. You two assholes should be ashamed of yourselves. But why am I surprised? I mean, it's always been about you two. You practically sucked the life out of Dad. Gregg—the washed-up football god turned lush, and Mark—the sex and gambling addict."

Mark rolled his eyes. "Oh get bent, drama queen."

Given what happened next, I guess Wes had been Jan Brady'd one too many times in his life because he just snapped. He jerked a pistol out from inside his suit pocket. At the sight of the gun, pandemonium broke out. People began screaming and scrambling away. Immediately, I dug my phone out of my suit pocket and dialed 911.

"What the hell are you doing, Wes?" Gregg demanded.

"If you two aren't going to quit making a scene voluntarily, I'm going to make you."

"Like waving a gun around isn't making a scene, dumbass," Mark replied.

"It's probably not even loaded," Gregg mused.

Wes narrowed his eyes at Gregg before firing off a shot

21

at his feet. The screams and shouting rose up again as Gregg began moonwalking like he was in a Michael Jackson video. "Jesus Christ, are you crazy?"

"I couldn't get you to listen to me," Wes replied, his tone eerily calm.

When I tried to step forward, Wes swung his arm around to train the pistol on me. I skidded to a stop and quickly threw up my hands, sending my phone clattering to the pavement. "Wes, I understand that you're hurt and angry with your brothers, but surely, we can resolve this without violence," I suggested.

Wes cocked his head at me. "You've seen my family. What do you think?"

At that moment, Earl, one of our other attendants, appeared in the doorway with two stands of floral arrangements. From his horrified expression, I'm sure he had anticipated the flower van to be waiting on him, not a hostage situation.

The sight of the flowers put an idea in my head, and I didn't stop to question it. "Don't drop the casket!" I screeched.

With Wes and his brothers now distracted, I lunged over at Earl and snatched the tallest of the floral wreaths out of his hand. Using all the strength I had, I lobbed Wes in the back of the head with my floral weaponry. "What the—" he started to demand, but I whacked him in the face. As Wes sputtered and choked on a mouthful of football mums, I went for his crotch, making sure to bring the wire part of the

arrangement against his dick.

As he screamed in agony, the gun fell from his hands. I dropped the wreath, grabbed the gun, and pointed it at Wes as he writhed back and forth in pain.

"What a pussy," Mark muttered.

"Shut. Up," Wes huffed through his clenched teeth.

"Way to go, Liv," Todd mused.

With a wink, I replied, "All in a day's work."

Outwardly, I put on a façade of fake bravado while inwardly, I was wondering if I didn't need a clean pair of panties because I might've pissed myself from fear.

After the police came to arrest the Brown brothers for several misdemeanors, the small crowd that was left got in their cars for the procession to the cemetery. Amidst all the craziness, we still had to bury poor Mr. Brown. Thankfully, it went off without any more gun wielding drama.

By the time I arrived back at the funeral home from supervising the burial, I was emotionally and physically drained. When I entered my office, I found Allen sitting behind my desk with his feet propped up. He cradled the phone receiver between his shoulder and neck as he read from the folder in front of him. From the sound of it, he was calling in a claim on a life insurance policy.

I shot him a pissed look before flopping down on the

leather loveseat across from my desk. I moaned in ecstasy as I slid my heels off. Allen was not only my co-worker. He was also co-owner in the funeral home. It had been willed to the both of us upon our father's death. At the time, Allen was only twenty, and the last thing he wanted was to have anything to do with the death business. But over the years, he had slowly come to embrace it. Since he hadn't been to mortuary school, he used his finance degree to manage the financial side of the business. He also helped out with funeral planning as well as in the transportation department aka picking up the bodies.

Although Allen had yet to marry, his single status didn't seem to grieve our mother quite as much as mine did. Maybe it was because as a woman I was supposed to marry young while my brother was allowed to be a swinging bachelor sowing his wild oats before settling down. Quite a few ladies had tried to get their hooks in Allen, but so far, he had managed to evade them. While he would never admit it, I knew his heart belonged to Maggie, the local florist. Although it wasn't part of his job description, he was forever volunteering to go do floral pickups.

"Yeah, thanks, Bernie. Talk to you later." When Allen hung up, he rose out of my chair.

"Our newest customer is waiting for you in the prep room."

I stilled rubbing my feet. "Ugh, fabulous." Considering the afternoon I'd had, I wanted nothing more than a glass of wine and a warm bath, but it didn't look like I was going to get either of them.

An amused look twinkled in Allen's dark eyes. "So I hear you had a little scuffle while I was gone."

I rolled my eyes. "I'd hardly call it a 'scuffle'. Just one guy got punched. Well, two if you consider me hitting that fool with the floral arrangement."

Allen grinned. "First rule of Funeral Home Fight Club: No one talks about Funeral Home Fight Club."

"Har-fucking-har," I muttered, as I rose to my feet.

After walking over to my desk, I held out my hand, and Allen passed me the tan folder with the deceased's information. I glanced down at the folder. "Oh, no, it's Mr. Peterson." At Allen's blank look, I said, "Don't you remember trick-or-treating at his house back in the day? His wife always made cookies and candy for us."

Allen slowly nodded his head. "Damn, he got old."

"He was old back then. He's pretty much ancient now." I grimaced. "Well, he *was* ancient."

That was one of the hardest aspects of being a mortician in the town you grew up in. You pretty much knew ninety percent of everyone who was laid out on the mortuary table. Sometimes it was easier aspirating organs and draining blood from people you didn't know. It had been excruciating, but I had forced myself to prepare my father. I felt I had owed him that much for all the love and support he'd given me over the years, not to mention teaching me all I knew.

25

I tucked the folder under my arm before heading out the door. My footsteps echoed through the silence as I made my way down the familiar hallway lined with family portraits. Allen and I had been the third generation of Sullivan's to live in the house. My grandparents had bought the sprawling Victorian monstrosity when my dad was just a baby. Because of my grandfather's gift at body preparation, the other funeral home in town quickly went out of business.

It wasn't too long before people from surrounding counties started bringing their deceased to him. Business boomed as did my grandparent's family. After trying to corral five children in the upstairs area during visitation and funerals, my grandmother insisted on a home of their own. Since my grandfather did everything she asked out of both love *and* fear, they bought the house next door to live in, leaving the family quarters abandoned for almost twenty years.

As the oldest son and heir to the Sullivan Funeral Home empire, my dad was offered the living quarters when he married my mom, and they had happily accepted. Well, my mom had been less than thrilled at first, but she knew when she married my dad that the death business was part of his life. He had sweetened the pot by having the upstairs gutted and remodeled to make a separate living room and kitchen along with three bedrooms and two baths. He also had the back staircase redone, so that she could get upstairs to our house without having to go through the funeral home.

After pouring myself a cup of coffee in the community

kitchen, I walked back down the hall to the door labeled *Employees Only*. I typed in the code on the keypad before stepping into the preparation room where Mr. Peterson awaited me. Turning on the switch to my right sent the florescent lights above my head humming to life.

I'm sure most people would imagine a body preparation room that resembled something out of Dr. Frankenstein's laboratory. Sadly, that wasn't the case. You had one wall of cabinets filled with everything from cosmetics to replacement eyeballs. In the center of the room was a stainless steel mortuary table that sat over a drain. Beside the table were the machines for embalming.

Before I went over to the table, I flicked on the stereo system. Whenever I worked on a body, I made sure I had music. Being a mortician was kind of lonely work. It wasn't like you could carry on meaningful conversations with the deceased. So having music not only helped to pass the time, but it helped to fill the silence. Since my father had been a huge lover of the oldies, I tended to lean towards Motown. Out of respect for the dead, I didn't play anything that could be perceived as offensive.

As the upbeat tempo of The Temptations *Ain't Too Proud to Beg* pumped through the speakers, I got down to business working on Mr. Peterson. Considering he was a ninety-year-old stroke victim, the prep was fairly easy. You did your standard wash down with antiseptic soap. It wasn't just about giving the deceased that final shower or bath before the beyond—it was also meant to kill any bacteria. The death process wreaked some nasty shit on a body.

Once that was finished, it was time to drain the body of blood. In my father and grandfather's day, they liked to go through the femoral artery in the thigh up to the heart. For me, that was too much guess work, and the last thing I wanted to do was flood the chest cavity with blood.

Just like I was instructed in school, I inserted the cannula, or small tube, into the jugular. Once the blood was drained, it was then time to pump in the embalming fluid. I liked to use a mixture of formulas to ensure the finest finished quality. The death business was highly competitive, and even though we were the only funeral home in town, people wouldn't hesitate to send their loved ones to the next county.

"You're only as good as your last body," my grandfather would say.

I had just started putting on the moisturizing skin rub on Mr. Peterson to even out the embalming fluid when a knock came at the door of the other preparation room. "Come in," I called over my shoulder.

At the click-clack of heels on the linoleum, I knew it was my cousin, Jill. While she owned her own salon down on Main Street, she had been doing hair and makeup here at the funeral home since we were in high school. She was two years older than me and was the wild-assed sister I'd never had.

"I just finished up with Mrs. Laughton."

I glanced up to give her a wry smile. "Do we have any hairspray left?"

Jill snorted. "Maybe a little. I'm pretty sure I just contributed to the further depletion of the ozone layer. Not to mention I jacked that shit so high you might not get the casket lid closed."

I laughed at Jill's description considering how Mrs. Laughton was as well known for her bouffant hair style as she was her blue-ribbon chocolate pies.

Jerking her chin at Mr. Peterson, Jill asked, "You almost done with him?"

"I just finished putting on the buffer."

"Good. You better let Todd do the casket transfer, so you can go get ready."

Instantly my mood deflated. "Oh damn."

"Don't tell me you forgot about your mother's shower?" Jill asked.

"I didn't forget. I just have selective amnesia where it's concerned."

Jill crossed her arms over her purchased Double D's. "I thought you were cool with your mom getting remarried."

Three years after my father's death, my mother had finally abandoned her widow's weeds and started dating Harry Livingston—a retired mortician who I often brought in to help when we were slammed with bodies. After a year of dating,

Harry had popped the question, and my mother had happily accepted. Don't get me wrong. I was happy for her. She deserved all the happiness in the world, as did Harry who had lost his wife the year my dad died. But was there a small part of me that tap-danced with the green-eyed monster of jealousy that my mother was getting married a second time before I did the first? Sure. I mean, I'm only human.

What really had me wigged out was attending tonight's lingerie shower. Any eternally single girl would rather walk on hot coals than attend a bridal shower of any sort. Make it your mother's *lingerie* shower, and it was a whole new level of torture.

"I am totally cool with her and Harry getting married. It's just been a hell of a day after the craziness at the Brown funeral, so the last thing I want to deal with is her cronies and their endless barrage of questions about my marital status."

"Yeah, I heard about the brawl."

"It was hardly a brawl."

Jill shrugged her shoulders. "That's just what Bessie Thompson told me when she came in for color."

I rolled my eyes once again at how fast the fires of gossip were fanned when you lived in a small town. By the end of the day, people would probably be saying that someone had been pistol-whipped after flashing their junk or something bizarre like that. "Trust me. It wasn't a brawl, and it's been taken care of."

"I told Bessie I wasn't too surprised they showed their

asses considering they're from Summit Ridge. Nothing but a bunch of meth-heads or rich snobs come from there."

"Not all people from Summit Ridge are bad. Besides, we've had our fair share of people from here showing themselves," I argued.

"Whatever. I knew they were going to be trouble after you told me how the wife wore all those diamonds but tried to be a cheapshit when it came to the casket and vault. I'm just glad you got to say 'Bye Felicia' to that epic twatwaffle."

I laughed. "You know as well as I do that it isn't truly over until the bill is paid." I put the cap back on the lotion and went over to the sink to wash my hands. I threw a glance at Jill over my shoulder. "Will you go remind Allen that he's in charge of the Laughton viewing since Mama and I will be gone?"

"Sure will."

"Thanks. I need to run on home and get ready."

"Why don't I come with you and do your hair and makeup?" Jill suggested.

"Do you really think that's necessary? It's not like I'm going clubbing."

"But you could after the shower. After all, there will be a fresh crop of men up there." When I started to protest, Jill shook her head. "Men who know nothing about your sexual history. Men who you don't ever have to see again after you've taken their dick for a spin."

I couldn't help snorting at Jill's summation. She did have a point. My mother's shower was being held at her best friend's cabin an hour away. The cabin was way up in the mountains and almost on the Georgia/Tennessee border. I didn't know a single soul from there. "I'm pretty sure they don't have clubs up there."

"Maybe not, but I sure as hell bet they have a bar." Jill waggled her auburn-colored brows. "You could find someone to help end your sex drought."

As I dried my hands, I considered what Jill was suggesting. The irrational side of me thought it made perfect sense. Of course, I very rarely listened to my irrational side. "I don't know."

"Come on, Liv. You swore that you would end the drought before your thirtieth birthday, and now you're two months over and still nada."

"I'm well aware of that."

"So do something about it before you end up with a plastic yeast infection from your vibrator."

I wrinkled my nose in disgust. "Um, ew."

Jill laughed. "Sorry. But you know me. I tell it like it is."

"Yes, unfortunately."

"Here's what we're going to do. I'm coming home with you to do your hair and makeup." At what must've been the wounded look in my eyes, she added, "Not that you don't do a great job yourself. It's just you need something special for tonight."

"Okay. Fine."

"Then I'll pick you out something sexy that you can change into when you leave the shower."

"You aren't coming along on the manhunt?"

Jill shook her head. "Chase is coming by at nine. I've been instructed to be wearing nothing but my black hooker heels."

Chase was Jill's on-and-off again boyfriend. Well, he was actually her ex-husband, but they just couldn't seem to quit each other. It wouldn't surprise me one day if she called in from Vegas to tell me they'd gotten remarried.

My rational side began arguing how dangerous it was to go out alone, but then I tried reminding it that I carried a gun and had been through self-defense training. I would make sure to only have one drink to calm my nerves and to make sure I didn't accept anything to drink from a man.

"All right. I'll do it."

Jill's green eyes widened. "Oh. My. God. Really?"

I laughed. "Yes, really."

She squealed and threw her arms around me. "You've just made my day, Livvie!"

"I'm so glad that me having sex with a stranger makes your day."

Jill pulled back and winked at me. "You getting some for the first time in almost seven years is enough to make more than my day. Hell, it makes my week."

With a shake of my head, I pulled out of her embrace. "Come on. We need to get going."

In a sing-song voice, Jill said, "Olivia's gonna get some dick!"

Oh, lord. It was going to be a long, long night.

CHAPTER 2

I'm pretty sure when Dante penned *The Inferno* with its nine levels of Hell, he couldn't fathom such horror as I currently found myself in. I'm sure if he could have, he would have deemed it necessary to devote another level *just* for me—my very own tenth circle of Hell. No, I wasn't frozen in a lake of ice or encapsulated in flaming tombs. Instead, I was being forced to watch my fifty-seven-year-old mother unwrap gifts of heat-activated body oils, edible underwear, and toys of the vibrating nature. No one, and I sure as hell mean *no one*, should ever have to imagine their mother using such things, least of all see them in her hands while she flushed crimson and giggled like a school girl.

"Won't Harry look sexy in these?" she asked, holding up a pair of bikini briefs in one hand while fanning herself with the other.

At that moment, I literally threw up in my mouth some of the decorative penis cake I had just eaten (Instead of the typical icing flower, I'd ingested part of the balls). The sugary bits of scrotum burned my throat. I realized then that regardless of how much of an asset he was to the funeral home, I was going to have to fire my future stepfather. There was simply no way in hell I could successfully embalm a body across from him while imagining him sporting red bikini briefs under his work apron. Come to think of it, I could never hand off an Anal/Vaginal plug to him without wondering if he had actually used the "Fun Factory Booty" butt plug my mother's oldest friend had given her.

Needing something to drink in more ways than one, I rose out of my seat and started for the kitchen. As much as I wanted to drown my sorrows, I had to pace myself if I was going to be able to go man-hunting after the shower. Not only that, but considering the cabin was out in East Bumblefuck, I needed to be on my game to find my way around.

I was splashing some vodka into my cranberry juice when I was unceremoniously knocked out of the way by my

grandmother's cane. "Where the hell is my Fireball?" After she eyed the liquor bottles on the table, she huffed in frustration. "I guaran-damn-tee one of those alleged teetotaler Garrett girls stole it."

Yes, ladies and gentleman, that pint-sized, foul-mouthed, octogenarian with teased silver hair and a chaw of snuff in her jaw was none other than my grandmother, Pease. Her real name was Eloise but very few people actually called her that. She even insisted on her grandchildren calling her Pease, rather than your typical "grandma" or "nana." It was just one of the many aspects of vanity that she possessed. Being called "grandma" meant you were old, and that was the last thing she wanted to be.

You would never know it by looking at Pease, but back in the day, she'd actually been a debutante who had come out at the exclusive Piedmont Driving Club in Atlanta. Of course, considering she liked to do everything to excess, she hadn't really fit into the society circle.

When she set her sights on my grandfather, he never stood a chance. He was everything she wasn't—a quiet, reserved guy from a poor mountain family who was at college on a football scholarship. Of course, it didn't hurt that he looked like Paul Newman. She left her highfaluting family, as she called them, and never looked back, even when my grandfather blew out his knee and decided on becoming a mortician.

"I'm going to need another drink if I make it through the afternoon. I mean, having all this sex bullshit shoved in my face just makes me remember that it's been five years since I've gotten any."

"Granddaddy died fifteen years ago," I corrected.

Pease pursed her lips at me. "I'm well aware of that."

"Then that means…um, ew," I replied.

Pease rolled her eyes. "Honestly, Olivia, if you don't stop being a prude, you're never going to get rid of those cooter cobwebs of yours."

I bit my tongue to keep from telling her that I planned on having my alleged "cooter cobwebs" swept squeaky clean tonight. Instead, I splashed a little more vodka in my cup.

When I came back into the living room, my mother was holding up her final gift, and fucking hell was it a doozy. A pair of red pasties with matching crotchless panties. She waved them at me as she waggled her brows. "Look, Olivia."

Yes, I see it. All the bleach in the world couldn't wipe out that image from my eyes. I forced a smile to my face. "Harry's not going to know what hit him," I said, as I took the empty seat beside her.

She giggled. "Before we leave for the honeymoon, I'm going to have make double sure he has his heart pills packed. Wouldn't want to give him a heart attack."

The allusion of a sex-induced heart attack instantly made me think of Eric, and an ache spread through my chest. I bit my lip and ducked my head.

Mama leaned over to take my hand in hers. "Oh, Livvie Boo, I'm so sorry. I wasn't thinking," she apologized.

"It's okay."

Thankfully, the rest of her friends were too busy hooting and hollering at the gifts they were passing around to notice our conversation. She placed her fingers under my chin and tilted my head to look at her. "You know, I'd give anything in the world if it was you getting married instead of me."

"Aw, Mama, you don't mean that."

She shook her head. "I do. More than my happiness, I want you to be happy."

"But I am happy," I protested.

Mama pinched her lips together in disapproval. "It's not polite to lie to your mother."

"I'm not lying. I'm perfectly happy with my life."

Okay, so I was lying through my teeth. I wasn't just desperate to be boned. I was even more desperate to have someone to call my own. For spooning while sleeping in on Saturday mornings. For mundane conversations over homemade chicken and dumplings. For arguing over what to watch on television—football or Lifetime. For shuttling our children between sports practice and dance lessons. For all the little things that made average lives extraordinary.

Although at times I wanted to throw my arms up, toss my head back, and scream to the heavens, "WHYYYYY?!", I refrained. While I could have easily sunk deeper into the quicksand of my pity party, I chose to clamber my way out of the abyss. After all, this was supposed to be my mother's happy time. She'd been through enough after losing my father that she shouldn't have to see me limping along from a broken spirit.

"Seriously, Mama, I'm fine. I haven't given up hope that one day my prince will come. Right now, he's probably just being held captive in some foreign prison."

While she didn't appear to be completely satisfied by my argument, she did manage to give me a smile. "I pray every day, sweetheart. There's nothing more that I want in life than to see you and Allen settled."

"Now it's your turn not to lie. Secretly, you want us to get married, so we can give you grandbabies."

At the mention of my brother and me procreating, my mother's dark blue eyes sparkled with pleasure. "Okay, so maybe I'm dying for a grandbaby…or three," she replied, with a giggle.

"If it makes you feel better, I've been toying with the idea of having my eggs frozen. You know, to be able to use later on in case the man doesn't show up."

My mother's happiness instantly evaporated. "That's not what I had in mind."

Pease poked my mom's leg with her cane. "What about that, Maureen? You can start telling everyone you're expecting a grandbaby as soon as it thaws out."

Mama rolled her eyes. "Excuse me that I don't get

excited over the prospect of a grandcicle."

Pease chortled. "As much as Allen dips his wick with stray ass, you'll be a grandmother before you know it." When both Mama and I shot her a horrified look, Pease shrugged. "It's the truth."

"I don't even want to ask how you know about Allen's love life," Mama said.

With a wink, Pease replied, "I never reveal my sources."

"Thank God," I murmured, which earned me a whack on the knee from Pease's cane.

"Ow!"

"I'd pay good money if my sources had anything juicy to reveal on you," she harrumphed.

"Leave Olivia alone, Eloise," Mama warned.

Pease leaned in on her cane. "I'm just stating facts about Olivia's lack of a love life."

I pinched the bridge of my nose as a headache began to form. I began to repeat *Do not bitch slap your grandmother. Do not bitch slap your grandmother* in my head. "I need some Advil," I said, rising to my feet.

"Oh, don't be such a candy ass, Livvie. You know I was only teasing," Pease called as I started back to the bedroom where the coats and purses were.

Resisting the urge to shoot her a bird, I chose the high road instead and ignored her. As I started in the bedroom, Jill was shrugging into her coat. "Are you leaving?"

"Yeah, I better hit the road if I'm going to make it back in time to meet Chase."

"I think I'll follow you out."

My words sent her hips gyrating into some epic pelvic thrusts. "Ooh, yeah baby, Livvie's gonna get her some."

"Shh!" I hissed as I threw a panicked glance over my shoulder to make sure Mama or Pease hadn't followed me.

"Any ideas where you're going to go?"

"I was thinking about doing a Google search. See if anything is around here."

"Well, good luck on that one."

"What's that supposed to mean?"

"It's just I didn't notice anything on the drive up here."

"It's been my experience that no matter how backwoods a place is, there is always a watering hole somewhere."

"Let's just hope at this 'watering hole', as you call it, there's a moderately decent looking guy with a working cock."

I   grinned.   "Fingers   crossed."

CHAPTER 3

After leaving Mama's shower, I pulled over at a Texaco station about a mile from the cabin. It wasn't for gas but to change into my sexy attire to hit a bar. Jill had deemed my wardrobe "too matronly", so she had promised to bring me a dress from her closet to the shower. And hot damn, Jill had really come through for me on a flaming red dress with spaghetti straps that hit mid-thigh. I loved the heels the most with their crisscrossing rhinestone straps.

I realized I'd made a serious mistake with my choice when after finding the outside bathroom locked, I was given the key, which was attached to a toilet seat lid. "Please tell me I'm not supposed to use this on the commode?" I questioned.

The attendant rolled her eyes. "It's to keep people from running off with the key."

Considering how the woman looked like she wanted to bitch-slap me, I refrained from saying, "Who in their right mind would want to hang on to it?"

Instead, I thanked her and headed back outside. Once I stepped into the bathroom, I knew why the key disappeared. People were so mentally scarred by what they saw that they didn't want to waste the time going back into the station on their way home to get a scalding hot shower.

While I wiggled into the skintight dress, I tried my best not to let any part of my body touch the dirt-encrusted walls. When my pants accidentally touched the floor as I was taking them off, I decided just to toss them. It was either that or burn them when I got home, and I was pretty sure I didn't want to contaminate my car with any germs. As for my shoes, I would hose them off with some of the body disinfectant when I got home. Until then, I would throw them in the trunk.

After washing and drying my hands, I used a paper towel to open the door. I received quite a few looks when I reentered the station outfitted in my sexy dress. I managed to make it almost back to my car before I received a blaring catcall from a trucker, which was just the icing on the cake to a truly horrific experience. Considering all I had been through, I had more than earned some mind-blowing sex.

Once I was back inside the safety of my locked car, I picked up my phone and started my Internet search. But the one bar I had on my reception meant I wasn't able to find jack shit. I had two choices. I could go back inside and ask the asshat sales lady if she knew where I could get a drink and some dick, or I get back on the road and try to find a place with better cell reception.

With my decision made, I cranked up the car and fastened my seatbelt. I peeled out of the parking lot, thrilled to be leaving the hellhole goodbye. Of course, I began to regret my decision fifteen minutes later and further into East Bumblefuck. My cell reception wasn't getting any better, and I debated whether or not I should just turn around and go back to the Texaco since I hadn't come across any other gas stations. To be honest, I hadn't come across anything for that matter. The two-lane road was lined with thick trees and an occasional house here and there.

But as I rounded a sharp curve, my salvation finally loomed in the distance. Oh sweet heavens, it was a bar. Gunning the accelerator, I couldn't seem to get there fast enough. I feared it was just another mirage in the desert of my datelessness that might evaporate the closer I got. But then it stayed a shining beacon of hope as I whipped into the parking lot on two wheels.

That's when I got a good look at my alleged salvation, which at best could be classified as something from Nightmare on Hee Haw Street. I exhaled the breath I'd been holding in one frustrated pant that came off more like a grunt. Multicolored Christmas lights ran the length of the ramshackle roof that hung over a long, rectangular building. A giant sign hung over the top of the bar with some of its bulbs burned out, so instead of reading *The Rusty Halo*, it said *The Rusty Ho*.

See, this is exactly what happens when you go off half-cocked searching for cock. Shaking my head free of my self-deprecating tirade, I glanced in the mirror to survey my reflection. Okay, so the Rusty Halo/Ho wasn't exactly what I had envisioned on my quest to end my long-suffering sex drought. It was the epitome of every backwoods dive of a honky-tonk. But tonight, it was going to be Club 54 or whatever the hell the most happening hotspot was now. I was Dead Woman Walking when it came to sex—it was going down tonight and so was I.

Throwing open the car door, I grabbed my purse and then stumbled along the gravel pavement. Just as I passed a rusted-out Ford pickup, a hound dog bellowed in my ear, causing me to jump out of my skin and almost piss my panties. "Jesus!" I cried, glancing over at the long-eared hound dog. Sitting behind the wheel, it looked like it was waiting to drive its inebriated owner home at the end of the night.

Once I got my wits about me again, I made it to the

door. Smoothing down my hair and dress, I drew in a deep breath. *Okay, Olivia Rose Sullivan, get a grip and get in there and get some.*

With that internal pep talk, I pulled open the door and took a determined step inside. The moment my heels slid through the sawdust and peanut hulls that covered the floor, I knew I had made a terrible, terrible mistake. The happy hoots and hollers of the patrons brought my attention up from what had to be a blatant health code violation to the small stage across from me. As a Skynyrd cover band blared out the opening from *Free Bird*, lighters appeared out of the pockets of faded Wranglers and overall bibs, cutting through the hazy smoke rings. The firelight helped illuminate the room, giving me a good look at my male choices for the evening.

My raging libido instantly shriveled at the sight of what had to be the reunion crew of *Deliverance*. Instantly the tune of *Dueling Banjos* started to play in my head. No, no, no, this couldn't be happening. I could not bring myself to go home with a hillbilly, regardless of the state of tumbleweeds blowing through my nether regions. It was time I turned around, tucked my tail between my legs, and got the hell out of there.

And then the crowd parted, and the banjo music playing in my head screeched to a stop. Sitting at a table alone was the living and breathing embodiment of my fantasies. Even though he was sitting down, I could tell he was tall because his knees bumped against the tabletop. His wavy dark hair fell across his forehead, which seemed to cause him great irritation judging by how exasperated he seemed each time he pushed it back with his fingers.

Instead of Wranglers or overalls, he had on a suit. The jacket was draped across one of the extra chairs while the sleeves of his white shirt were rolled up at his elbows. His tie sat a little askew as if he had been itching to rip it off. Multicolored folders littered the table along with the foamy beer he was nursing.

Even though people bumped and jostled me in the crowd, I stood frozen to that spot, undressing him with my eyes. A wet spot formed on my chin, and I brought the back of my hand up to wipe it away. Oh yeah, I was drooling. After thinking of having to bed Toothless Joe, this was a dream come true.

As if Mr. Tall, Dark, and Sinfully Handsome sensed someone staring at him, he jerked his head up, meeting my gaze. Then the most panty-melting smile imaginable stretched across his drop-dead sexy face. And in that bright and shining moment, my poor, male- neglected vagina, which for so long had been flat lining on life-support, coughed and sputtered back to life. The same jolt of electricity shuddered through its long dormant walls as if the paddles from a crash cart had been administered and a doctor yelled, "Clear!" Through a miracle, I had actually found the Dr. Feelgood who was going to end my longsuffering sex drought.

Considering his smile as an invitation, I pushed myself

forward to close the gap between us. The sawdust on the floor, coupled with my nervously knocking knees, made it a little harder than I expected. Finally, after what felt like an eternity, I stood before him.

My heartbeat drummed wildly when he stood up. "Well, hello there," he said, his deep, rich voice sending a lightning bolt straight to my vagina.

"H-Hi," I stammered.

He motioned to the empty chair across from him. "Won't you join me?"

"Sure. I'd love to." After I sat down, I thrust my hand at him. "My name is Olivia Sullivan." I'm not sure why I felt the need to give him my full name. What was next? Rattling off my social security number?

When his hand touched mine, I literally felt a spark of electricity. The rational side of me argued that it was my heels rubbing across the sawdust floor that had caused it. "I'm Catcher Mains."

Embarrassment flooded my cheeks when I realized I was still holding his hand. I quickly dropped his and used my hand to sweep my hair over my shoulder. "Catcher? That's an interesting name."

"I like to think so."

"Let me guess. It's your nickname from playing baseball."

"You're right that it's a nickname, but it's not from

baseball."

"Please tell me it's not something cheesy like you're a real catch or you always catch the women you chase?"

Catcher threw his head back and laughed heartily. "You could say that's part of it."

"Seriously though. What's it from?"

"You see my parents were English teachers, so they named me after the main character in one of their favorite books—Holden Caulfield."

"From *Catcher in the Rye*."

Catcher's blue eyes lit up. "You know it?"

I laughed. "So I must look like some bimbo who doesn't have an appreciation for literature."

"No. Not at all. It's just I don't find that many people who get the reference."

After glancing around us, I cocked my brows at him. "Maybe you're hanging out with the wrong people," I suggested.

He grinned. "Trust me. This isn't my usual Friday night hangout."

"Mine either. I just happened to be passing through and was in desperate need of a drink."

"And you just happened to be wearing a banging-hot dress."

"You think my dress is banging?"

"Hell, yeah." With a wink, he added, "I know I'd sure like to bang you in it."

A nervous giggle escaped my lips. "I think you're getting a little ahead of yourself."

"Maybe I am. I should probably be more of a gentleman by trying to get to know you better. Then I can feel pervy telling you how much I'd like take you to the bathroom, shove that banging dress up above your hips, and fuck you senseless."

My mouth ran Mojave Desert dry at the image he had just painted for me. Of course, right on its heels came a flashback of the Texaco hellhole, and I shuddered. "No bathrooms," I whispered.

Catcher's brows rose in surprise. "Just no to the bathrooms? You mean you're not shutting me down on the rest?"

"Buy me a drink, and we'll see." His attraction had bolstered my confidence.

That drop-dead sexy grin slunk across his face. "It would be my pleasure. What's your poison?"

I was pretty sure *The Rusty Ho* didn't have an extensive mixed drink menu. "Just a cranberry and vodka would be great."

Catcher nodded as he rose out of his seat. As he walked over to the bar, my gaze zeroed in on the imprint of his finely sculpted ass through his pants. Oh yeah, it was the kind of ass you wanted to sink your teeth into.

Easy there. You need to pace yourself. If you keep up

the dirty thoughts, you'll be jumping him the moment he comes back to the table, and you're too big a prude to enjoy public sex.

Catcher returned and sat my drink in front of me. "Thank you," I said.

"You're welcome." Catcher had gotten his mug of beer refilled. After taking a sip of his beer, he leaned his elbows in on the table. "So, Olivia Sullivan, what is it that you do for a living?"

"I'm a m—" I snapped my mouth shut. There was no way in hell I was going to tell him the truth and send my potential sexathon down in flames before it even got started. I quickly recovered by tossing my hair over my shoulder. "I'm a flight attendant."

Catcher narrowed his eyes. "Bullshit."

"Excuse me?"

"There's no way in hell you're a flight attendant."

"Why would you doubt me?"

"Because I've undergone extensive training to unravel the many layers of deception. Therefore, I can see right through the façade of you flying the friendly skies."

A stare down then ensued. When I finally blinked, Catcher gave me a self-righteous smirk.

"Fine. I'm a mortician and county coroner." Wincing, I braced myself for him to run screaming from the table. But instead, he surprised the hell out of me by grinning.

"Really?"

"Yeah. Really."

"That is too fucking cool."

I cocked my brows at him in surprise. "You can't be serious."

"I am."

"Usually my profession is a mega turn off for men."

"You mean it's a turn off for pussies." He captured me with his hypnotic gaze. "I'm a real man, Liv. It takes a hell of lot more to scare me off."

"I-I'm glad to hear that," I stuttered. "And what do you do?"

"What do you think I do?"

After glancing at the folders in front of him, I tilted my head in thought. "I'm thinking some form of law enforcement or maybe the military since you mentioned your training."

Catcher flashed me that panty-scorching grin again. "You're right. I'm an agent with the GBI aka Georgia Bureau of Investigation."

"Wow, that must be an interesting job."

"It keeps me on my toes."

I motioned to the folders. "What brings you out this way?"

"Ah, see, that's confidential," he replied, before taking the folders and putting them in his briefcase.

"Oh, I'm sorry. Is it one of those 'if you told me you'd have to kill me' kinda things?"

"Maybe. And I sure don't want to kill you. Especially before I got to fuck you and make you scream my name."

My mouth gaped open at him once again being so brazen. "Um, okay," I replied.

"Don't play the prude with me, Olivia. We both know that you came in here on a search mission for cock."

"I-I don't know what you're t-talking about," I replied as I shifted in my seat.

Catcher snorted before taking another swig of his beer. "Babe, I could see right through you the moment you walked through the door. But hey, I get it. Just because you're a woman, it doesn't mean you don't have needs. I'm sure as hell not going to judge you for saving face by coming to some dive where no one knows you to get your dick."

I gulped down two sips of my drink before I responded. "Okay, you're right. I came here to get..." Somehow I just couldn't seem to say it aloud.

"Fucked, laid, banged, bonked, nailed, ridden, screwed—"

I held my hand up. "Yes, that pretty much covers it."

Catcher scooted his chair closer up to the table. "Just how long has it been?"

I glanced down at my hands in my lap. "A while."

"How long is 'a while'?"

Chewing on my bottom lip, I debated whether to be honest with Catcher. I already dealt with the day-to-day embarrassment of my lack of a love life. I didn't want him

judging me as some kind of frigid weirdo. "Can't we just leave it at awhile and call it a day?"

"We could. But I'd also like to know what I'm getting into."

I jerked my gaze up to glare at him. "I can assure you it's not so bad that you're going to have to sandblast open my vagina, okay?"

Catcher appeared to be fighting a smile. "That's not exactly what I was alluding to."

"Sure it wasn't."

He reached over and took my hand. "You're right that I was somewhat addressing your vagina, but it's not what you think. If it's been a long time, then I know I'll need to take some time with the foreplay. I can't just go plowing into you like I want unless you're ready for me."

I furrowed my brows at him. It had been a long, long time since I'd been in a bar or part of the hook-up scene. The last time a guy spoke this frank to me was in college, and I just assumed his bluntness was part of his immaturity. When it came down to the nitty gritty, did all men talk this way?

"Thanks...I think."

He dipped his head closer to mine. "Stop thinking so much. Let me and your body make the decisions."

"I can try."

Catcher's closeness, coupled with his sexy smile, ignited a wildfire between my legs. I pressed my thighs together to try to put it out.

"First thing we're going to do is loosen you up."

"Considering the conversation we've just had, I think I'm loose enough."

I sucked in a breath at the feel of Catcher's warm hand clenching down on the skin of my exposed thigh. He shook his head. "Talking about something and actually doing it are two separate things. And I'm only talking about one or two drinks. The last thing I want is you plastered."

"Wouldn't that make it easier?"

"Hell, no. I want you to enjoy every second of this. After all, you've more than earned it."

"You're right. I have."

"Good." Catcher then took my arm and led me out of my chair. We weaved our way through the crowd over to the bar. Catcher waved the bartender over. After slapping a twenty on the bar, Catcher said, "Give us two shots of tequila, please."

"You got it."

"I guess I should've checked first to make sure you liked tequila," Catcher said as the bartender poured our shots.

"I would have let you know."

Catcher grinned. "Yeah, I thought so. You don't impress me as the type of girl to suffer in silence about anything."

I jerked my chin up. "I speak my mind if that's what you're alluding to."

"As well as not taking any shit from anyone."

56

I couldn't help laughing at his summation. "That, too."

When the bartender set our shots in front of us, Catcher lifted his. "To speaking your mind and not taking anyone's bullshit."

I lifted my glass. "Here, here."

Catcher clinked our glasses together and then motioned for me to drink. "Ladies first," he insisted.

"Okay." I licked the salt on my hand before tipping back the shot glass. The golden liquid scorched a trail down my esophagus to my stomach. I sucked the lime into my mouth as my eyes watered. "Done," I said, my voice hoarse from the tequila.

To my surprise, Catcher didn't immediately down his shot. Instead, he shocked the hell out of me by taking the salt-shaker and dusting my chest with its contents. "What are you—"

He brought a finger to my lips to silence me. "Just go with it, babe."

Although I was still uncertain, I decided to follow Catcher's advice. After he took his finger away, he picked up the shot glass. I sucked in a breath as he placed it inside my dress between my breasts. With my dress's tight material, the glass was held suspended perfectly.

I exhaled in a rush when Catcher dipped his head. I gasped when his warm tongue slid across the skin above my breasts. Once he had lapped up all the salt, his mouth closed around the top of the shot glass. I shivered when I felt his lips lightly brush against my skin. Oh fuck me, did it feel good having his mouth on me.

With the glass securely in his mouth, he tipped his head back and downed the contents. He winked at me as he put the glass on the bar. "That hit the spot."

"I'm glad you enjoyed it," I said breathlessly. Jeez, if I stayed around him too long, I was going to need an oxygen tank to regulate my breathing.

"Think you're good, or you wanna do another?" Catcher asked.

"Maybe. You want me to do it out of your pants?"

He chuckled. "No, babe. No tit for tat on that one."

Not wanting to be outdone or unsexy, I added, "I could probably make it work." Of course, in this case it would be dick for tit but whatever.

Catcher grinned as he waved the bartender over. "Two more shots please."

Once the glasses were refilled, he passed mine to me and held his up. "Let's do these together."

"Okay."

"Bottoms up."

I had just brought the glass to my lips when Catcher added, "Just like I hope to have you before the evening is over."

My mouth momentarily formed the Minion "Whaaat?" before I tipped my head back and sucked down the tequila.

Somehow with Catcher's innuendo, I felt I was going to need it.

"Good. Now let's dance."

"Okay," I replied uncertainly. I had never been overly talented when it came to busting a move, so I was a little alarmed at making a fool out of myself in front of Catcher. Thankfully, the band's cover of Credence Clearwater Revival's *Rolling on the River* turned into the slow tune of Charlie Pride's *So Good When You're bad*.

Catcher snaked his arm around my waist and drew me flush against him. Damn, it felt good being so close to a man again. When the woodsy smell of his cologne filled my nostrils, I shivered. There was something about a delicious smelling man that was like liquid sex to me. I quickly brought my arms up to encircle his neck. My fingers couldn't help playing with the hair at the base of Catcher's scalp.

After a few seconds of swaying to the beat, one of Catcher's hands traveled from my waist to squeeze my buttocks. While he caressed my backside, his hips began to move against mine. As if answering a siren's call, my hips began to move with Catcher's, my core rubbing against his growing erection. He swiveled his waist to bring one of his knees between my legs. Catcher brought his lips to mine as our hands ran up and down each other's bodies. For a minute, I thought we'd been transported into a scene from *Dirty Dancing*. I expected to see Patrick Swayze and Jennifer Grey come gyrating by.

When the song ended, Catcher extricated himself from our embrace. "Where are you going?" I panted.

"Bathroom."

"Now?"

A wicked grin slunk across his face. "Trust me, babe, if I don't jerk this one out, I won't last one second when we get to a hotel."

I'm sure my mouth must've made a perfect "O" of surprise because that wasn't what I was expecting him to say. I realized then I had a choice to make. I could let Catcher go to the bathroom to jerk off, or I could go with him to the bathroom and help him out. It was a whole *Jerry Macguire* "Help me, help you" kinda thing.

When I finally found my voice, I breathlessly said, "I'll go with you.

Catcher's brows shot up in surprise. "What about the 'no bathrooms' claim you made earlier?"

I shrugged. "I changed my mind." With a coy grin, I added, "You changed my mind."

"I'm glad to hear it."

Catcher took me by the hand and led me through the crowd toward the bathroom. Before we got to it, he stopped at a door labeled, "Staff Only". After glancing left and right, Catcher tested the doorknob. When he found it unlocked, he dragged me inside the dimly lit storage room.

After Catcher closed the door, he locked it. "This okay?"

"Fine."

The next thing I knew Catcher pounced on me. It took me so off guard that I went reeling back. "Omph," I muttered when I crashed against one of the racks.

"Are you okay?"

I smiled as I brushed the dust off my ass. "I'm fine. I swear."

"Sorry about that." Catcher flashed me a sheepish look. "I got too excited by the prospect of finally getting to fuck you."

My confidence, which had initially been bolstered by the tequila, began to wane, and now a feeling of inadequacy began creeping in. "You sure are getting your hopes up that sex with me is going to be good."

"I just call it as I see it."

"I wish I shared your confidence," I mumbled.

Catcher swept my hair out of my face. "Olivia Sullivan, are you wet for me?"

I blinked at few times in disbelief at his question. "Y-Yes."

"Dripping wet?" Since my panties were soaked, I nodded. "So I've already managed to turn you on enough to get wet?"

"Oh yes."

"For me, there's nothing that makes sex good like a woman who is hot for me—who wants me mind, body, and soul."

As Catcher once again held me in his hypnotic stare, I said, "I'm seriously on fire for you."

He grinned. "Good. Now enough fucking chatter. It's time to get fucking."

"Um, okay."

Catcher dipped his head to kiss me. Within seconds, his mouth had consumed mine. All the heat from out on the dance floor fanned back to life. As Catcher licked and nipped at my neck, one of his hands kneaded my breast. When he reached for the hem of my dress, I suddenly had an overpowering flashback of being with Eric. The desire that had been racing through my body was soon replaced with panic. Catcher noticed the shift in my mood because he lifted his head to look at me.

"What's wrong, Liv?"

I plastered a smile on my face. "Nothing."

He quirked his brows at me. "Bullshit. You just went from scorching to frigid in the span of a minute."

"You said no more chatter." Since I desperately needed to change the subject, I reached out to cup his erection over his pants. Catcher groaned and closed his eyes. "Kiss me again," I demanded.

Catcher brought his mouth to mine in a punishing lip-lock. This time when he shoved the hem of my dress up to my waist, I didn't protest. His hand delved between my legs, causing me to moan. He began to furiously work me over my thong.

He jerked the fabric aside and thrust two fingers into my wet walls. My head thumped against the back of the rack, causing a bunch of Jack Daniels bottles to rattle. "Oh God," I murmured.

As Catcher's fingers worked their magic, he buried his head in my cleavage. He sucked and licked the tops of my breasts before using his other hand to push the material down and expose my breast. My nipple, which was already pebbled, grew even harder. When his mouth closed over it, I cried out and fisted my hands into his hair.

But even as my body surged with sexual energy, I couldn't push away the worry that gnawed at me. "Catcher?" I breathlessly panted.

"Yeah, babe," he replied, his warm breath fanning across my breast.

"Have you had a physical in the last few months?"

After giving my nipple a hard tug with his mouth, he pulled away to gaze up at me. "Is this when you start worrying if I'm clean? You can push that thought right on out of your pretty little head because I can assure you I wrap my shit up each and every time?"

"No, no. I was wondering about your general health."

Catcher gave me a funny look. "What are you talking about?"

"I mean, did your heart sound okay? Like no abnormalities?"

He pushed himself up to face me. "Why do you want to know?"

"I was just curious."

"You were about sixty seconds away from me stroking you to an orgasm, and you were suddenly curious about my ticker?"

"Look. It might sound stupid to you, but I need to know before we do this."

"Why could you possibly need to know?"

"Because I killed the last guy I was with!"

The moment the words escaped my lips, I clamped my hands over my mouth and shook my head wildly back and forth. "I can't believe I just said that," I mumbled behind my hand.

"What do you mean you *killed* the last guy you were with?"

I quickly related Eric's story in a few sentences. When I finished, I finally dared myself to look at Catcher. I expected at any moment for him to run like hell away from me. Or to laugh. But instead, he gave me a sincere smile. "So that's why you closed up shop?" When I nodded, he cupped my face with his hands. "Olivia Sullivan, I do believe you are unlike any woman I've ever met. I'm really sorry that happened to you, and it is totally understandable why you would be afraid about having sex again. But I want to assure you that I'm healthy as a horse. My last physical was two months ago, and I was given a clean bill of health."

"I'm glad to hear that."

"Now that you know I'm able-bodied for sexual activity, can I make you come?"

I blinked at him in surprise. "You mean after all that, you still want to have sex with me?"

Catcher grinned as he rolled his hips against mine. I gasped when I felt his hard length pressed against my core. "Does that answer your question?"

"Oh yeah," I panted. His hot cock touching me more than answered that question. It sent my battered and bruised self-esteem rising up to do a victory dance.

Once again my dress was pushed up over my hips while Catcher's masterful fingers dipped inside me. It didn't take long for him to get back to where we had been before. Suddenly, I felt like I had been running a marathon, my body weak from exhaustion, as the finish line loomed in the distance. It was all just too overwhelming. Then the hands and mouth of a man were too much for my neglected body and pussy. For the first time in six years, I came because of someone else. As my walls contracted around Catcher's fingers, I cried out a string of curse words. In my mind, I crossed the finish line with my arms raised in victory.

When I came back to myself, I realized that I needed Catcher inside me. Like *now*. I barely gave him a chance to take his fingers out of me before my hands started fumbling with the button on his pants. Once I got it undone, I unzipped him and started to reach for his cock, but he stopped me. "You do that, and I'll cream my pants like a teenager," he groaned.

He dug his wallet out of his back pocket and fished out a condom. I guess I should have been glad he had one on hand, but at the same time, I couldn't help thinking he must be a real manwhore to keep condoms on him at all times.

As he slid the condom down his impressive length, I couldn't help licking my lips. He was like the Goldilocks of Cocks...not too skinny, not to wide, not too short, and not too long. He was just right.

He reached out and grabbed me by the hips. "Jump up, babe."

I didn't have to be told twice. I hopped up and wrapped my legs around his waist. Catcher kept one hand under my ass as he guided his erection to my core. He looked me straight in the eye as he thrust into me. I bit my lip as he filled and stretched me.

"Good?" he asked.

"Mmm," was all I could reply at that moment. I'm not sure I could have formed intelligible words if I tried.

Catcher grinned as both his hands cupped my buttocks. He began to work me on and off him in time with his thrusts. God, it was soooo good. I'm pretty sure if my vagina could have put into words what it felt like, it would have broken out into singing the *Hallelujah Chorus*. Or maybe some Aretha Franklin's *You Make Me Feel Like a Natural Woman*.

Even though Jack Daniels' bottles banged against the

back of my head, I didn't care. All I cared about was the banging going on below my waist. I began to climb closer and closer to a big finale of an orgasm. As if Catcher could sense it, he propped some of my ass weight on one the shelves and brought a hand between us to stroke my clit. How he thrust and stroked, I have no idea. I didn't stop to question it because it was just too damn magical.

I didn't cry out as my walls gloriously clenched down on his pumping dick in a masterful multiple orgasm. Oh no, I screamed. Like ear-splintering loud. At the same time, my nails dug into Catcher's back through his shirt. He groaned and pumped even more furiously in and out of me. It wasn't long before he tensed and then a long, guttural groan erupted from him. "Fuck yeah," he muttered in my ear.

I could have stayed in that moment forever, but then Catcher pulled away.

He eased out of me and then set my legs down. They were so rubbery that I began to slide, and he had to hold me up by pinning my thighs with his.

"Thank you," I said sincerely.

Catcher chuckled. "That's a first. I don't think I've ever had someone thank me for fucking."

I grinned. "I was thanking you for not letting me fall. But when it comes down to it, people should give thanks for good sex. After all, it's the polite thing to do."

"Babe, I just fucked you up against a whiskey rack in

the storage room of a shithole dive. I think we left polite a long time ago."

"Maybe so."

Ever the gentleman, Catcher knelt down and pulled my panties up my thighs.

I slid a lock of hair behind my ear. "So," I said.

"So," Catcher replied.

"What do we do now?"

"Well, we get the hell out of here and go back to my hotel room for round two, which hopefully will be followed by rounds three and four."

"If I go three or four more rounds with you, I won't be able to walk tomorrow."

Catcher waggled his brows. "I'll carry you."

I laughed. "I don't know if my vagina has it in her, but she's willing to try."

"My dick is very glad to hear that your vagina has such a good work ethic."

I couldn't help staring at Catcher like he was some desert mirage. Like at any moment, he was just going to disappear. It was hard to believe a man like him actually existed. He possessed so many wonderful attributes. Good-looks. Strength. Intelligence. Sex appeal. A sense of humor. Magical fingers that played my clit like it was an instrument. And a masterful cock that hit all the right spots.

The knob on the storage room door jiggled. "Who the hell locked the storeroom door," a voice grumbled behind the

wood.

"Two horny fuckers," Catcher whispered with a grin.

I playfully smacked him on the arm. "Come on. We better get out of here before we get in trouble."

"I'm pretty sure I could flash my badge to make things right."

"Do you often use your badge inappropriately?"

He grinned. "When the need arises, I might be known to use it."

"That's not too surprising," I replied, as I started to the door. After I unlocked it, Catcher said, "Here, let me." He stepped in front of me to open the door. He stuck his head out and peeked around. "Coast is clear."

Thankfully, we were able to slip out of the storeroom without being caught. I jerked my thumb toward the bathrooms. "Let me go freshen up a bit, and then I'll meet you out front. Okay?"

Catcher leaned forward to nuzzle my neck. "I kind of like the idea of you smelling like sex as we walk out of here."

His words caused a shiver to run over me, and I shuddered. Truth was, I'd felt the same way. There was something erotic and elicit about having the smell of sex on me. But I opted for cleanliness and ducked into the women's bathroom.

After I did a lightning quick clean up, I left the bathroom. As I started across the floor, a fleshy hand grabbed hold of one of my butt cheeks. "Hey sugar, I saw you dancin' earlier. Let's you and me take a turn."

I tried prying his arm off, but it was locked in a viselike grip. Forcing a smile to my face, I said, "That's sweet of you to ask, but I have to say no."

His face clouded over. "You musta mistaken me. I wasn't askin'. I was tellin'."

When I opened my mouth in protest, he covered my lips with his, assaulting my senses with the taste of someone who drank an ashtray. I gagged when he thrust his tongue into my mouth.

With all the strength I had in me, I shoved him away. "I said no."

"And I don't give a shit, girlie. You're gonna give me the same lovin' you were givin' that highbrow dude."

My gaze frantically spun around the room, desperately seeking Catcher. When I didn't see him, I tried controlling my breathing as the panic rose in me. I had to do something. I couldn't just let this dickhead manhandle me and force me to "give him lovin'." I'd been through self-defense training for fuck's sake. I wasn't some shrinking violet.

I'd just formulated a plan to rage war on his balls when Catcher appeared out of thin air.

"Let her go," he demanded.

"Fuck you," the redneck replied as he tightened his hold on me.

Catcher's expression was murderous. "Trust me,

buddy. This isn't a fight you want to pick."

The redneck sneered at Catcher. "I got a good hundred pounds on you, pussy boy."

Catcher's anger visibly swelled at being called a pussy. The next thing I knew he was swinging his fist into the redneck's face. The force momentarily took him off guard, and I was able to pry myself out of his stronghold. "Olivia, get the hell out of here!" Catcher yelled.

Before I could argue that I wasn't leaving him to get beaten by this Neanderthal, the redneck came back with a punch to Catcher's head. The redneck's Confederate flag ring split open Catcher's eyebrow, and blood splattered onto my dress. Catcher didn't have a chance to recover before the redneck captured him in a chokehold.

"FIGHT!" someone shouted. The next thing I knew everyone was kung fu fighting. Okay, maybe not. But the entire place erupted into strangers kicking and gouging each other while glasses and bottles were being hurled through the air.

As Catcher choked and sputtered, I knew I had to do something, and that wasn't calling 911. I picked up one of the rickety chairs and smashed it across the redneck's back. "Fucking hell!" he shouted as pieces of splintered wood rained down on the floor.

While the redneck staggered back, I grabbed one of the sticks off the pool table. When the redneck whirled around, I jabbed him in the crotch with the stick like I was a native island spearing a fish. He squealed before falling to his knees. I then lobbed him in the back of the head. When I saw I had knocked him out, I quickly dropped down beside him.

"What the hell are you doing?" Catcher asked hoarsely, as he rubbed his throat.

"Checking his pulse." Thankfully, he still had one, so killing a redneck at the Rusty Ho wouldn't stain my otherwise perfect record. Even though it would have been self-defense, my conscience still would have eaten me alive.

Catcher grabbed me by the arm and pulled me to my feet. "Come on. We need to get out of here."

"Sounds good to me."

He drew me to his side and began leading us through the fighting fray. "Duck!" he cried. A beer mug narrowly missed us before smashing into the bar. We had to weave and bob like a cobra to miss getting punched or jabbed. On the way out, Catcher grabbed his jacket and briefcase.

When we got outside into the parking lot, I exhaled the breath I'd been holding. Catcher started leading me to his car when I tugged on his arm. "No," I protested.

"Excuse me?" he asked.

I shook my head. "Wherever we're going next, I'm going there in my own car. That way I can come and go as I please."

Catcher rolled his eyes and grumbled, "Fucking feminists." At the sound of busting glass, we both whirled around. A man lay cut and bleeding on the pavement from where he had been thrown through one of the windows. "Where's your car?" Catcher asked, never taking his eyes off the man.

"Two rows over."

After unlocking the driver's side door on his car, he reached into the side console and took out a gun. When I stared wide-eyed at him, he gave me a tight smile. "In case we need a little extra protection on the way to your car."

We had to step over the man on the ground. Thankfully, he was unconscious, so he didn't pose any threat. The last thing we needed was to have a rumble in the parking lot.

"Follow me. I'm staying at a Holiday Inn about a mile down the road."

"Okay." After Catcher put me in the car, I locked the doors. While he started back to his car, I quickly cranked up. Before I could back up, a chair came flying out of the broken window and narrowly missed hitting my hood. With shaking hands, I threw the car in reverse and squealed out of the parking space. I felt a little relief at the sight of Catcher's taillights a few feet in front of me. He put the pedal to the metal, and we thankfully left the Rusty Ho in our dust.

As I sped along the two-lane road in the dark night, I couldn't help wondering if this was some karmic retribution for having sex with a stranger. I tried ignoring the voice that questioned what else crazy might happen after I went back to

Catcher's hotel. Although I was concerned, it wasn't enough to keep me away from Catcher. Maybe it was the long-overdue, post-orgasmic haze that was eradicating all rational thought. He was like the ultimate drug—I'd had a taste and now I was hooked.

CHAPTER 4

I couldn't help sighing in relief when I saw that the Holiday Inn where Catcher was staying wasn't a complete dive like the Rusty Ho. That place was going to scar me for life. At the same time, it couldn't be classified as the Ritz. It appeared to have been built in either the late seventies or early eighties. In the end, the only thing that mattered was it wasn't a total shithole.

I eased my Accord into the space beside the black

sedan Catcher was driving. Although it didn't look like something he would drive, it screamed federal agent. He impressed me more as the type who would drive a flaming-red sports car. Not that he needed to compensate for his manhood. He had that in spades.

Catcher flew out of his car and was at my door before I could even open it. "How are you holding up?" he asked, his handsome face etched with concern.

My heart did a sappy pitter-patter at his concern. "I'm fine. It was nothing."

Catcher tilted his head at me. "You call being sexually assaulted and partaking in a bar fight nothing?"

"After the day I've had, it certainly pales in comparison."

Catcher chuckled as he shook his head. "As my late grandmother would say, 'Honey, you just won't do.'"

I laughed. "Sounds like something my grandmother would say. Well, if you threw in a few expletives." I motioned my finger at his eyebrow. "While I appreciate your concern, you're the one who is bleeding."

Catcher winced when he reached up to feel his busted brow. "Dumb fucker."

"Are you talking about you or the redneck?" I teasingly asked.

Catcher snorted. "It should probably be me since I didn't block that Neanderthal better.

Considering he was a lumbering idiot, he was surprisingly quick."

"I would have to agree since he came out of nowhere at me."

Catcher cuffed my chin playfully. "You're a tough cookie, Olivia Sullivan."

"Thank you, Catcher Mains."

We stood there staring into each other's eyes for what felt like an eternity. "Come on. Let's get inside, so I can get inside you again," Catcher said, in a husky, bedroom voice.

My-oh-so-sexy response to his naughty words was to trip over my heels and almost face plant on the sidewalk.

"Easy there. I need you to stay vertical." With a wink, he added, "Well, at least for a little while."

"Okay. I'll try," I replied.

Catcher threw an arm around my shoulder and drew me to him. We walked side by side into the lobby. Catcher ushered me in front of him to take the elevator to the tenth floor, which happened to be the highest floor. "Oh, you have the penthouse?" I teasingly asked.

"Oh yeah. Just wait until you see the killer views I have of the abandoned textile mills."

I laughed. "Swanky."

"I demand only the best whenever I stay at a Holiday Inn." Catcher slid the keycard into the slot and unlocked the door. "Ladies first," he said, motioning for me to go in.

"Thank you," I replied, as I walked into the room. After I sat my purse down, I turned back to him. "Do you mind if I take a quick shower? I desperately need to wash away the grime of the Rusty Ho."

Catcher grinned. "As long as I can join you."

"Sure."

"First, I think we need to clean your eye up."

"Can't I just hold it under the warm water, and call it a day?"

"It needs cleaning," I countered.

"Fine," he grumbled.

"Go sit on the bed," I instructed, as I dug my first aid kit out of my purse.

"You seriously carry a first aid kit with you?"

"Habit of the trade. More often than not, you have someone who gets hurt when investigating a death or when you go to pick up a body."

Catcher snorted as he flopped down on the mattress. "You are one hell of a woman," he mused.

I brought the kit over to him. "I'll take that as a compliment."

"You should. I don't think I've ever met such a fascinating woman who can fuck like a champ in a storeroom and then take down a redneck assaulter with a chair and a pool stick."

His summation of the night's events had me giggling as I brought the antiseptic wipe to his eyebrow. "I wouldn't say I was always so fascinating. Tonight has certainly been something out of the ordinary for me in many ways."

Catcher winced before saying, "I guess there's a first time for everything."

"You can say that again." I leaned forward and blew on Catcher's eyebrow to dry the antiseptic.

He took me off guard by bringing his hands to my thighs. I sucked in a breath as they slid my dress up over my hips. Dipping his head, he took one end of my thong between his teeth. When he jerked it, the flimsy material gave way. My legs began trembling as he kissed his way across my abdomen to the other side. When he repeated the process, the thong completely tore away from my body.

Cool air swirled around my inflamed core as I stared down at Catcher. He gave me a cocky grin as he swept my thong from his mouth. "You owe me a pair of panties, Mr. Mains," I said.

"Would you take an orgasm instead?"

I brought a finger to my chin in thought. "I guess that will have to do."

Catcher surprised me by flicking his tongue against my pussy. When I gripped his shoulders tightly and thrust my hips forward, he tilted his head at me. "You want to rethink that response."

I bit down on my lip and nodded my head, causing Catcher to chuckle. "Come on. Let's get in the shower."

When he rose up off the mattress, his hands slipped around me to find my zipper. With a quick tug, he had the zipper down my back. His fingers came to the spaghetti straps on the dress. He pulled them down my arms, exposing my breasts. My nipples instantly hardened under his heated gaze.

He must've grown impatient because the next thing I knew he was jerking the dress off my hips and down my thighs. When it lay on the floor, he stepped back to look at me. "Fucking hell, you're gorgeous," he murmured.

Warmth spilled across my cheeks and filled my core at his words and stare. I'd never had a man, least of all one I barely knew, make me feel so desired before. "I think it's your turn now."

Catcher grinned. "Ready to see me unveiled in all my glory?"

I laughed. "Yes. I am."

"I promise I'll live up to the fantasy in your mind."

With a roll of my eyes, I brought my hands to loosen his tie. "If you're not careful, we won't be able to fit that big head of yours in this room."

"I know where another big head of mine fits snug and tight," he replied.

My gaze flew up to his. "You're an egomaniac." Of course, I did love his dirty-talking mouth.

"Admit it. My big head felt really good in your tight pussy." His voice had dropped into that warm, husky tone again. The one that had both me and my vagina mesmerized. Like he was holding a swinging watch before us and hypnotizing us while saying *You're getting very horny.*

"I suppose it did," I answered as I unbuttoned his shirt.

"Ha, you suppose." Catcher dipped his head to where his breath scorched against my ear. "You and I both know how good you liked it. Your pussy had my cock in a death vise."

After unbuckling and sliding off his belt, I put the ends together and cracked it. "You should be spanked for the way you're talking to me."

Lust burned bright in Catcher's blue eyes. "Hmm, you like a little S&M?"

I didn't want to admit to Catcher the closest I'd gotten to whips and chains was the time in undergrad when I tagged along on a call to Club 1740 in Atlanta where a seventy-year-old dude had a heart attack after being hogtied and whipped. Since the guy had been a regular, he'd gone out doing what he'd loved, but at the same time, it was slightly horrifying to his children that their dad wasn't vanilla and had croaked in a sex club.

So I shrugged. "Maybe."

Catcher captured my chin between his fingers and tsked at me. "You're lying through your teeth."

Damn him and his GBI body language training. "Fine. I've been a hundred percent vanilla in my sex life. Happy?"

With a grin, Catcher said, "Don't feel bad, babe. It's not like I'm Master Mains, and I'm going to whip out a flogger. I don't need embellishment when I fuck. Now, if you wanna blindfold me or tie me up, I'm all for it."

"That's good to know."

"What about you?"

"What about me?" I asked as I slid his pants off his delectable ass.

"Do you want someone to tie you up and blindfold you?"

"Maybe...the blindfold more than the tying up." I wrinkled my nose. "I'd have to really know and trust a person before I let them tie me up."

"I think that's part of the whole BDSM idea thing. You know, trust and consent. I know I sure as hell wouldn't let just anyone tie me up."

"I'm glad you're good with just sticking with the basics."

"As long as I get to stick it in you, I'm good," Catcher teased with a grin.

"You're impossible," I muttered.

"Impossibly well endowed."

I laughed as I smacked his impossibly defined six pack. "Enough with the innuendo." My thumbs dipped into the waistband of his briefs. I tugged them down over his hips and legs. Once they were on the floor, I swept my gaze to his package. Although I had already seen *and* felt his masterful dick, I couldn't help admiring it once again.

It soon began to swell under my appreciative gaze. "There you go getting the big head again," I teased.

Catcher laughed. "It can't help himself. When a lady looks at him the way you were, he has to show his

appreciation."

Using my index finger, I tapped the bobbing erection. "You're going to have to be patient and let me get cleaned up before I show you any more attention." Then when I realized what I had just done, I swept my hand over my eyes. "Oh my God, you've got me talking to your dick."

"Don't feel bad. I talk to him a lot."

I peeked at him through my fingers. "You do?"

"Sure. Don't you ever talk to yours?"

"Well, since I don't have a penis, that would be no."

Catcher rolled his eyes. "Not a dick, your pussy."

"Um, no."

"Maybe you should start." He grinned. "After all, she deserves some compliments since she's an awfully nice pussy."

I laughed as I shook my head. "Thank you."

"I'm serious. I've known quite a lot of pussies in my day, and by far, yours is one of the nicest."

At the mention of his man-whoring, I reached over and pinched his nipple and not in a fun, sexual way. Although it was only about tonight for us, I still didn't like to hear him talk about other women...or other pussies.

Catcher winced. "Sorry. It is *the* nicest."

"Don't you know it isn't polite to brag about your sex life in front of me?"

"I wasn't bragging; I was just stating facts."

"Would you like a paddle to help you up Shit Creek in your douchecanoe?"

Catcher threw his head back with a laugh. "Liv Bug, I do love your sassy mouth."

"Does that mean you'll watch yours?"

"Yes, ma'am. I will." I started to nod when he added, "I'll watch my mouth go all over your body."

I groaned. "I give up."

Catcher chuckled and held out his hand. As I slipped my hand in his, I said, "Thank you."

"You're welcome." He then led me into the bathroom. While he bent over to turn on the shower, I ignored the urge to stare at his ass, and instead, I checked my reflection in the mirror. Even after the storeroom fuckfest, my hair and makeup were holding up remarkably well. I would have to give Jill some more thanks for her mad skills.

Once the water appeared to be just right, Catcher slid back the shower curtain and crooked his finger at me. Ever the gentleman, he helped me inside before following behind me. I moaned as the scorching hot water beat against my back.

"Hey now, save those moans for me and not inanimate objects," Catcher said, as he tore into one of the hotel's wrapped bars of soap.

"I'll try."

After lathering up his hands, Catcher went straight for my breasts. Kneading them, cupping them, squeezing them. It was seriously working me up. I gasped when he tweaked and pinched my nipples.

"Gotta make sure those are squeaky clean," he said, with a grin.

"I didn't realize I was such a dirty girl."

"Hmm, I plan to clean you up just to get you down right filthy."

I shivered in spite of the scalding water. With both Jesse and Eric, it had taken time for them to warm up to using dirty talk. Catcher, on the other hand, came right out swinging with it. And so help me, I loved it.

Catcher eased me back into the shower stream to rinse my breasts. When his hand dipped between my legs, I bit down on my lip to keep from moaning. "Don't do that."

"Do what?" I panted.

"Hold back. I want to hear you—every moan and groan, especially the screams." As if to elicit a quick response, his fingers stroked my clit harder. This time I didn't hold back. I threw my head back and groaned. "That's nothing. Wait until I get my mouth on you."

I whimpered. "Please. Now."

Catcher obliged me by sinking down onto his knees. His strong hands gripped my thighs and pushed them apart. He nudged my pussy with his nose before placing licks along my inner thighs. When his tongue lapped at my clit, I rewarded him with a hearty grunt. My torso leaned back against the shower wall while I propped one leg up on the ledge to give Catcher easier access.

The man must've graduated from the Academy of Pussy Eating with top honors. Maybe even the Valedictorian. I'm not sure how he was able to swirl his tongue around my clit while simultaneously sucking it. It was multitasking as its finest.

When he spread me apart with his fingers, I expected to feel them pumping inside me.

But he used his tongue instead while his mouth and even his teeth pressed down on my clit.

"I'm going to come!" I cried.

"Yeah, baby. Come hard around my tongue." His words vibrated around my pussy.

I wanted to argue with him that if I came, my already rubbery legs were going to give way. But instead, I rode out the pleasure like I was on the back of a bucking bronco. I held on for dear life not to miss a single thing. I made Catcher's face my bitch as my hips pumped furiously for added friction. If I thought the Rusty Ho storeroom orgasm was hot, this was like scorching hot magma pouring over me.

"Catcher!" I screamed, as the walls of my vagina clenched and pulsed.

Once I came back down from the epic high, I found Catcher standing before me with a pleased smirk. After flicking his tongue, he said, "Pretty good, eh?"

I swept my hand to my forehead to push the sopping wet hair out of my face. "Oh, yes."

He grinned. "Come on. Let's get out of here before I take you standing up again."

I bit my tongue from protesting that I wouldn't have minded. I didn't care where we had sex as long as we had it. We could bang on the bathroom floor, and I wouldn't have cared. Hell, I would've ridden him on the toilet at that point.

Catcher turned off the shower and then helped me step out. I grabbed a towel and started drying off. When I finished, I picked up a fresh towel. I turned to Catcher and held out the towel. "Want me to dry you off?"

"I'd love for you to."

I began at his chest, doing wide sweeps across his muscles. The fact he had a dusting of dark chest hair that spread over his pecs and then down his abdomen to his happy trail sent a tingle between my legs. At the same time, I was grateful he didn't have a hairy back or ass.

When I grazed his erection with the towel, Catcher sucked in a breath. Instead of giving it any attention, I walked around behind him to dry off his back. I was surprised to find in the center of his back a tattoo of a heart, cross, and gun intertwined. "Interesting ink," I mused aloud, as I rubbed the edible dimples above his ass.

"I got that after I graduated from the GBI academy. It's something to represent who I am—a man of faith, heart, and honor. I guess the gun is an odd choice to be with the others, but it represented my career in law enforcement."

"I like it."

Catcher threw a glance at me over his shoulder. "You ever thought of ink?"

"Actually I have."

Grabbing the end of the towel, Catcher jerked me around to face him again. "Where."

"Well, not a tramp stamp."

He laughed. "You don't look like the tramp stamp type." His fingers brushed against the skin above my breast. "You're not one for a tit-tat either."

I wrinkled my nose. "No." I was about to add I wouldn't have one on my ass either when his fingers swept across my abdomen. "Here?"

My revived vagina wanted to scream, "No *here*!" so he would touch me there. Thankfully, I managed to get ahold of myself. "I was thinking my shoulder blade or foot."

"Good choice. Classy but sassy."

I laughed. "If you say so."

"Can I say suck my dick?"

I widened my eyes at his request. In my hesitation, Catcher added, "Maybe you want me to beg for it?"

"Maybe I do."

He took my hand in his and brought it to his throbbing erection. "Olivia, baby, will you please suck my dick? Will you please run your lips and tongue over it like your hand and

fingers are doing right now?"

I'd never felt such intense desire to go down on a man before, but with his deep voice, and his rock-hard cock in my hand, I was actually salivating. It wasn't so much that I wanted to suck his cock. I *needed* to suck his cock.

I licked my lips. "Yes. God, yes. Here?"

"Where do you want to do it?"

Well damn. No one had ever asked me that question before. Although I'd only had sex with two men, I'd given more than a few blowjobs in my college days. With those, it had usually been the guy unzipping before doing the head push in the dick direction. If they'd thrown in a grunt, it would have been a total caveman act.

"I want you to sit on the bed."

"Yes, ma'am," Catcher replied. He brushed past me to leave the bathroom. He went straight to the king-sized bed and plopped down. He then widened his legs to give me room to get between them.

"Nice presentation," I teased, as I padded across the carpet.

"Why, thank you. I must say the view you're giving me is pretty fucking amazing, too. I mean, that dress didn't leave much to the imagination, but damn, you have one fine-as-hell body."

Instead of wearing his compliment with pride, my face warmed. "You really think I have a good body?" I knelt down before him on the carpet.

Catcher reached out to stroke my cheek. "Baby, I know you do." He shook his head. "You must walk around with a bag over your head to go so long without sex."

"Whatever," I mumbled. After all the years of being the town's dateless wonder, it was almost too hard for me to comprehend a man as good-looking as Catcher could actually think I was sexy. But he wasn't just throwing out some pretty words to get in my pants. His tone and his expression appeared truly sincere. And it made sense to reason that if he truly felt I was hideous, he would have run for the hills after our Rusty Ho storeroom bang.

"I mean it, Olivia."

Holy shit. It was as if Catcher sensed my self-doubt, although I found it hard to consider given he barely knew me. Well, he did in the biblical sense, but not in the vulnerable, insecure, chick way.

Bolstered by his compliments, I took his erection in my hand. Bending down, I ran my tongue along the main vein on the underside of his penis. When I got to the head, I swirled my tongue teasingly around the tip before I sucked the head into my mouth. Catcher groaned and fisted my wet hair as I began sliding up and down on his dick. He was the biggest guy I'd given a blow job to, so it took a few seconds to get used to his size. I bobbed up and down, hollowing out my cheeks. After a few minutes, Catcher began lifting his hips to work himself faster in and out of my mouth. One of his hands

fisted the sheets while the other stayed in my hair.

His groans of pleasure fueled me on. Just as I felt him tensing up, he eased me away. "Don't wanna waste it," he mused breathlessly. He helped me off my knees and sat me down next to him on the bed before reaching for his pants. This time when Catcher dug a condom out of his wallet, he came back with a strip of three.

"Aren't we cocky?"

Catcher smirked at me. "You should know since you've had me in both your mouth and pussy."

I rolled my eyes. "I meant you're cocky to think we're going to need that many condoms."

"I like to keep you guessing." He leaned in to graze my bottom lip with his teeth. He then suited up in a condom. "I'm calling in that bottoms up from before."

"Huh?"

"When we were drinking earlier, I told you I'd have you bottoms up before the night was over."

"Oh yeah."

"So I wanna see that perfect ass in the air."

"As you wish." I grinned as I pushed myself back to the center of the bed. Then I rose up on my hands and knees. When I felt the mattress dip, I glanced over my shoulder to see Catcher scooting over to me on his knees. Feeling flirtier than usual, I swayed my hips back and forth. "Is this how you wanted me, Agent Mains?"

"Hell, yes." Catcher brought his palm down hard on one of my ass cheeks. I jumped at the pleasure-filled pain. When I stared back at him, he winked. "Thought I'd throw in a little S&M."

"I liked it."

Catcher's response was to smack my other cheek. Just as the stinging began to slightly wane, he slammed hard into me, causing him to grunt and me to whimper. After that first thrust, he brought both his hands to my hips. He began a punishing rhythm of slamming into me while jerking my hips back to meet him. If there were any cobwebs left, they were getting fully and thoroughly swept clean.

His hands left my hips to come to my shoulders. He eased me up to where I was sitting on my knees. He continued pumping in and out of me, but now he had access to my breasts and pussy. As one hand squeezed and kneaded my breast, the other went to tease my clit.

I dipped my head back for him to kiss me. *Damn, I loved his kisses.* His tongue swirled and danced with mine as his dick kept working its magic. I could feel another orgasm building. *Holy fuck. This is what I had been missing out on all these years?* After Catcher, I would never be able to go without sex six weeks, least of all six years. It wasn't long before I cried out as the third orgasm—yes, third—of the night came charging through me like a locomotive.

Catcher maneuvered my limp body around to lie me on my back. He gave me a sexy smile as he brought my legs up to rest on his shoulders. "Fuuuuucccck," he groaned when he thrust back into me. With a determined expression on his handsome face, he began pounding me relentlessly. We both cursed and groaned and moaned with ecstasy before Catcher's body tensed, and he came with a thunderous yell.

He collapsed onto the mattress beside me. His chest heaved as he fought to catch his breath. He swept an arm across his forehead. "Damn," he muttered.

"Yeah."

He propped up on one arm to stare at me. "That was seriously amazing."

"Yeah," I repeated.

Catcher laughed. "Is it always like that for you? You can be honest."

"Trust me, it's never been like *that* for me." If he only knew. Well, he knew about Eric, but that was only part of my sad sexual history.

Instead of the "I am the man" look I expected to flash in his eyes, Catcher appeared serious. "Same for me. There's something to be said for a chick who has gone without."

I snorted. "Thanks a lot."

He stroked his chin in thought. "But it must be more than that because even though the storeroom sex was hot, this was mind blowing."

"I thought so, too."

Catcher's intense gaze held mine as he searched my

eyes. "Olivia Sullivan, where have you been all my life?"

"Lost. Searching," I answered honestly.

Catcher leaned in to give me a lingering kiss. When he pulled back he groaned. "Damn that mouth of yours." He grinned. "One kiss and you've already got my dick up and running for another round."

"Really?" I nibbled my bottom lip as I worried about having sex three times in one night. I wasn't sure my vagina could take it. All I could picture was it starting to smoke from overuse, or it having an electrical surge and shorting out.

"I want you riding me this time with those perfect tits bouncing for me to see."

At Catcher's naughty words, my vagina pulled herself off the floor, dusted herself off, and got ready to ride again. Yippee-ki-yay!

CHAPTER

5

For the first time in my life, and hopefully the last, the sound of a rooster crowing jolted me out of a deep sleep. The grating noise sent me shooting straight up in bed. Frantically, my drowsy gaze spun around the room, desperately taking in my unfamiliar surroundings. The shitty polyester curtains, pressed-wood furniture, and the overall funky smell permeating the air meant only one thing.

I was in a cheap hotel/motel room.

And then as it hit me, a groan of shame escaped my lips. I slapped my hand over my eyes, trying to shield myself from the mortification as last night's events played through my head like an X-rated movie complete with the seedy bow-chicka-wow-wow music. I couldn't help wondering what the hell had gotten into me. Yeah, I'd been in a sex drought, but last week, I would have never allowed a stranger to take me home—well, to a hotel room. What made last night any different? Then I remembered my mother's lingerie shower, coupled with my talk with Jill, and I realized where things had gone wrong.

When I glanced over my shoulder, my mistake was stretched out on his stomach, his muscular arms wrapped around the pillow. His broad back rose and fell with lumbered breaths. Heat coiled between my legs with the sheet doing a provocative peekaboo with his delectable ass. It took everything within me not to pounce on him for another round.

A big O for the road. A farewell fuck. A "see ya never again" screw.

No, no, no. I couldn't do that. I'd been enough of a brazen hussy in the dark, but now in the light of day, I had to get a hold of myself and my raging libido. I silently thanked God Catcher was still asleep, and I could make a clean getaway.

With my limited sexual experience, I'd never dealt with a walk of shame in real life, but I had seen plenty on television and in the movies. I knew with my bird's nest hairdo from going to sleep with wet hair and outfitted in my sexy dress, I was going to look like the Queen of Walk of Shames.

Slowly, I started shimmying across the mattress. Once I got to the edge, I eased off the bed and dropped to the floor like I was in stealth ninja mode. I picked up my dress and threw it over my head. I gave a muted grunt as I fought with the tight material. As I rolled around on the floor, I probably looked like a caterpillar stuck in its cocoon. Or a sausage being stuffed.

The thought of a sausage made me think of the fine piece of Grade-A sausage that was just a few feet away. Ugh, I was seriously pathetic. I patted around the cheap carpet for my panties. And then I remembered what had happened to them the night before. RIP Victoria's Secret Chantilly Lace red thong.

When my hand reached out for my heels, an ache spread between my legs. Once again, a bow-chicka-wow-wow flashback assaulted my senses. I could see, and if I concentrated hard enough almost *feel*, Catcher's tongue sliding across the arch of my foot, sucking on my toes the same way he did my clit. I shook my head as the heat in my vagina spread through the rest of my body. If I let myself continue the stroll down memory lane, I would combust.

It took everything within me not to go jump Catcher. After I got myself together, I rose up from the floor. Catcher still slept soundly. As I gazed at him one last time, a different ache entered my chest. Besides the sex, I had enjoyed my time with him. He had been interesting to talk to—smart, funny, kind, and a king of addictive, filthy talk. Basically, he was everything I was looking for in someone to date. Unfortunately, that could never happen now because you just didn't turn one-night-stands into lasting relationships.

As I tip-toed across the threadbare carpet, I held my breath hoping with me being so close to a getaway, I wouldn't wake Catcher. When I finally stepped outside the hotel room, I exhaled in relief. I tucked my head to my chest, so I wouldn't have to meet any potential judging eyes. I even kept my resolve when the lady at the front desk called, "Good morning."

"Morning," I mumbled as I powerwalked by her and out the mechanized doors.

I didn't feel completely safe until I was locked into my car. Since I didn't want to give Catcher the chance to catch me, I gunned it out of the parking space. I kept a led foot on the two lane roads. When I got to the interstate, I glanced back into the rear-view mirror.

"Bye Catcher Mains. Thanks for the memories. And the laughs. And the mind-blowing and life-altering sex. And the five orgasms. But most of all, thanks for showing my vagina what it was born to do.

After getting home from Bumblefuck, I managed to shower

and get ready in record breaking time. When I finally wheeled into the funeral home parking lot, it was after ten. I powerwalked to the backdoor before plowing into the kitchen. I didn't want to have to deal with anyone until I had at least one cup of coffee, preferably two. Without proper caffeine consumption, I could not be held accountable for my actions.

I had just poured a steaming cup of Joe when a voice behind me caused me to jump out of my skin, sending scalding coffee onto my hand. "Shiiiiiit!" I screeched.

"Where have you been?" my mother demanded.

Ignoring her, I brought my hand to my mouth and sucked on the burning flesh.

"Olivia Rose Sullivan, you answer me."

I turned around to find her, hand on hips and sporting her most pissed-off expression. The worst part was the fact Pease stood behind her looking equally as pissed.

I sighed. "I'm not avoiding your question, Mama. I'm a little busy at the moment tending to the third-degree burn on my hand from where you scared the ever loving shit out of me."

"I must've called you ten times."

I'm pretty sure if my mother ever wanted a career change, she could find it in interrogating suspects for the government. She was seriously relentless. Forget forms of torture—she would just nag them to death. "I didn't answer the phone because I was trying to get ready for work, and I didn't want to be any later than I already was."

"You could have at least picked up to let me know you were fine, or you could have sent me a text. You can't imagine the horrible scenarios running through my mind at what could have happened to you."

"Once again, I'm sorry. It won't happen again. Okay?"

While my mother might have appeared satisfied with my apology, she wasn't quite ready to let me off the hook. "What happened to make you so late?"

I apathetically shrugged my shoulders. "Just overslept."

Mama's brows furrowed. "But you never oversleep—you're always early. That's exactly why I was so worried earlier."

Pease hobbled over to me. After giving me the once-over, she leaned in and took a giant whiff of me. A triumphant look flashed in her eyes. "Hot damn, you've been with a man!"

Her exclamation sent a jolt through me like I'd been tasered. I stood there with what probably was a total deer-in-the-headlights expression. "Um, excuse me?"

With a smirk, Pease replied, "Don't play coy. You heard me the first time."

After glancing between her and Mama, I shook my head. "I'm sure I don't know what you're talking about."

Pease huffed out a frustrated breath. "Trust me, I know the smell of sex."

"Ew. How is that even possible when I showered?" I blurted before I could stop myself.

"Aha. I knew it," Pease gloated as she snapped her gnarled fingers.

When I dared to look at my mother, she stared back at me with a puzzled expression. "But you were at the cabin until seven."

"I stopped at a bar to have a drink."

"With a side of cock," Pease replied.

I pinched my eyes shut and willed the floor to open up and swallow me whole. At my mother's strangled cry, I opened them. "You mean, you went home with some strange man?"

At that moment, I had a choice. I could lie and say I met up with an old college boyfriend or high school acquaintance. Or I could tell the truth and further horrify my mother. While she might've appreciated crotchless panties and body oils, they were only to be used within the sanctity of a relationship. No one would ever see her in pasties without a commitment. Her sexual ideas also extended to me.

I decided for today honesty would be the best policy. My breath exhaled in a nervous rush as I placed my hand on her shoulder. "Yes, Mama, I went home with a 'strange man'. Except I didn't go home—we went to the Holiday Inn off Route 53. And as the night progressed, he wasn't that much of a stranger—"

"I'd hardly say anyone you knew in the Biblical sense could be considered a stranger," Pease remarked.

After shooting her a look, I continued. "His name is

Catcher Mains, and he's an agent with the GBI."

My mother blinked a few times as she processed my words. "Will you be seeing him again?"

"I don't think so considering I snuck out this morning."

Mama sighed. "But why?"

"You really want me to answer that question?"

"Yes. I do. I never thought a daughter of mine would do such a thing."

Pease crossed her arms over her chest. "Oh lighten up, Maureen. It was a one-night stand, not armed robbery or murder."

Mama rolled her eyes at Pease. "I mean it. What if you get an FTD?"

"That's STD," I corrected.

She waved her hand. "Whatever." Her eyes widened. "What if he got you pregnant?"

"I might be sexually naïve, but I'm not stupid. We used protection, not to mention I'm on birth control."

Mama looked slightly relieved, but then her hand went to fiddle anxiously with her pearls. "Is this something you're going to be doing on a regular basis?"

I laughed. "No, Mama. It was a one-time thing—a way to put the past behind me."

"You just needed to scratch an itch, right?" Pease suggested.

"If you must put it that way, then yes."

A knock came on the kitchen door. I snorted

102

contemptuously at the sight of Brandon Jenkins, Taylorsville's newest Sheriff's deputy, standing in the doorway. Sweeping a hand to my hip, I narrowed my eyes at my mother. "You seriously called the law on me when I didn't answer the phone?"

She shook her head in protest when Brandon stepped forward. He took his hat off before speaking. "Sorry to bother you, Ms. Sullivan. But there seems to be a situation over at Mr. Dickinson's house."

I furrowed my brows in confusion. "A situation?"

Brandon's fingers played along the brim of his hat. "He's been murdered."

An incredulous chorus of "Murdered?" came from me, Mama, and Pease.

"Yes, ma'ams. It does appear that way."

I swallowed hard, trying to suppress the rising anxiety that tightened my chest. Taylorsville hadn't had a murder since the seventies, and that was back when Dwayne Bassey pulled double duty as the chief of police and coroner. Now it was all on my shoulders.

Mama swept a hand over her heart. "That sweet man. Who could possibly want to kill him?"

"Some disgruntled Medicare customer who was pissed they couldn't afford their medicine anymore?" Pease suggested.

Randall "Randy" Dickinson owned the only drug store in

town. He'd been the kindly pharmacist my mother consulted whenever Allen and I were sick. He also sang bass in the First Baptist choir. Although he was seen from time to time having dinner with some of the widows in town, he'd always been a confirmed bachelor, which was surprising since he wasn't a bad looking guy. If you put him and nine other men in town in a lineup, he would have been the last one I would have ever imagined being murdered.

After downing the rest of my coffee for fortification, I drew my shoulders back and got in the coroner zone. "You guys called the GBI?"

Brandon frowned and shifted on his feet. "Um, not that I know of."

"Seriously? You guys should know as well as I do that whenever there is a suspicious death the G-men are called in."

"Ralph coulda called it in while I was on the way here."

"Whatever. You can double-check on the way back to the crime scene." I turned to Mama and Pease. "Can you guys hold down the fort with Mrs. Laughton? Her family should be back at noon for today's viewing."

"As a proud member of PAM, I'm happy to serve," Pease replied with a grin.

I snorted. PAM stood for Professional Association of Mourners. It was an unofficial club that Allen had come up with for Pease's group of silver-haired ladies who considered it a good time to hang out at the funeral home. It didn't matter if they knew the deceased well or not. They still came and paid their respects as well as swiping some of the food that churches or family friends had provided. While it had started out as a joke, Pease's group had embraced it so much they had T-shirts made with PAM on the front and their names on the back.

I laughed. "I'm glad to hear it. Brandon, let me grab my bag, and we'll go."

CHAPTER 6

Randy Dickinson lived on five wooded acres on the outskirts of town. He had a beautiful cape cod with a wrap-around front porch. One side of his property met the banks of the Etowah River. As we made our way down the long drive, Brandon informed me that Randy was known to lodge a few complaints from time to time about people trespassing on his land to fish. I filed that comment away for future reference when it came to potential suspects.

When we pulled up in front of the house, I found Ralph Murphy, our local sheriff, and two of his deputies standing on the front porch waiting for us. Since I had called the GBI in the car, I hadn't expected to see any agents yet.

As I started up the front walk, Ralph came to meet me. He was the epitome of the stereotype of a small-town sheriff—kinda like Jackie Gleason's character in *Smokey and the Bandit*. Instead of thrusting out his hand, he pulled me into a bear hug. It was the kind of greeting you got when you lived in a town like Taylorsville, which was basically a modern-day Mayberry. "Morning, Olivia."

"Morning, Ralph. What happened?"

After spitting out a stream of shit-colored tobacco juice, Ralph shifted his chaw to his left cheek. "Well, around nine this morning, Blondine Cook, Randy's cleaning lady, arrived. Although she could see his car in the garage, the front door was locked. So, she used her key to get in. She went back to the bedroom to start cleaning, and she found him in the bed deader than a doornail. Gunshot to the chest."

"Got any idea of what kind of weapon we're looking for?"

"We were waiting on you to do measurements. But from the looks of the wound, it's a relatively clean shot in close range. Clearly it's not a shotgun. I'd guess a pistol. We haven't moved him yet to see if the bullet got lodged or exited the body."

I nodded. "Any idea how the suspect got in?"

"I had Frank and George checking the points of entrance and exit, and all doors and windows are locked up nice and tight."

"Hmm, the ol' locked room mystery rears its head."

"Huh?" Ralph questioned, his bushy brows creasing.

"Oh, you know how in old detective stories there was always a room locked from the inside, so how could the murderer or thief gotten in? The craziest one was in Poe's Murders in the *Rue Morgue* where he had an orangutan be the killer that got in through a window." When Ralph continued to stare at me, I waved my hand dismissively. "Never mind."

"It appears the security system was disarmed, too."

"So we're looking for somewhat of a professional."

"It would appear so."

Turning around, I peered at the gravel drive. "Any sign of footprints or tire treads?"

My question turned Ralph suddenly sheepish. "Oh yeah that." He scratched the back of his neck. "To be honest with you, we really hadn't thought of that yet."

While I could have let him squirm a little, I decided to let him off the hook. "No problem. That's probably something the GBI will want to look at."

Ralph's face appeared momentarily relieved that he hadn't screwed up the investigation, but then it clouded over. "G-Men are coming?"

I nodded. "I made the call on the way over here.

Thankfully, they had some agents in the area, and they were going to dispatch them here."

Ralph spit out another stream of tobacco. "Well, I ain't really a fan of the G-Men, but I guess it's good that we have someone more knowledgeable on the case. Hell, it's been twenty years since I've been involved in a murder investigation."

"At least you've been involved in an investigation first-hand. I've only witnessed them as an observer when I was in college."

"Well, let's don't let the G-Men show us up too much. I'll get my boys busy photographing the scene and dusting for fingerprints."

"Sounds good. Now let me get a look inside."

Ralph nodded and held the front door open for me. Before I stepped into the house, I traded my heels for tennis shoes and then put on the paper booties to cover them. Once I walked inside, my senses went on high alert as I took in the particulars of Randy's house. Even the smallest detail could mean something big to the case. The living area was gorgeous with floor-to-ceiling windows that faced the woods. If you looked closely, you could see the river in the distance.

The inside of Randy's house was warm and inviting, much like his personality. He owned several impressive pieces of art as well as oriental rugs and porcelain. Some of it surprised me since it seemed a little out of a small town pharmacist's budget. At the thought that Randy might've had a darker side, I couldn't help laughing at the absurdity of the thought. Since he never mentioned his family, he most likely had inherited the pieces or the money to buy them.

"Do we have a timeline of Randy's actions?"

Ralph nodded. "Somewhat. He closed up the pharmacy at six last night like usual. Then he stopped in at The Hitching Post to have dinner, which he does on the nights he handles closing instead of one of the pharmacy techs. Thelma said he left probably between seven and seven forty-five."

"So we're looking at anywhere from eight last night to this morning for a time of death?"

"Pretty much."

"Fabulous," I muttered. As I started out of dining room, the photographer's flashbulb momentarily blinded me. "Easy there, Newt," I said, as I fought the black blobs dancing before my eyes.

"Sorry about that, Olivia."

"Can I have you come back to the bedroom to photograph the body while I do my investigation?"

"Sure thing."

Newt and I were almost to the bedroom when I heard Todd call my name from the front door. "Back here," I called.

He came jogging down the hallway. "Hey. Your mother and Pease said that with Harry and Earl, they had the Peterson and Laughton visitations covered, and I should come here to be with you."

I rolled my eyes. Leave it to my mother and Pease to think my thirty-year-old self was incapable of handling my coroner duties. "Thank you, Todd, but I think I have it under control. And since the GBI will be taking Randy's body to the crime lab, I won't need the hearse for transportation."

Todd held up his hands in surrender. "Got it. You don't mind if I stay and watch do you?" Curiosity danced in his brown eyes. "I've never been part of a murder investigation before."

I smiled. "Of course, you can stay. I can use your help in a minute when it comes to turning Randy over."

"What about Ralph?"

With a roll of my eyes, I whispered, "He's always conveniently down in his back and can't help lift even a finger."

Todd chuckled. "Nice."

As I stepped into the bedroom, a coppery, metallic smell invaded my nostrils. It was one I had grown accustomed to whenever blood loss was involved in the death. I once again did a visual sweep of the room. The expensive TV and computer system remained in place. None of the drawers in the bureau had been disturbed or rifled through. It was certainly not a robbery-motivated attack. Since everything was meticulously in order in the bedroom, I felt it safe to assume there hadn't been a struggle.

When I walked up to the bed, it hit me how different Randy looked. Sure, he was going to look different considering he was dead, but it was more about how I was

used to seeing him. Gone was the crisp, white lab coat he sported over a button-down shirt and tie. In its place was a whole lot of pasty-white flesh. I never would have pegged Randy for someone who slept naked. He seemed more like the pajama type, even in summer.

I reached into my pocket and took out my voice recorder. After clearing my throat, I pressed the button and began speaking. "Today is February Eighth, 2015. Time is ten forty-five am. Victim is a male, Caucasian between sixty and sixty-five years old. Preliminary cause of death appears to be a gunshot wound to the left pectoral at close range. The wound is about an inch to an inch and a quarter in diameter."

I then turned my attention to reporting on Randy from the head down. After lifting one of Randy's eyelids, I said, "No signs of petechial hemorrhaging, so he wasn't choked or strangled before he was shot." As I examined the rest of his face, I didn't notice any cuts, scratches or bruising.

I picked up one of his hands and eyed it curiously. "No defensive marks or wounds." I massaged Randy's forearm before lifting it. "From the rigidity of the muscles and range of motion in the arm, the victim appears to be in peak rigor mortis." Rigor Mortis was an easy way for coroners to estimate the time of death. It usually set in two hours after death, and it reached its peak at twelve. By fifteen hours, the muscle fibers began to break down and would loosen up again.

I cut the recorder off and looked at Ralph. "He

obviously didn't put up a fight. From the looks of it, someone just came in and shot him after he'd gone to bed."

Ralph sighed. "If that's the case, I guess there are some small mercies in the fact he wasn't tortured or beat up. Maybe he never even knew what was happening. Just went to sleep and never woke up."

"Unless he woke up to someone standing over him with a gun, which considering the shot range wouldn't be surprising," Todd countered. When Ralph and I both looked at him in surprise, Todd gave us a sheepish grin. "Sorry. I watch a lot of *Law and Order.*"

"Yeah, well, they do things a little different up in New York City," Ralph said.

I lifted my gaze momentarily to the ceiling. I could tell the animosity rolling off Ralph toward Todd was about more than just a television show. Todd had grown up north of the Mason Dixon line, so to Ralph, he couldn't be trusted because he was a Yankee.

"Let's not turn this into a Yankee vs. Southern thing, okay?" I said.

"Whatever," Ralph grumbled.

"All right, let me check his lividity to see if I can pin down a possible time of death." Lividity happened when the body's blood supply stopped moving after the heart stopped pumping. You could gage how long someone had been dead by the way gravity caused the blood to settle. It presented in deep purple discoloration. Since Randy was lying down, I

would need to examine the blood discolorations on his back.

I reached to pull the sheet away from Randy's body when a male's voice boomed from the hallway. "Hello? GBI."

Ralph groaned. "Great the G-Men are here."

I wagged a finger at him. "Be nice. We owe it to Randy to find his killer by having a smooth investigation without animosity."

"I will as long as they are. But if they start that holier than thou bullshit, the gloves are coming off."

I didn't bother arguing with him anymore. Instead, I left Randy's bedside and started for the door. I got halfway there before I froze on the spot. Like I seriously looked like something out *Despicable Me* with the freeze ray.

When I was in second grade, I fell off the monkey bars. As I had lay in the grass, I'd tried desperately to catch my breath, but I couldn't. I had the wind completely knocked out of me. I had never experienced the feeling like a flattened tire because my lungs wouldn't inflate.

That's exactly the same way I felt when Catcher Mains waltzed through the bedroom door.

CHAPTER 7

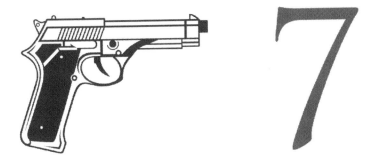

As I continued standing there like a statue, Catcher reached into his coat pocket for his badge. "Afternoon. I'm Holden Mains from the GBI and this is Elias Solano." He motioned to the tall, Latino standing next to him.

It was then as he gazed around the bedroom that he finally saw me. And then that smile—that drop-dead-sexy smile that had made me throw my inhibitions to the wind and my panties to the floor—stretched across his face and managed to de-thaw my frozen status. "Well, well, well. Olivia Sullivan. Fancy seeing you again."

Glancing between Catcher and me, Ralph questioned, "You two know each other?"

Catcher licked his lips. "Oh yes, I know Ms. Sullivan very well."

I shifted nervously on my feet. "Oh, I wouldn't say it was that well. We just seem to run into each other from time to time."

A wicked gleam burned in Catcher's blue eyes. "Yes. I would say it's been at least three times, wouldn't you?"

A strangled cry erupted from my lips at the fact he was alluding to the number of times we'd had sex last night. My mouth had already run dry with nerves, so it took me forever to find my voice. "Might I have a word with you, Agent Mains?" When I felt Ralph and Todd's eyes on me, I quickly added, "So I can discuss the case with you?"

He crossed his arms over his chest. "Sure. Go right ahead."

I narrowed my eyes at him. "Alone."

Catcher glanced at Elias and the others. "Agent Solano, while Ms. Sullivan is briefing me, why don't you talk with the officers?"

Agent Solano nodded. When we stepped into the hallway, I ran into one of the deputies dusting for fingerprints. "That room is clear?" I asked.

"Yep," he replied, as he moved on to the bathroom.

I took Catcher by the elbow and dragged him into the bedroom. After crossing my arms over my chest, I tilted my head at him. "What the hell are you doing here?"

"Um, I believe it's called an investigation."

"Don't be a smartass."

"I was just answering your question."

"Yeah, well, there's the fact that you didn't look too surprised to see me."

"You ran out on me this morning," Catcher accused.

I scrunched my brows in confusion. "Yes, I'm aware of that. But what does that have to do with you being here?"

"Everything."

After throwing my hands up in frustration, I glared at Catcher. "Why must you be so infuriating?"

"Because I don't like waking up alone after a night of amazing sex."

"Oh, really well—" I had already started to argue with him, but his reply stopped me cold. "Whether the sex was good is not the issue at the moment," I argued feebly.

Catcher quirked his brows at me. "Correct me if I'm wrong, but did I not give you—" He paused to wiggle his fingers at me. "Five orgasms over the course of the evening?"

Ah, that would be a yes. Five of the best orgasms of my life actually. I rolled my eyes at him. "You already know the answer to that, so why are you asking me?"

He grinned. "Because I just like to hear you

acknowledge it."

"Fine. You gave me five orgasms. Are you happy now?"

"No. Since my record was seven in one twelve-hour span, I'd like for us to get together again to see if I can beat it."

I wrinkled my nose at him. "You're seriously disgusting."

"And you're still avoiding the question."

"You answer mine first."

Catcher swept his hands to his hips. "Fine. I was working on my case when the call went out about a murder in Taylorsville. When I heard the name Olivia Sullivan mentioned, I had ulterior motives in volunteering to help out Agent Solano and his team." When he took a step towards me, I eased back until I bumped against the door. "The truth is I wanted to see you again."

"Because you've always been the first to run out after a one-night stand," I countered.

He shook his head. "Because I had a good time with you last night."

I couldn't tell him I had the best sex of my life last night. The same went for telling him what a good time I'd had with him outside of the storeroom and Holiday Inn bedroom I could, but it would only encourage him. There wasn't any joking in his expression either. I knew that face. Did he really want more? With *me*?

As my traitorous heart soared at his words, I gave a resigned sigh. "Last night was wonderful. It really was. But let's acknowledge what it was—a one-night stand." When he started to argue, I held up a hand to silence him. "I will always be grateful to you for ending my sex drought, but there's really nothing more."

"Bullshit."

"Excuse me?"

Catcher closed the gap between us, causing me to shrink back against the door. Suddenly, he was just too close, too built, and too sexy. If I didn't get out of there soon, I was going to end up mauling him for more sex.

"You and I both know that we had a good time outside of the sex," he stated determinedly.

"I usually don't rate dates on whether or not we win a bar fight."

Catcher's blue eyes flared. "You can't blame a groping redneck and hillbilly brawl on me. And deep down, you know that's not what made last night memorable. It was me fucking you up against the storeroom rack and then all over the hotel room."

At a knock on the door, I covered Catcher's mouth with my hand. "Yes?" I questioned weakly.

"Oh, I was looking for Agent Mains," Agent Solano said.

Catcher removed my hand from his mouth. "I'm in here, E."

"Look. I'm going to take Agent Capshaw and do a perimeter check."

"Sounds good," Catcher replied. At the sound of Agent

Solano's retreating footsteps, Catcher pressed against me. "There's not just a spark between us. There's a full-on raging inferno." He rolled his hips against mine. "Don't put it out."

It took everything within me not to attack his face with my lips and tongue. And I do mean every ounce of self-control. The man smelled mouth-wateringly delicious. The heat rolling off his body singed my exposed skin. I wanted to melt my body against him. Sans clothes. The truth was I didn't know why I was fighting him. Something within me just screamed "Caution" like one of those annoying flashing yellow lights.

When I shook my head, Catcher growled into my ear, which drenched my panties. "Dammit, Olivia. Why are you being so stubborn?"

"Look, I can't talk about this anymore." After prying myself away from him, I whirled around and fumbled for the doorknob. I fled the guest bedroom and started back into Randy's.

Unfortunately, Catcher was right on my heels. "This isn't over. Not by a long shot," he hissed behind me.

"Excuse me, but I have a job to do." I threw back at him. Ignoring the curious looks from Ralph and the others, I stomped over to the bed. "Newt!" I called.

I heard some hustling in the hallway before Newt appeared in the doorway. "Yeah, Olivia?"

"I'm ready for you to photograph the body."

"Sure thing. I got two more shots in the bathroom, and

I'll be right there."

"Fine." I grabbed the sheet bunched at Randy's waist and tugged it to the floor. The horrified chorus that rang around me sent me jumping out of my skin. My hand flew to my chest to still my erratically beating heart. While still rubbing my shirt, I glanced back at the others. They had all paled slightly and wore a look of horror on their faces.

"Sweet Jesus, Mary, and Joseph," Todd said while crossing himself.

"I'll be damned," Ralph muttered while Catcher merely blinked a few times. He appeared so shaken that he had lost the ability to form words. Ha, I bet that was a first.

Considering the trio consisted of a funeral attendant, a sheriff, and a GBI agent, I couldn't imagine what could have possibly freaked them out so much. I mean, they had to have seen their fair share of traumatizing things in their careers. And then when I looked down at Randy, I truly understood the horror.

Just like with Jesse's latex-allergy-induced eggplant dick, what I saw would haunt me for years. It would be one of those things that after you fluffed your pillow, snuggled under the cozy covers, and turned out the light, you would suddenly want to scream out in terror because it was emblazoned on the back of your eyelids. It was a vision all the bleach in the world wouldn't remove. It would be the thing when you were old and grey that strangers curiously asked if you really saw.

Like your own version of Big Foot or the Loch Ness Monster.

Protruding from an overgrowth of dark pubic hair was not one but two penises. I furiously blinked several times as if I could somehow wake myself out of my stupor of a bad dream. How was this even possible? Our victim, Randy Dickinson, mild-mannered pharmacist, civic volunteer, and bass in the church choir had two penises. Or was it peni? He was packing two schlongs, two meats and four veg, double dongs, a duo of dicks, a couple of cocks, twin trouser snakes, two tallywackers. I shook my head to try and get a hold of myself. I wasn't someone who was easily shaken on the job, but Randy and his two dicks had me absolutely gobsmacked.

Curiosity got the better of me, and I leaned forward for a better look. Although they began at the same base, they grew separate of each other. Neither one was circumcised, which considering Randy's age wasn't too surprising. I couldn't help wondering if they were both functional for urination…and for sex. How in the world does one have sex with two dicks?

"One in each orifice or maybe double-dicking one hole?" Catcher suggested.

Mortification filled me not only because I had somehow managed to verbalize my inner monologue, but at how Catcher had answered. I didn't want to imagine anyone "double-dicking" a hole, especially not Randy. It was hard enough picturing him having missionary sex least of all something kinky like that.

Damn. No wonder he had never married.

It was then I realized the others had crowded around the bedside to get a closer look at Randy's endowments. Both Todd and Ralph wore the same expressions of wide-eyed wonderment. I guess I couldn't blame them. Considering how men felt about their manhood, this would be like hitting the Powerball in the penis lottery.

Todd blinked a few times before asking, "Uh, Olivia, have you ever seen anything like that?"

"No. I haven't."

"Doesn't that—" Ralph paused to motion to Randy's crotch area, "have a name?"

"Diphallia," I replied at the same time Catcher said, "Freak."

I shot him a scathing look. "Don't you even have a shred of decency in you?"

He grinned. "Sorry. It got shot to hell the moment I saw the dude had two dicks."

Catcher's comment, coupled with the absurdity of the moment, caused the others to break out in hysterical laughter. I rolled my eyes at their antics. "Excuse me, gentleman, but regardless of the victim's endowments, I still have a job to do. So, if you'll please give me some room."

"By all means," Catcher replied.

"Thank you." Not wanting to appear weak in front of Catcher, I rolled Randy over myself. Once he was on his side,

I examined his back lividity. Here's some fun forensic facts for you. When a body had been dead between two and eight hours, you could press the skin, and the color would disappear. With a body that had been dead twelve hours, the color stayed. It was kind of crazy that poking around a corpse could reveal so much.

I pressed the four fingers of my right hand onto Randy's back. I was immediately met with the icy cold that takes over a body within one to two hours of death. The clinical term was Algor Mortis.

When I removed my fingers, the colored remained. I glanced back at the others. "We're looking at least at twelve hours."

"So maybe the murder took place sometime around nine last night?" Ralph suggested.

"Yes. Let me take his temperature." After I dug my thermometer out of my bag, I started to spread Randy's butt cheeks when Catcher stopped me.

"Do you seriously have to do that in his ass?" he asked with a disgusted look.

I rolled my eyes as I thrust the thermometer into Randy's rectum. "Yes, Mister Big Shot Agent Man, I do. Just like when you're alive, rectal temperature is the most accurate."

Catcher shuddered. "I've only seen it done under the arm when I've been on investigations in the past."

Choosing to ignore him, I focused on reading the

numbers. "He doesn't have two assholes, does he?" Ralph asked.

"No. Just the one."

I heard Ralph exhale in relief. In the first twelve hours of death, the temperature would decease 1.4 degrees Fahrenheit every hour while after twelve it went to .7 degrees. Once I measured Randy's temperature, I used the calculator on my phone to determine the equation. "Based on both Rigor and Algor mortis, I would guess the murder took place sometime between nine thirty and ten PM."

Both Ralph and Catcher nodded. "That gives us something to go on until he comes back from the crime lab," Catcher said.

When I eased Randy onto his back, a sense of déjà vu filled me when another horrified chorus echoed through the room. But this time, I screamed with them. Both of Randy's dicks were at full attention.

"Hold the phone. Is he not dead?" Todd demanded.

"Why he's deader than a doornail," Ralph replied.

Now that I'd had a moment to collect myself, I felt silly for my over-the-top reaction. "Postmortem erections, while rare, do occur."

Catcher shook his head. "I've seen people who shit and pissed themselves, but that's a new one."

"I guess when I put Randy on his side, the shifting lividity sent the blood forward to his penises."

After scratching his chin, Catcher asked, "So if they both got hard post mortem, does that mean they were both functional when he was alive?"

"I would assume so. But since blood isn't pumping through the cardiovascular system, it's hard to tell."

It was at that moment with the four of us standing around eyeing Randy's pumped up peckers, that Agents Solano and Capshaw came into the bedroom. Both of them skidded to a stop, their expressions frozen in disbelief.

"What. The. Hell," Agent Solano said while Agent Capshaw appeared to be trying not to vomit.

"You guys look surprised. Don't tell me you've never seen a dead guy with two hard cocks?" Catcher grinned, amusement dancing in his eyes.

"That would be not just no, but hell fucking no," Agent Solano replied while Agent Capshaw merely shook his head.

"Did you two find anything during your perimeter check?" Catcher questioned.

Agent Solano nodded. "Looks like the perpetrator came via the river."

"They did?" I questioned.

"There are disturbed places along the shoreline where a boat was kept. We found a few shoe prints that we'll make a cast of. I'll go get the kit and get started."

"Thanks, E."

Agent Capshaw picked up Randy's phone off the nightstand. "We'll need to take this with us to crack the combo

code to get into his contacts."

Catcher nodded. "Put it in the bag with the laptop and computer that Solano found in the office. We'll need to check all the files."

"Got it," Capshaw replied before starting out the bedroom door.

"Any idea about a next of kin?" Catcher asked.

Ralph adjusted his chaw. "That's a good question. I don't think I've ever heard him mention any family. He always closed up the pharmacy on holidays and went out of town. Where I have no clue."

Catcher nodded. "Did you check the nightstand for a little black book?"

"Although we didn't check, I'd be damn surprised to find one. Randy was not that type of man."

Catcher tilted his head at Ralph. "Considering the man was hiding two dicks in his pants, I think it's safe to say whoever you thought he was is a lie."

"Well, damn," Ralph muttered as the realization finally hit him. He proceeded to start rifling around in the nightstand drawer. "Aha!" he cried.

"You found a black book?" I questioned. I hoped it was something as innocuous as that. I didn't think my heart could take it if Ralph pulled out Randy's hot body oils collection or a pocket pussy. Well, I guess in Randy's case it would have been two pocket pussies.

"Actually, it's something better." He held up something that resembled a credit card. As I leaned forward to peer at it, I read *Emergency Contact Card.*

"Let me see," I said, holding my hand out. Ralph passed me the card. It looked like something that had come with a prescription, which made a lot of sense considering Randy's profession. After years of reading Randy's handwritten prescription instructions, I would have recognized his handwriting anywhere. He had personally filled out the particulars that he had no allergies or major illnesses. Under the person to notify in case of an emergency was:

Patricia Crandall.

1801 Bare Haven Dr.

Hawkinsville, GA

678-953-9451

Without hesitating, I dialed the number. Two rings in and I got an annoying monotone voice in my ear, causing me to grimace. "It's no longer a working number," I announced to the others.

Ralph snorted. "Why am I not surprised? This just keeps getting weirder and weirder. In all the years I've been in law enforcement, I think I've only had one or two cases where there wasn't a clear next of kin, and those were both indigents who ended up buried in the pauper's field out in Monroe."

I sighed. "It certainly has me stumped. I guess the only thing I can do it try to talk to this Patricia Crandall and see if she can make sense of all this." I looked at Catcher. "You G-

Men could do a reverse address to try find a current phone number, couldn't you?"

"Sure we could. But there's something even better you could do."

"What's that?"

"You can go with me to talk to Patricia Crandall."

I blinked at him. "Are you joking?"

"Nope. A hundred percent serious."

"What about Agents Solano and Capshaw?"

"What about them?"

"Doesn't protocol dictate that they should be the ones helping question Patricia Crandall rather than a small-town coroner?"

"I'll be the one interrogating Ms. Crandall. You'll simply be informing her of her obligations as Randy's emergency contact and next of kin. Besides, Solano and Capshaw need to be here working the scene."

After crossing my arms over my chest, I eyed him suspiciously. "Why do I think this is just a ploy to get me to be with you?"

Catcher appeared insulted. In a low voice, he said, "Surely you don't think I'm suggesting anything inappropriate, Ms. Sullivan?"

"Oh please."

He ducked his head to whisper in my ear. "Mmm, I do love when you beg."

I shoved him away. "Fine. I'll go with you to talk to Ms. Crandall. Since I need to know where to send Randy's body when he leaves in the crime lab in forty-eight hours, it's imperative to find his next of kin."

Ralph glanced between the two of us. "You sure you're all right going, Olivia?" He gave Catcher the stink eye. "I could always go in your place to talk to Ms. Crandall."

"Thank you for the offer, but I'm fine."

Catcher motioned to the door. "Shall we?"

"I need to finish up here."

With a nod, he said, "I can wait."

"Okay. Thanks."

I then went back to finishing up my investigation of Randy's body. The final part being that there was no exit wound. Therefore, the bullet was lodged somewhere in his chest cavity, and it would need to be recovered during the autopsy to help locate the type of gun used on him.

After finishing my write up, I turned to Ralph. "Can you wait with Randy until the crime lab arrives?"

"Of course."

"Thanks. I'll let you know what I find out."

"I appreciate it."

With Randy's Emergency Card in my hand, I threw my bag and purse over my shoulder and headed out of the bedroom with Catcher close behind me. After pounding down the front stairs, I walked over to Catcher's standard issue G-Man car. I was immediately assaulted by a flashback of seeing the car the night before when it was in the parking lot of the Rusty Ho. Not to mention the Holiday Inn.

As I buckled my seatbelt, Catcher cranked up and started down Randy's drive. "Poor fucker. He sure did have a nice house and land," he mused.

I peered curiously at him. "You like this?"

"Yeah. I do."

"Interesting."

"Why do you say that?"

"You don't seem like the kind of guy who likes roughing it out in the boonies."

Catcher chuckled. "Exactly what kind of guy would you say I was?"

"For starters, you seem much more urban."

"Do I?"

I nodded.

"And that's where you would be wrong, Miss Sullivan. I'm sure it'll surprise you that I live on two acres in Dahlonega."

"You do?"

"Yes, I do. Since I work out of the eighth district, our regional office is in Cleveland, so I wanted somewhere relatively close by." He smiled. "Not to mention that's where my family is from."

"So you have a house and not a condo?"

"Even better than having a house is the fact my brother

133

and I built it."

My eyes widened as this news was certainly unexpected. "How interesting."

"Yeah, I can't take all the credit. My younger brother, Jem, is a contractor."

"Jem? As in Jeremy Atticus Finch from *To Kill a Mockingbird*?"

Catcher grinned and bobbed his head. "Yep. Another one of my parents' favorite books."

"It's mine, too. My father was a huge fan. He always kept a copy in his desk drawer at the funeral home. Whenever business was slow, he would take it out and reread it. It was the only book I ever saw him reread. Well, except for the Bible."

"He *was* a huge fan?"

I bobbed my head. "He passed away five years ago. Pancreatic Cancer."

"I'm so sorry."

"Thank you."

Our once easy-flowing conversation became strained, like so many times whenever grief or loss was mentioned. Although the great equalizer, death was always the pink elephant in the room—the one sure-fire mood and conversation killer. Pun intended.

"So..." Catcher said breaking silence.

"So what?"

"Are you finally going to answer my question?"

I furrowed my brows in confusion. "What question?"

"Why did you run out on me this morning?"

I shifted in my seat. "Not that again."

"Oh yeah, that. And since we have at least half an hour in the car, I'm not going to let you avoid it again."

"You're such a pain in the ass," I grumbled.

Catcher turned to grin at me. "Come on, Liv. The truth shall set you free."

"Fine. If you must know, I was embarrassed."

"Of fabulous sex?"

With a roll of my eyes, I replied, "Last night was unchartered territory for me. I've never done anything sexual with someone outside of a relationship. Well, at least, several dates." I shook my head. "In the light of day, I realized what a mistake last night was."

"You seriously need to get your head checked if you think mind-blowing sex is a mistake." When I started to protest, Catcher held up one of his fingers. "So what if you didn't know me that well. You can get to know me before the next time."

"Next time? I think you're the one who needs his head checked if you think we're having sex again."

"Trust me, babe. It'll be on like Donkey Kong the minute I have you alone again."

"Did you honestly just compare our sex life to a video game?"

"Maybe." He turned and pinned me with his gorgeous baby blues. "Seriously, Olivia, I meant what I said about last night being special. I really do want to see you again and not just for sex."

I stared at him for a moment, waiting for the punch line or for him to say, "Psych!" But he didn't. I desperately tried to find a reason to tell him no. But I couldn't. My heart, mind, and vagina all pleaded with me to give Catcher a chance. Of course, I think my vagina was putting up the greatest argument.

My mind convinced me that the man was intelligent, driven, quick-witted, and pretty freakin' phenomenal in bed. My heart recalled his moments of absolute kindness and empathy, his defense of me at the bar. Those things were emotional kryptonite to a female heart. Especially one who had been through a dating wasteland.

And my vagina? That greedy little bitch had found the best piece in the candy store and definitely wanted another lick, suck, and swallow.

"So what do you say?" Catcher asked.

"Okay. Why not."

A pleased smirk curved on his lips. "I knew you wouldn't be able to say no to me."

Rolling my eyes, I shook my head at him. "You sure make a girl second guess herself."

He laughed. "My apologies, Miss Sullivan."

The GPS instructed us to turn off the main highway.

After we drove down a secluded road for half a mile, Catcher mused, "It seems one thing Randy and Patricia had in common is living in the sticks."

When we turned a curve, a guard shack loomed in the distance. "Hmm, a gated community. The plot thickens."

"Maybe it's some kind of resort."

"Maybe it's some kind of commune for genital freaks. Like there's women with three tits or something."

I rolled my eyes. "You have got to stop calling Randy a freak. He was a really nice man who deserves better than to be made fun of because of his special endowments."

Catcher held up his hand. "Fine, fine. I'll try to be more respectful."

"Thank you."

As he drove the car up to the guard shack, Catcher eased the window down and then reached into his jacket for his badge.

"Can I help you?" a man's voice asked.

"Yes, I'm Agent Mains of the GBI. We're here to speak with one of your residents—a Patricia Crandall."

When Catcher turned to flash his badge to the guard, he jumped in the seat. "What the fuck, man?"

I leaned forward to get a better look out the window. "Oh my God!"

For the second time in the last twenty-four hours, I had the *privilege* of seeing a man's junk. Well, the third time if you considered that I'd also seen Catcher's. Or was it the fourth since Randy had two dicks? Whatever the exact number, it had turned into an all-out penis-palooza.

The naked man held up his hands. "I'm sorry to shock you both. My apologies you were unaware that Bare Haven is a clothing optional resort."

"Excuse me?" Catcher asked

"You mean this is a nudist colony?" I questioned incredulously.

The man, who looked like he was wearing one of those fur vests from the sixties with all his chest and back hair, shook his head. "We really prefer you don't use the word 'colony'. It has such a derogatory feel. You know like a cult or something."

"I'll try to remember that," I mumbled in reply.

Catcher was handed a sheet of paper. "This is your guest parking pass. I'll radio the clubhouse and let them know you're coming. Ms. Crandall is one of our full-time residents. If she's home, they can have her meet you there."

"Thank you. I appreciate your help."

"No problem. Have a nice day."

"Same to you," Catcher replied before the car screeched away from the guard shack.

"Oh. My. God," I muttered.

Catcher snickered beside me. "Looks like we're not in Kansas anymore, Dorothy. We've entered the Bucknekkid City of   Oz."

CHAPTER 8

"Siri, play *Bad Moon* lby Creedance Clearwater Revival," Catcher instructed.

"*I see a bad moon risin'. I see trouble on the way.*"

I turned my head to cock my brows at him. "You really had to go there, didn't you?"

Catcher chuckled. "Of course I did."

As Jim Fogerty sang, we drove down the winding road leading into the resort. At the sight of two naked landscaping guys with leaf blowers on their backs, I shook my head. "I seriously cannot believe this."

Catcher cut his eyes over to me. "That places like this exist, or that Randy patronized them?"

"If I'm honest, I'd have to say both. I mean, I knew places like this existed. I just never imagined one practically in my backyard." I grimaced. "Right now, I cannot possibly fathom the idea of seemingly shy Randy Dickinson frolicking around here with his naked fanny showing."

"Don't forget his two dicks flapping in the wind."

I covered my face in my hands. "Ugh. Thanks for reminding me. I'm going to be haunted by that the rest of my life."

With a grin, Catcher replied, "Me too, babe."

"Babe?"

Catcher's brows popped up. "What? Are you one of those chicks who doesn't like terms of endearment?"

"No, no. I like terms of endearment."

"Let me guess. You're just not a big fan of 'babe.'"

I shrugged. "It's okay." What I wasn't able to say is that he continued to take me off guard by using terms of endearment so soon. I mean, we were just one day off a one-night-stand. I didn't imagine that sort of thing usually happened. At least he wasn't using the word in a demeaning way.

With a grin, Catcher said, "All righty then. *Babe.*"

I turned my attention away from him and back to the

140

road. Bare Haven's actual complex was about a mile down the road. It made sense that it was far off the beaten path to keep prying eyes away. When we came to a roundabout, we went to the right, which took us a sprawling clubhouse. I blinked a few times in disbelief because it resembled something you might see at a country club.

As I reached for the door handle, I drew in a few deep, cleansing breaths. After the crazy events of the past twenty-four hours, I could've used a Xanax the size of my head. It seemed wise to gird my strength for what further insanity I was about to be subjected to.

When we started down the sidewalk, a tall, lanky man with all his naked twig and berries glory came striding toward us. He thrust out his hand to Catcher. "Hello. I'm Barry Gideons—the day manager here at Bare Haven."

Catcher shook Barry's hand. "Holden Mains. GBI." He motioned to me. "This is Olivia Sullivan, Merriam County coroner."

Barry's smile faded slightly. "What brings you here, Agent Mains? Surely, we're not in violation of anything."

"No, no. It's nothing like that. I'm actually here as part of a homicide investigation."

Barry's gray eyes widened. "You are?"

Catcher nodded. "We need to speak to Patricia Crandall. She seems to be the victim's next of kin."

Barry swept a hand over his heart. "Oh poor Patty. How

terrible. I've already sent someone out to her condo to get her. Considering the news, let me go and meet her."

"If you don't mind, we would like to tell her the news ourselves." When Barry gave Catcher an odd look, he replied, "Just following procedure."

"Yes, of course. I totally understand."

When we reached the front door, a naked bellhop opened it for us. Considering he was young and incredibly built, I couldn't help staring at him as I passed by. Catcher snorted at what must've been my blatant ogling.

"Bite me," I muttered under my breath.

"With pleasure," he replied.

I shot him a murderous glare as Barry led us across the lobby and over to the bar. "Why don't you wait here for Patty?"

Catcher nodded. "Sure."

"And please have a drink on the house."

Catcher smiled. "Thank you for the hospitality, but I'm afraid I have to refuse since I'm on the clock."

I nodded in agreement. "But yes, thank you."

The phone he was holding in his hand rang. "Excuse me," he said before answering it. He grimaced. "Okay. I'll be right there." He hung up and gave us an apologetic look. "There's something I have to take care of in my office. But I'll be back just as soon as I can to check on Patty."

"We appreciate your help," Catcher replied before shaking Barry's hand again.

After he shook my hand, Barry headed barefoot and

bare-assed down the plush carpeting to his office. While Catcher quickly hopped up on one of the bar stools, I wrinkled my nose. "What is it?"

"I have two words for you: slug trail."

Catcher snickered. "I'm pretty sure they clean and disinfect the fabric."

Although he made a good point, I still took one of the linen napkins off the bar and draped it across the top of the stool. Once I was seated, I looked up to find the bartender staring at me. While he didn't look like he was judging me, I still managed to blurt, "Sorry. I'm just a bit of an OCD clean freak."

"Actually, we have a towel rule here at Bare Haven."

"A towel rule?" Catcher questioned.

"You have to place one down before you sit."

"Ah, I see," I murmured.

"Would you like something to drink?" the bartender asked.

"Water would be wonderful. Thank you," I replied.

Catcher shook his head. "I'm fine. Thanks."

When the bartender went to fill my request, Catcher grinned at me. "Throat run dry from staring at all the naked men? Or *nekkid* as we say in the South."

I rolled my eyes. "Oh please. It's not like I haven't seen a bunch of dicks in my day. When you've seen one, you've seen..." My voice trailed off at the sight of a twenty-something man coming toward us.

Catcher leaned forward and craned his neck to see where I was looking. "Well fuck me," he murmured.

"Not without a gallon of lube," I replied absently.

At the man's combined length and girth, I'm pretty sure my cervix shriveled up and died. Kinda like the scene in *Wizard of Oz* when the Wicked Witch of the East's feet curl up and go under Dorothy's house. I swallowed hard as I tried to fathom the logistics of how you would even begin to give him a blow job. Talk about "just the tip."

If the man realized we were staring wide-eyed and open-mouthed, he didn't let on. He just kept on walking. However that was even possible when he was weighed down with such a meatstick. "I wonder how he fits that into a pair of jeans?" Catcher questioned.

"Maybe that's why he lives here at the nudist colony. I mean, resort."

Our conversation was interrupted by an attractive, fifty-something woman walking up to the bar. Her chestnut hair was streaked with silver and reached the top of her breasts, which were remarkably perky for a woman her age. Of course, my attention was naturally drawn to the seventies porn bush she was sporting. Ladyscaping must not have been big around here. Guess they spent a fortune on vacuum cleaners to suck up the stray pubes.

She extended her hand. "Hello. I'm Patricia Crandall. Barry called and said you were looking for me."

Catcher shot off his stool and shook her hand. "I'm Holden Mains with GBI." I noticed he always used his given name of Holden, rather than his nickname, when he was doing business. Jerking his thumb at me, Catcher added, "And this is Olivia Sullivan, she's the coroner for Merriam County."

Patricia frowned as she shook my hand. "Isn't Taylorsville in Merriam County?"

"Yes, it is," I replied.

After sucking in a harsh breath, Patricia glanced between Catcher and me. "Has something happened to Randy?"

Sensing I was the one best to handle this, Catcher nodded his head at me. I cleared my throat. "Ms. Crandall, I'm very sorry to have to tell you that Randy was found dead this morning at his home. It appears to be a homicide."

Patricia swept one hand to her heart and the other went over her mouth. She shook her head furiously back and forth. "No, it can't be true. I just talked to him last night. We made plans for this weekend."

"I'm so very sorry." I motioned to one of the couches across from the bar. "Why don't you sit down?" I suggested.

Patricia's response was to burst into tears. I glanced around for some way to comfort her. "Catcher—erm, Agent Mains, why don't you grab Ms. Crandall a water?"

"Coming right up," Catcher replied before waving the bartender over.

Taking Patricia by the elbow, I led her over to the couch. Once she was settled, I reached into my purse for a handkerchief. Not only was carrying an embroidered handkerchief part of working in the death industry, but it had also been impressed upon me by my very manners-conscious Southern mother.

"Thank you," Patricia said when she took the handkerchief from me. She dabbed her eyes before staring mournfully at me. "I can't believe I just broke down like that."

"Please don't apologize. It's only natural when you've lost someone you love."

Tears once again overran her eyes. "I did love Randy. Very much. He's been a part of my life since I was eighteen years old."

"That's a long time."

"Yes, it is," she replied wistfully.

Catcher returned with a water for both Patricia and himself. After handing one to Patricia, he eyed one of the chairs beside the couch before sitting down.

"I have to be honest with you, Ms. Crandall—" I began.

"Please call me, Patricia."

I smiled. "Okay, Patricia. I've known Randy for twenty years, but since his death, it seems like I didn't know him at all."

A bark of a laugh came from her lips. "I'm assuming you mean you didn't know he had a—" she made air quotes with her fingers, "freaky side to him?"

"Um, well, I wouldn't exactly call it freaky," I answered.

"I would," Catcher replied, before winking at Patricia.

I shot him a murderous look, but Patricia merely giggled. "I'm sure it had to be quite shocking when you saw his endowments."

Shifting on the couch, I replied, "If I'm truly honest, I would have to say I was pretty surprised."

"I can't say I blame you. I was pretty surprised the first time I saw King and Kong."

Catcher snorted. "Excuse me?"

"Those was the nicknames he gave his penises."

Good lord, the man had actually named his dicks.

"I see," Catcher replied, amusement twinkling in his eyes.

"So you and Randy dated?" I asked.

"Oh, we more than dated."

"Considering you saw King and Kong, I assumed you did a whole lot more than dated," Catcher remarked with a smile.

Patricia shook her head. "No, I mean, we were married."

My mouth gaped open in surprise. "But in the twenty years he's been in Taylorsville, he never mentioned being divorced. He led everyone to believe he was a life-long bachelor."

"That's probably because we were barely married. We

were just a pair of twenty-year-old flower children who got hitched during the Summer of Love by some shaman. It wasn't even legal. But all these years later, he liked to call me his wife from time to time."

My mind tried to wrap itself around the image of Randy with long hair, wearing tie-dyed shirts, dropping acid, and saying "Groovy" while making a peace symbol. "Randy was actually a hippie?" I questioned incredulously.

"Yes. We both were."

"I apologize if that sounded like I was looking down on him or you. It's just Randy seemed a little too square, for a lack of a better word, to have been a part of the swinging sixties."

"Trust me. He did quite a lot of swinging. Two and three women at a time."

"Oh my," I murmured.

Patricia twisted the handkerchief in her hands. "His appetite was one of the reasons why we didn't stay together. I just couldn't keep up. I mean, King and Kong always seemed up for it, and there's only so much your orifices can take."

Catcher choked on his water, sending it spewing over his lap and onto the floor. Once he recovered from a coughing fit, he held up his hand. "My apologies."

As Patricia stared at Catcher in shock, I tried focusing her attention on me. "I can imagine that must've been difficult both for him and for you," I said.

Patricia looked from Catcher to me before nodding.

"Yes. It was. More so on me at first, but then when I went on to get remarried, it was hard for Randy. He experienced some dark years then when he truly began to despise King and Kong. He wanted more than anything to be normal."

"Do you think it could have been Randy's sexual proclivities that led to his murder?" Catcher questioned.

"No. Most of the people he was with were peaceful, loving people. Like myself, many were Buddhists who wouldn't believe in hurting a fly, least of all Randy."

"What about a non-peaceful person who was perhaps jealous of Randy's endowments?" Catcher suggested.

Patricia smiled. "While that could have been possible, I would seriously doubt it. Although he caused quite a stir when he first came here, people got used to seeing King and Kong." Patricia turned to me. "You know as well as I do what a sweet, personable man Randy was."

I nodded. "Yes, he was. It's hard for me to imagine anyone would want to kill him."

Catcher cocked his brows. "And you're sure he was completely honest with you about his sex life after the two of you broke up?"

"Even when I remarried, Randy and I were never truly apart. Although I remained physically faithful to my husband, I was emotionally unfaithful. Because of our relationship, I know without a doubt that he wasn't involved in something sexual I didn't know about."

"Can you think of anyone who might've had it out for him enough to want kill him?" Catcher asked.

Patricia nibbled on her bottom lip. I could tell immediately that while she might've had an idea, she was hesitant to say. Since I knew she loved Randy and wanted his killer found, I had to assume she was holding back out of fear.

"In many ways, Randy was the mild-mannered pharmacist who enjoyed singing in the church choir. It wasn't just a clever façade he concocted to hide his other side. It's just that his wild side was much more dominant. In fact, it often even bled into his professional life."

Catcher's dark brows knitted together. "How so?"

"Although Randy did well as a pharmacist, it didn't totally fund his lifestyle. He loved traveling to exotic locations like Bali and Tahiti. He started using his chemist skills with other avenues."

"Are you trying to say that Randy was selling drugs?" I asked.

"In a roundabout way, yes. But it wasn't anything like cocaine or meth. It was his own…concoctions."

"Concoctions?" Catcher and I both questioned in unison.

"He didn't like to tell me all that he delved in. By keeping me in the dark, he felt he could keep me clean in case there was any blowback."

"He was that worried about his safety?" I inquired.

"You must not have gotten a good look at his house.

That place is armed like Fort Knox."

"I did notice the extensive security cameras and door locks," Catcher said

"His need for excellent security was in part because of what he was into as well as how he was running away from his past. That's why he chose Taylorsville—he needed a small town to disappear in."

"So he had been making 'concoctions' for quite a number of years?"

"Yes. He had. Apparently, one of them went horribly wrong, and he had to disappear."

Catcher and I exchanged a glance. The fact that Randy was hiding out from someone meant a huge deal to the case. "He never told you any of the specifics about why he relocated to Taylorsville?" Catcher inquired.

Patricia shook her head. "It was one of the few secrets he kept from me. I think he felt it was protecting me in some way."

"Do you have any names you could give us who were clients of Randy's?"

"Zeke Chester. He's a deacon at the Full Zion Church."

Catcher's brows shot up in surprise. "Randy had a holy man on his client list?"

"I don't know many of the details. I walked in on a conversation a few months ago. Randy wouldn't tell me anything more than he had been working on something for

Zeke to be used in his brother, Ezra's, services."

Catcher scribbled his name down in his notebook. "Do you know anything else about this Zeke Chester besides he was a customer of Randy's?"

"Just that his brother has gained quite a following to his Friday and Saturday night tent revivals."

"You know a location of those tent revivals."

"Randy said they were forty-five minutes from here over in Dawson County."

Catcher nodded and then glanced up from his pad. "I appreciate you speaking with us, Patricia. If you remember anything else about Randy's concoction business, please let me know." He then reached into his suit pocket and produced a business card that he gave to Patricia.

I leaned forward on the sofa. "Before we go, I have to ask about Randy's next of kin. Do you know anything about his family?"

"He was an adult orphan—his dad died when he was seventeen, and his mother when he was twenty-three. His older sister lives in Tennessee, but they rarely saw each other. His family became our circle of friends."

"I see. Do you know if he had a will?"

Patricia nodded. "Yes. I have a copy of it at the condo somewhere. I'm the executor of his estate."

"Oh good. I was hoping he had left instructions of what he wanted when he passed away."

"Yes. It's all there from being cremated to having the

service here at Bare Haven's chapel.

"You have a church here?" Catcher blurted.

Instead of being offended, Patricia merely smiled. "We're not godless people, Agent Mains. We're just clothes-less."

Catcher returned her smile. "My apologies. This is all very new to me, but it's no excuse to show intolerance."

"Thank you."

I dug in my bag for the necessary paperwork for Patricia to fill out. "As the executor of Randy's estate, you can sign for me to release the body to the crematory. Of course, I'll need you to fax me over a copy of the will."

When I handed her the paperwork, she stared at it absently for a moment. Once again, tears began streaming down her cheeks. Tentatively, I reached out my hand to pat her shoulder. One of the first lessons I'd learned about the bereaved was not all people want to be touched.

But apparently Patricia wanted it. The next thing I knew she dove into my arms and began weeping inconsolably. It took a few moments to get my bearings since it was the first time I'd had a naked woman pressed against me. But any embarrassment I might've felt melted away, and all I could do was focus on giving comfort to Patricia. After all, she'd lost the love of her life unexpectedly and violently.

"Maybe you should get Barry," I whispered to Catcher.

He nodded before shooting off the couch. Like a mother

with her child, I rocked Patricia back and forth, speaking soothing words of comfort. Catcher returned with Barry, and he sat on the other side of Patricia on the couch.

"Patty? I'm here, sweetie," he said.

His voice seemed to cut through Patricia's storm of grief. She pulled away from me. Swiping her cheeks, she gave me an embarrassed smile. "I'm so sorry for falling apart like that."

"Please don't apologize. It's totally understandable given the news about Randy."

"You're very kind." She inhaled and exhaled a few deep breaths and then pulled her shoulders back. "I think I'm able to do the paperwork now."

I pointed to the paper on the table in front of us. "Just sign this." Once she scribbled her name across the form, I took the papers back. "Thank you."

Patricia glanced from me to Catcher. "You will find who did this, won't you?" Her chin trembled a bit, and I feared she might start crying again.

He gave a firm nod of his head. "Yes ma'am. We sure will."

"Good."

She rose off the couch and gave us a weak smile. "If you don't mind, I'm going to head back home. I need some time to process all this. And either a glass of wine or a Xanax."

Catcher and I stood up. "Of course. As soon as we know anything, we'll let you know," Catcher replied.

"I'll appreciate that." After shaking our hands, Patricia let Barry lead her down the hallway and out of the clubhouse.

When Catcher continued to stare thoughtfully after her, I asked, "You don't think she's hiding anything, do you?"

He shook his head. "No. She gave us all she had."

"Then why the stare down?"

A mischievous glint burned in his eyes. "I was just trying to imagine her, Randy, and King and Kong getting it on."

"You're disgusting," I replied, as I shoved my paperwork back in my bag.

"Oh come on. Don't tell me you weren't wondering about them?"

I slung my bag over my shoulder. "No. My mind isn't that warped." The truth was the thought had gone through my mind when Patricia was talking about how King and Kong were just too much for her.

Catcher grinned. "You're lying, Liv."

Once again, I wanted to throttle him and his special agent training. "Fine. Maybe I entertained the thought."

He laughed. "It's a hell of a thought to entertain. I'm pretty sure that today will go down as the craziest case I've ever worked on."

"I'm pretty sure I would have to agree with you," I said, as the naked bellhop held the doors open for us.

As we started to the car, Catcher asked, "Before King and Kong, just exactly what was the craziest thing you've ever seen on a case?"

I tilted my head in thought. "Probably when I was in undergrad at UGA and shadowing the Clarke County coroner." I opened the car door and tossed my bag inside.

"So what happened?" Catcher asked as he placed his elbows on the top of the car.

"We receive a homicide call to an apartment complex. When we get there, we find a male and female deceased in the bed. Blood is everywhere. It literally looks like that scene in *The Shining* when the elevator doors open, and blood comes flooding out."

"Jesus," Catcher muttered.

"Anyway, the bodies both have exit gunshot wounds, but for the life of the investigators, they can't find an entrance wound on the bodies. And I don't where the hell it came from, but suddenly, an idea pops in my head. Before I can stop myself, I blurt out, "Check their assholes."

Catcher snorted. "You did?"

I grinned. "Yeah, I did. A quick peek between the cheeks, and it turned out I was right. The murderer had stuck the barrel of the shotgun up their ass before shooting them."

With a wince, Catcher said, "That's one sick fucker."

"Turns out it was the woman's jealous husband. He came home from a hunting trip and found his wife and best friend screwing. He just snapped." I dropped down into the seat, and Catcher followed.

After he cranked up, he turned to me. "And I thought

my goat-fucking story was wild."

"Excuse me?"

He laughed. "I was part of a narcotics bust on this guy who lived out in the boonies. He was running a meth lab out of an abandoned travel trailer on his property. Anyway, we get there, and when we knock, the guy yells, "Just a minute. I'm almost there." Well, we all look around at each other like what the hell is he talking about? After a few more times knocking, we get the same response. So we end up having to use a battering ram on the door to get it down. When we get inside, we find the guy, high as a kite, and fucking a goat."

I gasped. "Oh my God. That poor goat."

"Exactly. So we're all standing there with guns drawn, and he just keeps nailing the goat. He almost got his ass shot off because he kept holding us off so he could come."

Slowly, I shook my head back and forth. "That is the most disturbing story I think I've ever heard."

Catcher nodded. "Yup, it was my second year out of the academy, and I can still remember it like it was yesterday."

"I can see why. Something like that would scar you for life."

"Kinda like Sir Randy of the Two Dicks."

I laughed. "Randy's case is shocking…I'm not so sure it would be as mentally scarring as seeing a guy violating a goat."

"You have a point there." Catcher glanced over at me.

"Speaking of Randy, I've been thinking about his concoctions."

"What about them?"

"I'm assuming Harry Potter must've had a place at his house where he was doing his potion making."

I nodded. "He certainly wouldn't have done it anywhere else than in the privacy of his home. Makes sense that his house was so secure. That way he didn't run the risk of anyone finding it."

"Except all that security didn't help him in the end."

"True."

"When we get back, do you wanna have a look at Randy's place with me? See if we can find his secret concoction lair?"

I whirled around in the seat to stare at him in surprise. "You want me to investigate with you?"

"Sure. Why not?"

"Call me crazy, but I just thought that was something for you and your fellow agents to do."

"Solano just texted me that he and Capshaw were taking the boot treads to the field office along with some of the other evidence they gathered today. Since it'll just be me, why not?"

"You won't get in trouble for having a civilian along with you?"

Catcher grinned. "But you're not a civilian. As the county coroner, you're a member of law enforcement."

"Oh yeah. Right." Duh. Why hadn't I thought of that?

Talk about a powerful penis presence. Being around Catcher was making my mind a scrambled mess.

When we approached Randy's driveway, a sheriff deputy's cruiser was parked in it. Catcher pulled up alongside and rolled his window down. When the deputy followed suit, Catcher flashed his badge. "Agent Mains, GBI. We're going to have a quick look in the house."

"Okay," the deputy replied.

Catcher rolled the window up as we coasted down the driveway. Although I normally wasn't one to be spooked, I was kind of glad it was still daylight. Sure, I'd had to go on body pickups and unexplained deaths after dark for both the funeral home and coroner's office, but there just seemed to be something a little creepier about this case. Maybe it was because Randy's house was so far off the road. Maybe it was because I'd never handled a murder case all on my own. Or maybe it was because of Randy's two dicks and an ex-wife who lived in a nudist colony, erm resort. Better still, there was the creepiness of his concoction making business. All of those maybes meant I wasn't too sure what other freakiness lurked within his basement.

As we pulled up in front of the garage, I saw where the yellow crime scene tape had been wrapped around the doors and front porch. After Catcher grabbed his kit from the backseat, we headed to the house. Catcher and I had to dip under the caution tape to get into the house. When we found the door locked, I asked, "Do I need to call Ralph to see about getting inside?"

Instead of answering me, Catcher took his wallet out of his back pocket and dug out a credit card. He stuck it in the doorjamb and jiggled it around. At the sound of the lock popping, he turned back to me and grinned.

"Impressive," I mused.

"I am a man of many talents."

"As well as an inflated ego."

Catcher chuckled as he opened the front door for me. One solitary lamp in the living room lit the way for us. "Since I didn't do the searching earlier, I'd wager the basement door is off the kitchen," Catcher said.

I had peeked my head in the basement door earlier in the day, but I hadn't gone all the way downstairs. "Yup. You're right."

"Lucky guess," Catcher said as we walked into the kitchen.

Just as my hand reached for the knob, the sound of the refrigerator door creaking open stopped me. I whirled around to see Catcher's head stuck inside. "Please tell me you aren't raiding Randy's fridge like some scavenger?"

Catcher peeked his head around the refrigerator door. "I'm starving."

"It's stealing," I countered.

With a scowl, Catcher replied, "Since he's dead, I'm pretty sure he's not going to be needing it."

"That's so unprofessional." I swept my hands to my hips and cocked my head at him. "Can't you get in trouble for that?"

A feeling of paranoia caused the hairs on the back of my neck to rise. I quickly glanced up at the ceiling to see if I could see any mounted cameras. Randy had been such a security freak I wouldn't have been too surprised if every room in his house was wired up. I exhaled a relieved breath when I didn't see anything.

"Jesus, it's not like I'm looting his house for electronics. I'm just making myself a quick sandwich. It's all going to have to be thrown out anyway."

"You're impossible."

Catcher's head disappeared back into the fridge. He returned with a container of luncheon meat and Coke. "For a skinny dude, Randy sure did eat a lot. He also must've spent some of his concoction money on food because he's got some highbrow shit in there."

"He does?" Although my stomach rumbled at the sight and smell of the turkey, I couldn't bring myself to eat Randy's food. I would just have to wait until I got home.

After tossing back a few slices of smoked turkey, Catcher replied, "Hell yeah. Imported cheeses and even some caviar."

I wrinkled my nose. "I hate caviar."

Catcher paused in rolling more turkey up and gave me a curious look. "Hmm, I would have never pegged you to be a connoisseur of caviar."

"When I was in college, I worked a side job waiting tables at the Athens Country Club. This guy I was crushing on dared me to eat some off one of the plates, so I did." I shuddered. "To this day, I could still throw up when I think of the way they popped and crackled in my mouth. Not to mention the crush never really gave me the time of day."

Catcher grinned at me as he finished off the turkey. "I, myself, have never had any, and after your glowing review, I think I'll pass on swiping one of the jars." He cleaned his hands with a napkin and then threw the turkey container away. After popping the top on the Coke can, he said, "And the guy you were crushing on was an absolute dick. One for being such an immature prick that he dared you to do something like that, and two, for not staking a claim on you the moment he met you."

I fought the urge to call for the smelling salts since I felt all swoony from Catcher's statement. Instead, a dippy smile formed on my lips. "Do you always flatter the women you're with?"

"Only if they're deserving."

Warmth rushed to my cheeks, and I quickly mumbled, "Thank you."

"You're more than welcome." After chugging down the Coke, Catcher let out the most unattractive belch before walking over to the basement door. "Ready?"

"As I'll ever be," I replied.

Once he flipped on the light switch, Catcher pounded down the stairs with me close on his heels. "Nice digs," he remarked.

The basement was one large room with only one door, which led outside and not to Randy's concoction lair. It was the epitome of a man cave with a giant-screen TV, a pool table, and even a bar. Of course, the two things that piqued my interest was one wall of floor-to-ceiling bookshelves and the 1950's era juke box.

As Catcher stood in the middle of the room, he scratched his chin. "There has to be a secret passage of some sort."

"The bookcase?" I asked, as I patted around some of the shelves.

"That would seem too obvious." He jerked a thumb at the massive oil painting on the wall. "Just like I'm sure that doesn't swing back to reveal a tunnel."

Since I wasn't entirely convinced, I kept shifting things on the bookshelf. Catcher went over to the light switch. When he plunged the room into darkness, I whirled around. "What the hell are you doing?"

Catcher took a flashlight out of his kit. "If there are cracks in the walls, they'll be easier to see with the lights off."

"If you say so," I replied uneasily.

It wasn't completely pitch black considering some light was creeping in through the one set of windows as well as the glass on the door. Catcher started focusing the beam of the flashlight on the walls. He covered the front wall closest to the stairs before walking over to the bar. "Did you know there are three parts to a bar?"

"Um, no. I didn't."

Catcher nodded. "The front, back, and under bar. The front is where your customers congregate and drinks are served. The back is where most of the bottles are stored along with a mirror. And then the under is below the front bar and where drinks are mixed."

"When did you become so knowledgeable about the interworking of a bar?"

"I did some bartending during my last year of college."

Catcher stepped behind the front bar. He started patting down the wall where the wood met the back bar. He gripped one of the ornate carvings and pulled, sending the back bar swinging out. Instead of a gaping hole in the wall, there was a door.

"Holy shit!" I cried, as I scurried over to join him.

"Eight years as an agent, and this is my first secret passage." He turned to me and grinned. "I feel like I'm ten and stuck reading some of the *Hardy Boys* mysteries at my grandparents' house."

I laughed. "I had some Nancy Drew forced on me as a kid, too. But it was more reading about the secret passage at Dawn's house in the *Babysitter's Club* books."

"Oh yeah, my little sister used to read those."

164

It was at that moment I realized Catcher and I were purposely avoiding entering the passageway. We just stood there in the doorway, staring down the length of the tunnel. "Guess we better check it out, huh?" I prompted.

"Yeah. I guess so." After digging out two pairs of rubber gloves from his kit, he passed one to me. Once we'd put them on, Catcher then reached over and flipped on the light switch, but nothing happened. "Dammit. The bulb's burned out."

But then we both still stood there, staring into the darkened abyss. When Catcher placed his hand on my shoulder, I jumped. "Ladies first," he suggested.

"Oh that's okay. You can go first."

"That would be ungentlemanly of me."

"Are you telling me that a strong, strapping GBI agent like yourself is scared of the basement?"

"I'm not scared of the basement. I'm just not a fan of creepy tunnels."

I snorted. "That makes you sound like a real pussy, Agent Mains."

Catcher scowled at me. "The truth is I get a little claustrophobic in confined places. It's not something I like to spread around since agents aren't supposed to have a weakness."

"Fine, fine. I'll go first," I said. After I drew in a deep breath to fortify my strength, I took a tentative step into the tunnel with Catcher close on my heels.

We'd crept a few feet when Catcher said, "This kind of reminds me of that scene in *Silence of the Lambs* when Jodi Foster is in the basement and Buffalo Bill turns the lights out on her."

A shiver ran through me. "You seriously had to bring that up *now*?"

Instead of answering, Catcher leaned forward and went "pffffffffft" in my ear like Lecter after his Chianti and fava beans line. I elbowed him in the ribs. "You're an asshole."

Catcher chuckled. "Sorry. I had to do something to get my mind off things."

"I could think of a thousand other ways to do that."

"Hmm, maybe a few hundred of those could be sexual?"

I rolled my eyes. "Spare me."

At the end of the tunnel was another door. Although I imagined it having some kind keypad and code to get in, I was shocked to find it unlocked. Considering both the tunnel and room were hidden, I guess Randy didn't think he needed to lock it.

When I swung it open, the fluorescent lights overhead flashed on, illuminating the four walls of the small, windowless room. In the center was a large table filled with different kinds of pharmaceutical tools like mortar and pestles and pill tiles. On one wall was a floor to ceiling shelf filled with different prescription bottles. Some were filled with pills while others contained liquid.

Catcher took a few in his hand, and we both peered at them. Instead of a having a person's name, they just had numbers written on the labels for identification. "I guess that's one way to keep things ultra-secretive," Catcher said.

"I wonder if he has the numbers written down with the corresponding drugs, or if he just committed all that to memory."

After looking at the shelf again, Catcher said, "Since there only looks like five to ten types of drugs, he most likely committed the preparation of them all to memory. Most likely this whole operation was based on memory. Without a paper or computer trail of ingredients or descriptions, he made it impossible for someone to steal his business. Not to mention if he was caught, it would make it hard on the authorities to prove what he was cooking up down here without extensive testing."

"Pretty ingenious," I remarked.

"It sure as hell was." Catcher reached into his kit and pulled out a few plastic baggies. "I'm going to take a few of these, so our lab can analyze them."

As Catcher bagged the bottles, I searched the room for anything else vital to the case like a record book. But I came up with nothing. Randy really ran a very tight and secretive ship.

"Okay. I think that's everything. Let's get out of here," Catcher said.

I nodded and followed him out of the room and down the tunnel. When we got back to the basement, Catcher took out his phone to call in what he had found to the GBI field office.

As he talked to one of his supervisors, I went over to the juke box. I ran my fingers enviously over the buttons. If I ever allowed myself to make an impulse buy, it would be for a juke box of my own filled with the oldies, especially Motown. It seemed Randy and I had similar tastes.

I had been so enthralled by reading the musical selections that I hadn't heard Catcher come up behind me. His voice caused me to jump. "I gotta go run these into the lab tonight since we have a technician working late."

My fingers hit the buttons before I turned around, and before I knew it, *Runaround Sue* by Dion began playing. "*Here's my story. It's sad but true...*"

Catcher groaned. "Of all the songs."

"You're not a fan of the oldies?" I asked while my heart shriveled a little.

"It's not that. It's just the song itself." He exhaled a deep sigh. "The girl who tore out my heart and stomped the poor bastard flat was named Sue."

Instantly, my interest piqued at the mention of the Ex Files. So far Catcher hadn't had too many specifics to say about his love life. I had begun to question if he had a love life or just a sex life.

"How old were you?"

"Twenty-two."

"Ah, just a baby."

"Pretty much."

Leaning back against the jukebox, I asked, "So what happened?"

He ran his hand over his face. "You seriously want to go there."

"I told you about my embarrassing past with Eric dying on me."

"Fine, fine. I found her in bed with some guy the night before I'd planned a romantic wedding proposal."

My mouth gaped open in shock. "You were that serious?"

Catcher gave me a rueful smile. "I thought we were."

"Damn. That sucks."

"Yeah, it does. Or it did. It's been ten years, and I've definitely moved on."

"I'm glad to hear that. I mean, that you've moved on, not that you had your heart broken."

"What about you?"

"Have I ever had my heart broken?" When Catcher nodded, I said, "Sure, I have but not from cheating." I gave a mirthless laugh. "It seems everything in my life is tied to death including my heartbreak. I don't know if I was in love with Eric, but it broke my heart when he died. Especially the manner in which he passed away."

169

Catcher grimaced. "That had to be horrible."

"Yeah. It was."

After tossing the samples on the pool table, Catcher held out his hand to me. "What?"

"Can I have this dance?"

I laughed. "You really want to dance with me?"

"Yes."

"In the basement of a crime scene."

"That would be a big hell yeah." He pointed at the jukebox. "No need to waste the opportunity."

Although we weren't in the best setting possible, the romantic possibilities of this moment weren't lost on me. So, I silenced my inner voices of doubt and slid my hand into Catcher's.

He tugged me to him before wrapping his other arm around my waist. We then began to bop around like we were at a sock hop or something. Seriously, that's the only way I can even begin to describe it. Catcher would sling me out and bring me back. As the song came to an end, he dipped me. I was out of breath from both our exertions and laughing.

When he pulled me back up, he ducked his head to bring his lips to mine. The record changed over to Smokey Robinson and The Miracles *You Really Got a Hold on Me,* and hot damn, if we both didn't get a real hold of each other. I slid my hands down Catcher's back to cup his ass while pressing my pussy against the ridge of his growing erection. He groaned into my mouth before bringing a hand to squeeze my

breast. Our grip followed suit when the song deemed, "tighter, tighter."

We staggered back to the pool table before collapsing on it in a tangle of arms and legs. Our mouths stayed fused together as our tongues slid in a tantalizing dance against each other. Catcher's hips pumped his erection against my core, and I could feel myself growing wet. Although it was morally and ethically *wrong* on so many levels and I should have been ashamed of myself, I wanted nothing more than for Catcher to fuck me on dead guy's pool table in the middle of a crime scene.

"Olivia?" someone called from the top of the stairs.

As I recognized Ralph's voice, I jerked my lips from Catcher's and tried desperately to catch my breath. "Yes?" I shouted back.

"I was just heading home when I got the call that you and Agent Mains were in the house. I thought I would stop by and see what you guys found out with Randy's emergency contact."

"Sure. One second and I'll come up." I pushed Catcher off me before scrambling to my feet. In that moment, I silently thanked the fact that Ralph was lazy or else he would've come down the stairs and caught Catcher and me in make-out city.

"I think he planned that," Catcher grumbled as he straightened his tie and shirt.

I stared at my reflection in the mirror over the bar. "Oh,

be serious."

"I am. I think he was on the way home when suddenly his cock-blocking senses went into overdrive. Interrupting us has nothing to do with the case, and everything to do with making sure no one is getting any."

I laughed. "It was a good thing he interrupted us."

"Blue balls and a shriveled erection are not good things, babe."

"It would have been bad for both of us to have gotten caught getting it on at a crime scene."

Catcher scowled. "I guess so."

"You know so. Now come on."

Reluctantly, he followed me over to the stairs. Ralph stood at the top, peering curiously at us. "What were you two doing down there?"

"Investigating Randy's hidden lair," Catcher replied.

Ralph's eyes widened as he stepped aside to let us pass. "What the hell does Randy have a lair for?"

"I'll fill you in on the way home."

"You will?" both Ralph and Catcher said.

I nodded. "Ralph can take me home since you need to run those samples to the lab."

Catcher's expression soured. I guess he had thought we could have a quickie after he took me home. "Peachy," he muttered.

I bit my lip to keep from laughing. "Give me one sec, Ralph. I need to get my purse from Catcher's car."

"Sure thing, Liv. I'll lock up."

As we walked out onto the front porch, Catcher gritted his teeth. "Epic cock-blocker."

"Would you take a rain check on what we started tonight?" I asked on the way to his car.

Catcher's brows shot up questioningly. "Really?"

"Of course."

A pleased smiled stretched on Catcher's lips. "Okay. I'll call you tomorrow."

"But don't you need my number?"

He winked at me. "I'll get it. I don't have access to cell phone records for nothing."

"That is totally stalker creepy."

Catcher laughed. "Talk to you later, Olivia."

"Goodbye, Agent Mains."

After I closed the door, Catcher took off, and I stood with a goofy smile on my face as I watched his tail lights disappear in the distance.

CHAPTER 9

Although only twenty-four hours had passed since Randy's death, it felt more like a week. Last night after I left Randy's house and Catcher, I had come home, taken a long, scalding-hot shower, and then fell into bed at seven without even bothering to fix dinner.

It had been my phone dinging, not my alarm, that had woken me up this morning around seven. After I rolled over and picked my phone off the nightstand, I almost fell off the bed when I saw it was Catcher, rather than a body pickup.

Mornin' Beautiful.

As I stared at the screen, my heart did a funny flip-flop that made me both giddy as well as contemplating making an appointment with a cardiologist. *Morning.*

Did u have sweet dreams of me last nite or nitemares of Randy's dicks?

I snorted. *No nightmares, thank God.*

No sex dreams either?

Sorry but no.

Such a pity.

Did u need me for something?

Nope. Just wanted to say hi.

Once again my heartbeat went kaka crazy. *Glad you said hi.*

Talk to you soon. Bye.

Bye.

Catcher's text had me on Cloud Nine for the rest of the morning. Now I found myself supervising Mrs. Laughton's funeral. Instead of the chapel at Sullivan's, the service was at the First Baptist Church.

The second minister had just stood up to eulogize Mrs. Laughton when my phone buzzed in my coat pocket. I quickly ducked out of the sanctuary to check my message. My heartbeat did its erratic flutter when I saw it was once again Catcher.

Need 2 check on holy roller lead 2nite. Can u come

with?

Hmm, he was actually inviting me to tag along for part of the investigation. That was certainly an interesting development. *Sure. What time?*

Pick u up @6 at your place.

K

I started back into the sanctuary when my phone buzzed again. "Oh God!" I cried at the sight of Catcher's erect dick pic. I jerked my head up from the phone and hastily glanced around. Thankfully, the hallway was empty, and no one but me had seen Catcher's throbbing member.

Seriously? I'm working a service!

I wish u were working me in & out of that delicious mouth of yours.

A squeak escaped my lips before I typed, *Catcher, please.*

Mmm, I like it when you beg. Would u let me cum in ur mouth? Or on ur fabulous tits.

His dirty talk sent a flush ricocheting over my body, causing me to feel scorching hot in more than just my face. I pressed my thighs tight together to try to relieve some of the growing ache between my legs.

Maybe u would rather me be working on u. Licking all the cream off that perfect, pink pussy.

"Mmm, oh yes," I moaned at his words and the visual. Then it hit me like a lightning bolt out of the sky where I was.

177

Although it wasn't in the Ten Commandments, I'm pretty sure, "Thou shalt not sext in the house of God," was pretty high up there on the list of no-nos.

Stop it.

That's not what u said the other nite.

Yeah, well, I'm not usually in a church's sanctuary!

Ever role play? I could totally play a priest, & u the innocent nun. Damn, I'm so fucking hard thinking about running my hand up under your robe & pumping my fingers in and out of you til u came screaming my name.

At that moment, I felt the flames of desire, rather than Hell, licking at my feet. But then I once again got a hold of myself. There were just somethings I could not do, and regardless of how hot it was, I could *not* sext while in a church. Least of all at a funeral. Not to mention one that I was in charge of.

Enough. Can't do this now. Talk 2 u later I furiously typed.

Fine. But wear a skirt. I wanna finger-bang you on the road.

Good lord, the man was relentless. Instead of responding, I shut off my phone and ended the temptation. I eased back inside the sanctuary. When I glanced up at the altar, it appeared the face on the massive stained glass Jesus was giving me a disappointed look. "I'm so sorry," I murmured to him.

A few people on the bench in front of me turned around

to peer curiously at me. Trying to save face, I quickly said, "Yes, I'm so, so sorry for your loss."

One of the women bobbed her head like she sincerely appreciated what I had said. When they turned back around, I rolled my eyes and exhaled.

It was then that Todd came from the right side of the sanctuary to join me. "Are you okay?" he asked.

"I'm fine. Why?"

"Your face is all red, and you seem to be out of breath."

"I'm fine," I reiterated.

I was so going to kill Catcher. Well, I would at least screw him again. Or maybe twice. I might even try to let him break his eight orgasm record on me.

Then   I   would   kill   him.

CHAPTER 10

After Mrs. Laughton's burial, I drove the hearse back to the funeral home to get my car. Since it was close to four and we didn't have any visitations that night, I locked up both my office and the funeral home before heading to my house to get ready for my date. I mean, I assumed it was a date. Of course, Catcher hadn't mentioned anything about getting dinner, a drink, or any of the other usual date-like occurrences. Just that he wanted me to go with him to check out this lead.

Oh and he wanted to finger-fuck me while we were on the road. Yes, I certainly didn't want to forget that little detail.

I took a quick shower before doing my hair and makeup. Since we would be outdoors at a tent service, I slid on a plum-colored silk blouse and paired it with a black skirt with a flaring hem that hit at my knees. With the February chill in the air, I put on a pair of thigh highs along with my black knee boots and pulled on my black jacket.

My doorbell rang just a few minutes before six, sending Motown into a barking fit. "Easy boy," I cajoled as I started down the hall.

After unbolting the door, I threw it open to find Catcher dressed to kill in a navy suit. My gaze dropped from his handsome face to his hands where he held a book, rather than a usual bouquet of flowers.

I crossed my arms over my chest and grinned at him. "Are you going to throw the book at me, Agent Mains?"

He smirked at me. "Not quite. I wanted to do something nice like bring you flowers, but I imagined that after working in a funeral home, you might get tired of the smell."

My mouth dropped open in surprise at both his thoughtfulness and insight. Whenever men had given me flowers in the past, I would merely smile and say thank you. The truth was I so associated the sickeningly sweet floral smell to my job that I hated to be around them anywhere else.

"You're right I do."

Catcher's face lit up. "I knew it." He held out the book to

me. "I thought you might like this better."

After taking the book, I glanced down at the cover. When I saw it was a hardback of *To Kill a Mockingbird*, tears stung my eyes as my hand flew to my mouth, which caused the book to fall to the ground. "Shit!" I muttered.

Catcher and I both leaned forward to pick it up and ended up bumping heads. "Ow!" I cried as Catcher said, "Fuck!"

With shaky hands, I picked up the book. Once again my vision blurred with tears as I ran my fingertips over the cover.

"It's a first edition."

I tore my gaze from the book up to him. "Catcher, this is too much. I can't accept this."

"Sure you can."

Holding the book out to him, I protested, "But this is worth a lot of money."

He waved his hand at me. "It's like a hundredth printing of the first edition. And it's not even signed. You probably couldn't even get a hundred bucks out of it."

Overcome with emotion, I threw my arms around his neck and squeezed him tight. When I pulled back, I gave him a long, lingering kiss. I then cupped one of his cheeks with my free hand. "From the bottom of my heart, thank you."

He grinned. "Hell, I'll give you a book a day if it means I'll get this kind of attention."

I laughed. "Do you have a never-ending pile of the

classics stashed away to woo women with?"

"Not exactly. My maternal grandmother was a librarian in Monroeville."

"Where Harper Lee lived?"

Catcher nodded. "You could say she got a little sneaky with the copies sometimes."

I laughed. "Are you telling me this is a hot copy?"

After Catcher took the book from me, he opened up the front flap. When I gazed down and read *Property of Monroeville Library*, I snorted. "Once again, I think our grandmothers would have been the best of friends."

"Probably so."

"Regardless of how you came to get the copy, I'm very grateful."

"You're welcome." With a wicked grin, he added, "Now why don't you show me again just how grateful you are?"

I smacked him in the chest with the book. "Nice try, but we have work to do, remember?"

Catcher groaned. "Being an agent is so cock-blocking."

"Come on in. I just need one second to grab my purse."

Catcher started into the foyer when a woof of greeting from Motown had him skidding to a stop. After getting a good look at the somewhat gnarly looking pit bull, Catcher took a step back. "It's okay. He won't hurt you."

When Motown gave a low growl, Catcher cocked his brows. "You sure about that?"

"Positive. Trust me, he's the biggest pansy and worst

guard dog ever. He just wants to lick you to death."

With apprehension in his eyes, Catcher stepped inside. He held out his hand for Motown to sniff. Instead of getting a whiff, Motown proceeded to lick and slobber all over Catcher's hand. Catcher grinned. "I think he likes me."

"He does. You would know it if he didn't."

"I thought you said he was a bad watch dog?"

"He is. When he doesn't like someone, he just pees on their leg and walks away."

"Wish I could do the same sometimes."

I laughed as I walked down the hall to the living room. After grabbing my purse, I came back to see Catcher sending Motown into doggy heaven when he started scratching behind his ears. "You know, I never would have imagined you with a dog like this."

"Why is that?" I asked.

"First off, you really seem more like a cat person."

I snorted and rolled my eyes. "Because I'm thirty and single aka a future cat lady in the making?"

"No. That's not it at all. You just seem like someone who likes small, cuddly things."

"Motown might be eighty pounds, but he's a real cuddle bug."

"Yeah, I also didn't see you as someone with a pit bull that looks like he's been through the wringer."

"He has. After he started hanging around at the funeral

home, I took him to the vet. She confirmed that he'd been used as a bait dog in a dog fighting ring."

Catcher's face clouded over with anger. "Bastards."

"If I had my wish, anyone who attended dog fights or participated in them would have a machine gun fired at their genitals."

With a bark of a laugh, Catcher said, "Easy there, Terminator."

I gave him a sheepish look. "Sorry. I tend to get a little violent about people who hurt animals, children, and the elderly."

"Don't apologize. I totally agree with you about machine-gunning genitals of abusers. It's just I'm not used to seeing all that rage come from you." He brushed his thumb across my cheek. "It was a little scary and a little sexy at the same time."

I laughed. "I think you're one of the few men who find my scary side even remotely sexy."

"They don't know what they're missing," Catcher replied.

As we stood there staring at each other, palpable electricity swirled in the air around us—the kind that made the hair on the backs of your arm and neck stand up. Even Motown sensed it because he came up and nudged his nose between us.

Catcher chuckled as he patted Motown's head. "Easy there, boy, I'm not trying to take her away from you. Can we

share?"

Motown glanced between Catcher and me before burrowing deeper between us. "Hmm, guess the answer is no."

"We should probably get going," I said. It wasn't so much that I cared about tracking down the Ezra and Zeke Chester lead as it was I feared if I didn't get some distance between Catcher and me, I would rip his clothes off and bang him on and off the furniture in my living room. There was also that nagging voice in the back of my head that it was about so much more than sex with the two of us. That we had a deep connection that had nothing to do with connecting my vagina with his penis. Although that part was certainly very nice.

After slinging my purse over my shoulder, I looked at Motown. "Be a good boy while I'm gone." He licked my hand in acknowledgement before grabbing his bone and hopping up on the couch. I turned to Catcher. "Ready?"

"Yup. Let's go get our holy on."

I laughed. "Fingers crossed that this is an uneventful evening."

Catcher snorted. "Babe, I think it's safe to say that there is not going to be anything uneventful about this case."

And once again, Catcher was right.

Ezra Chester held his tent revivals about forty-five minutes from Taylorsville. After getting off the interstate, we spent most of the drive on two-lane roads. It was fifteen minutes after we left the nearest town and any semblance of civilization that we came to our turn. Catcher grimaced the moment the gravel on the road started kicking up on the sides of his car, which I had been right in guessing was a convertible. It was a fire-engine red Mustang.

The road ended at what appeared to be some abandoned fairgrounds. There were so many people in attendance that the cars overflowed onto grass lot and were parked along the roadside. In the middle of the field, two giant tents had been erected. "Looks like quite the crowd," Catcher noted.

I unbuckled my seatbelt. "Yeah, well, Patricia did say he had a big following."

"My question would be how the hell does a guy like this get a following, least of all a big one? I mean, this doesn't impress me as the type of thing you advertise in the newspapers or on Facebook. And I didn't see any billboards on the way."

Catcher was right. The only advertisement of any kind had been the small signs that said *Tent Revival Ahead.* "I guess word of mouth," I replied, as I shut the door.

After coming around the side of the car, Catcher took my hand in his, which of course made me all goofy feeling, and we started walking down the road. We then cut through the high grass in the field.

Once we reached the tent, we found the rows of metal chairs had been filled, and it was standing room only. At the right side of the tent, a few musicians armed with banjos, guitars, and a fiddle were playing a hymn. In front of them was a small, wooden floor with a microphone stand in the center. Two middle-aged men in black suits with salt and pepper hair stood on the stage, surveying the people coming in. From time to time, the tallest one would throw up a hand in greeting and smile. Sometimes he would nod.

"I guess that's Ezra and Zeke Chester," I said to Catcher.

"It would seem so. With the tall one being Ezra. He seems to have that evangelist vibe about him."

I laughed at Catcher's description. A few minutes passed before Ezra walked over to the microphone stand. The buzz of conversation from the crowd began to die down. "Good evening, folks. It sure does my heart good to see so many of you have come out tonight. I hope each and every one of you gets an amazing blessing. First thing, I want us to get the service started by singing a song." He turned back to the musicians. "Boys, let's sing *I Saw the Light.*"

The guitar, fiddle, and piano struck up an upbeat tune. Almost simultaneously, people in the crowd started clapping and stomping their feet in time with the beat. "I wandered so aimless life filled with sin."

I jerked my gaze from peering at the front of the tent to

stare wide-eyed and open-mouthed at Catcher.

He turned to me and grinned. "What?"

"You're singing."

"Yes, I'm aware of that."

"You're good."

He winked. "Why, thank you. I excel at many things both inside and out of the bedroom."

After rolling my eyes, I questioned, "So how is it someone like you knows the words to this song?"

Catcher swept a hand to his chest in feigned indignation. "Are you insinuating that I'm not a spiritual person?"

"Maybe."

"I'll have you know when I was growing up, I was in church every time the door opened."

"Really?"

Catcher nodded. "And Bible school every summer."

"I'm impressed. What denomination?"

He quirked a brow at me. "Guess."

"Hmm, Baptist?"

"Close. Both my daddy and mama's families were sprinklers."

I laughed. "Ah, Methodist."

"Yup. What about you?"

"I'm a dunking Baptist."

"I would have probably guessed that."

"Do I have a Baptist look about me?"

"Not exactly. It's more about the fact you grew up in a small town in the Bible Belt. I'm sure Taylorsville doesn't boast many non-Protestant denominations."

"You'd be right."

The song came to an end, and Ezra once again took the microphone. "Once again, I just wanna thank everyone for comin' out tonight. It sure does my heart good to see so many God-fearing people with the desire to hear the preached word and to feel the Holy Spirit."

I jumped when the man beside me thrust his arm into the air and shouted, "Amen, brother!"

Ezra smiled at the man. "The Lord tells us not to have fear. It is because of my faith that I fear nothing. To illustrate to you how I'm truly under the protection of our Father, I will physically take up serpents."

It wasn't until that moment I noticed a box sitting at foot of the altar. I held my breath when Ezra threw back the cover. Then the air was filled with the distinctive clicking sound of rattlesnakes. "Oh my God, he's a snake handler!"

Snake-handling churches were something of a legend in the Southern backwoods. Since you mainly heard whispers about them, you started to even doubt their existence. The crux of the church doctrine being that people handled poisonous snakes to allegedly prove their faith. They took Mark 16:18 about "taking up serpents" a little too literally. If you held the snake and didn't get bitten, you got an A + for being faithful. If you did get bitten, you would get a big ol' F, and most likely you'd be hospitalized or die for your blatant lack of faith. Snake-handling churches were illegal in Georgia, and they had all but disappeared from sight. I had no idea any were still in operation.

Zeke paled slightly "I don't think you should tonight."

Ezra shook his head. "But where is your faith, brother?"

"It is with you as always. It's just I believe we should devote all our time tonight to the salvation of lost souls."

As Ezra started toward the box, Catcher leaned over to whisper in my ear. "Get ready. Shit's about to get real."

I shoved him away and shot him a disapproving look. "Don't curse in the house of the Lord."

"This is a tent, Liv."

"Same thing."

I couldn't argue with Catcher anymore. Instead, I was riveted by what was going on with Ezra and the snakes. Without a moment's hesitation, Ezra shoved his hand inside the rattling box. He whirled around to the crowd and thrust two snakes into the air.

"Oh, hell no," Catcher murmured under his breath. This time I didn't bother chastising him since he was echoing my particular sentiment.

The musicians struck up a fast-paced hymn, and Ezra danced around, swinging the snakes around in sync with the music. At the same time, his brother wrung his hands and wore a petrified expression.

Leaning over to Catcher, I said, "What's up with Zeke?"

"You mean is the fact he looks like he's about to shit himself with fear part of the show? Like to amp up Ezra's level of faith?"

"Exactly."

"If it is, he should win an Oscar for his performance. The dude is actually breaking out in a sweat."

With his back to the crowd, Ezra suddenly skidded to a stop. When he spun around, his face had contorted in agony. He stared at the congregation for a moment before his gaze dropped to his hand.

"Oh shit!" I exclaimed. The sight of one of the rattlesnakes fangs buried in Ezra's right hand had made me forget my resolve about not cursing in church.

A scream erupted from Ezra's lips as he flung the unattached snake in his left hand to the ground while he tried slinging off the attached one. The musicians cut the song abruptly short as they glanced around at each other.

"I don't understand. He's been bitten before," the man beside me said.

"He has?" I questioned.

The man nodded. "But he's never acted like that."

When Ezra staggered back, he tripped over the box of snakes, sending it toppling over. The altar became filled with slithering rattlers. Screams broke out then as people started turning over chairs to try to get away.

"Fuck this," Catcher said as he reached in his suit pocket. I widened my eyes when he produced not one but two pistols. He then started pushing and shoving his way through the crowd to get to the altar. Since I didn't want to lose him, I grabbed hold of the back of his suit and followed along.

When we reached the altar, Catcher began firing at the snakes in rapid succession. This caused even more pandemonium to ensue. As Catcher went Dirty Harry on the serpents, I ran over to Ezra who was still held prisoner by the rattler on his wrist. My gaze spun around for a weapon. I grabbed the microphone stand and then began beating the snake off of Ezra.

Thankfully, it released its fangs, and using the stand, I flung it over to where Catcher was doing his High Noon shoot-out.

I turned back around to see Ezra collapse onto the stage. I jabbed a finger at Zeke. "Call 911. *Now.*"

Zeke jerked his cell out of his pocket and dialed while I knelt down beside Ezra. "First off, you need to keep still. The less you move, the less the venom can spread."

He bobbed his head in acceptance of what I had said. "Ambulance is on its way," Zeke said as Catcher came over to us.

I looked up at him and Catcher. "I need a sling to tie around his arm to keep the wounds immobile so the venom can't spread as easily."

"Handkerchief?" Zeke suggested as he started to reach

for his back pocket.

"Too small."

The next thing I knew Catcher jerked off his suit jacket and tie before ripping off his shirt. Seeing his sculpted bare chest rendered me immobile like being shot with a tranquilizer gun. At the sound of my name, I shook out of my stupor. "What?"

"I said use my shirt."

"Oh, sorry. I zoned out for a moment."

"That seems to happen to you whenever you see me without a shirt," Catcher replied with a grin.

I narrowed my eyes at him. "I was mentally going over a checklist of what to do next."

"Sure you were."

"Whatever. Make yourself useful by folding that into a triangle for the sling."

While Catcher went to work, I took Ezra's arm and folded it across his chest. Once the shirt was ready, I slid it under Ezra's back and arm. I brought the ends together at his collarbone and then tied them. "Okay, that's all we can do for now. You'll have to get to the ER to be administered the antivenin."

"Okay. Thank you," Ezra said weakly.

"Should I pee on him?" Zeke suddenly asked.

Catcher stared open-mouthed at Zeke. "Have you fucking lost your mind?"

Zeke swept his hands to his hips. "Old-timers used to say pissing on snake bites helped to dilute the venom."

I shook my head. "Neutralization of venom by urination is just a myth."

"Thank God. The last thing I need to see is his dick," Catcher muttered.

Zeke opened his mouth to say something to Catcher, but he was interrupted by an ambulance's wail. It came tearing through the clearing, kicking up dirt and clumps of grass. It screeched to a halt to the right side of the tent. Catcher ran over to escort them over in the continuing chaos of the crowd.

Of course at the sight of the paramedics and their stretcher, the crowd parted like it was Moses with the Red Sea. I scrambled to my feet and got out of their way so they could start working on Ezra.

As they started an IV line, one of the paramedics glanced up at us. "We're just going to stabilize him here. We need to get him to the hospital as quick as possible so they can administer the antivenin. Who is the next of kin or power of attorney?"

Zeke raised his hand. "I'm his brother."

The paramedic nodded. "You can ride along with us if you'd like."

"I would. Thank you."

As the stretcher carrying Ezra was shuffled back to the ambulance, Catcher placed a hand on Zeke's shoulder. "I've got more than a few questions for you."

Zeke narrowed his eyes at Catcher. "And just who are you?"

After fishing his badge out, Catcher flashed it at Zeke. "GBI."

Zeke winced. "Follow me to the hospital, and I promise I'll answer whatever you want to know."

"I'm glad to hear that. I would've hated to have you arrested for obstruction of justice."

After giving us a sheepish grin, Zeke said. "Yeah, considering I'm on probation, that would have really sucked."

"And the plot thickens," Catcher mused.

"Yeah," Zeke replied. He gave a short wave before he hopped in the back of the ambulance. As the doors shut, the wail of the ambulance kicked up.

Catcher jerked his chin toward the hillside where we'd parked. "Let's get going. There's no one else here I need to question. Zeke and Ezra are the ones with the answers."

I nodded. Catcher and I weaved our way through the crowd of onlookers that were hanging around the edge of the tent. When they saw us, people stopped talking and stared wide-eyed. I guess Catcher's snake shoot-up had them a little shaken.

"Bless you, ma'am," an elderly man said.

The comment took me so off guard that I tripped over my own feet. "Um, thank you."

A heavy-set woman in a faded housedress stepped in front of our path. Her hands were clasped like she was about to start praying. "Might I touch the hem of your skirt?"

While slightly recoiling back from the woman, I glanced around the anxious faces. "I don't understand."

"The scriptures say that the woman with the blood issue was healed by touching just the hem of Christ's garment."

197

My eyes bulged at her statement, and I held my hands up. "I'm sorry, but you're mistaken. I don't have any mythical healing properties."

"But you saved Pastor Ezra from the serpents," a twenty-something looking guy in overalls protested.

"By using common medical knowledge that I learned in one of my college classes. I'm just a coroner." When they still stared earnestly at me, I shook my head. "Seriously. I just work with dead people. I've never been able to resurrect any of them."

My response didn't seem to sway the people's respect. I forced a smile to my lips. "We have to go now. But thank you."

I then started powerwalking away from the tent with Catcher on my heels.

Once we were inside the safety of the convertible, I reached over to lock the door before I buckled my seatbelt. Catcher chuckled. "Are you really afraid of those holy rollers?"

"Yes, as a matter of fact I am. We're talking about people who risk their lives by taking the Bible so literally that they physically handle snakes, rather than just symbolically."

"I don't think you had anything to worry about considering they were ready to worship you. I'm the one who should've been worried considering I've known you in the biblical sense."

"False religious adulation by whacked-out people is pretty damn scary. I mean, look at Jonestown and the Branch Davidians. Shit gets epically crazy when they realize that you're a fake and then turn on you."

As he pulled the car onto the road, Catcher reached over and took my hand in his. "Don't worry. I won't let the crazy Bible Thumpers get you."

I giggled while trying not to swoon like a lovesick school girl at his words. "Thank you."

He winked. "Anytime."

True to his word, Zeke was waiting on us outside the emergency room

doors. "How is Ezra?" I asked.

"Doctors haven't been out yet, but the paramedics told me while he has a rough twenty-four hours ahead of him, he should be fine." He smiled at me. "Thanks to you."

I held up my hands. "There's no need to thank me. I'm just grateful I paid attention in that seminar during my forensic science degree on wildlife injuries and deaths."

Since the waiting room was packed with people, Zeke gestured for us to go outside. We followed him out the mechanized doors and over to a secluded side of the hospital.

Catcher cocked his brows at Zeke. "Is all this secrecy necessary?"

"Yes and not just because I'm on probation." He reached into the back pocket of his pants and pulled out a pack of cigarettes. After we refused his offer of one, he lit up and took a long drag. He glanced left and right before exhaling a puff of smoke. "Our entire ministry is a lie."

"You don't say?" Catcher responded, amusement twinkling in his eyes.

"There's nothing spiritually different about Ezra. You see, all his life he's been a faithful guy. About fifteen years ago, he felt the calling to start preaching. He tried to start several churches, but they all eventually failed. It all boiled down to the fact there just isn't anything special about him. After visiting a snake-handling church, he decided that was his true calling." Ezra shook his head as he took another drag on his cigarette. "I tried 'til I was blue in the face to talk him out of it, but he was bound and determined to do it. As luck would have it, it was around that time I ended up being thrown in county lockup for public drunkenness."

Catcher snorted. "Nice."

Ezra stomped out his cigarette. "Hey, I never said I was the overly faithful one. You could call me the prodigal son at best."

"Gotcha. So what happened when you were in lockup?"

"I shared a cell with this guy who had been arrested earlier that night for public lewdness." At what must've been my curious expression,

199

Zeke said, "He was screwing women on a pool table at the local bar."

Heat flooded my face. "Oh," I murmured at the same time Catcher questioned, "Women?"

Zeke nodded. "Apparently, he'd done two already and had a line of volunteers waiting to be next."

"Interesting. And I have to say I'm on pins and needles to find out how the fuck this relates to a snake-handling ministry."

Zeke scowled at Catcher. "I'm getting there. Anyway, so after banging two chicks and being arrested, the guy is still hard as a rock. He tells me that it's this male enhancement drug he'd been using. It could keep him going for hours, not to mention it gave him an extra inch."

Catcher crossed his arms over his chest. "Really?"

"Yeah. Really. Since I'm curious about the product, I asked him where he got it. Said some guy he met at this nudist colony—"

"They actually prefer nudist resort," I argued. Both Catcher and Zeke shot me a look. "Sorry."

"Like I was saying, he'd been to a party at the nudist colony, and he met this guy who was a pharmacist and made his own drugs."

Catcher cut his eyes over to me before looking back at Zeke. "Did he mention what the guy's name was?"

"Yeah. He gave me his name and private number—Randy Dickinson."

My breath hitched at hearing Zeke speak Randy's name. I glanced at Catcher to see how he was going to handle this development. "Did you meet up with Randy to get some male enhancement?"

"I wasn't just interested in that. It was more about what Randy could do for the ministry. You see, I figured if Randy could make a man enhancer, then he might be able to make an antivenin, so that Ezra could handle snakes but not get killed."

Ah, now it was all starting to come together. "So Randy made you an antivenin?"

Zeke nodded. "The best part was he made it where it would be a

preventative measure, not after the fact. That way Ezra never knew. I just slipped a few drops into his water every day, and bam, he was good to go. When he started getting bitten and not dying, word grew of his gift. The crowds at the tent meetings doubled, even tripled, overnight. We started collecting lots of money in love offerings."

Catcher cocked his brows at Zeke. "I'm sure more money was spiritually rewarding for you."

"It's never been about the money for me—it's about Ezra's happiness." When Catcher gave Zeke a pointed look, he held up his hands. "Fine. I'd be a hypocrite if I didn't admit that the money was an added plus. But let me assure you that Randy's shit doesn't come cheap either."

"But if Ezra was taking the antivenin, why did he react the way he did tonight?" I questioned.

Zeke grimaced. "I ran out of antivenin two days ago. I've been trying to get ahold of Randy for two days, but he's not answering his phone."

"That's because he's dead," Catcher dead-panned.

After staggering back, Zeke clutched his chest. "Randy's dead?"

I nodded. "Murdered."

Zeke ran both his hands through his hair as he shook his head. "Holy shit. I can't believe it."

It was pretty clear at that moment that Zeke wasn't our killer. Neither was his brother considering Ezra had no idea who Randy was. Unless Zeke had any information for us, we were back to square one.

Zeke gave a mirthless laugh. "Without Randy, our ministry is screwed."

"Your ministry was screwed the moment Ezra's snake bite was called into law enforcement. They'll be patrolling the fairgrounds now to ensure you guys are closed down. In case you missed it, snake handling is illegal in the state of Georgia."

"Yes, I was aware of that. Ezra was always safe."

"Yeah, what about the kids I saw there? Were they drinking the antivenin too?" Catcher demanded.

Zeke averted his gaze to the ground. "No. They weren't."

"You seem like a nice guy, so I'm sure you wouldn't have wanted a dead kid on your conscious if one of the snakes had gotten away from Ezra."

"No. You're right. I get it. I guess I'll have to tell Ezra the truth," Zeke lamented.

With a shrug of one of his shoulders, Catcher said, "You could, or you could simply lead him to believe that the law will no longer allow him to handle snakes." At both Zeke's and my curious expression, Catcher added, "The man almost died tonight. Don't kill his faith as well."

While Zeke did a slow bob of his head in agreement, my amorous feelings for Catcher amped up a notch. How was it a good-looking, sex machine could have such a deep side? It was almost as much of a mystery as who killed Randy.

"Before we go, I need to ask if you know any of Randy's other clients?"

"Nope. Randy was really good about maintaining your privacy, which was a plus for me. In fact, all the bottles of antivenin just came with a number. My name was never on the bottle, nor was it labeled *antivenin*."

"And what number was that?"

"Seven."

Catcher scribbled that down on his notepad. "So you don't know anything about anyone else affiliated with Randy?"

After thoughtfully scratching his chin, Zeke replied, "There was this one time when I asked him how the hell he came up with all this stuff. He said he collaborated some with the Granny Witch Thornhill."

"A witch?" Catcher questioned, stilling his pen.

"Not a witch, but the Granny Witch Thornhill."

"All-righty then," Catcher replied. His tone alluded to how ridiculous he found the turn of the conversation. I couldn't blame him since it was all

too bizarre. I guess now we could add witches to the craziness of nudists and snake handlers.

"She's not a black hat and spells kinda witch. Granny Witch is the name given to mountain women who practice folk healing." At what must've been Catcher's and my blank expression, Zeke said, "You know, women who did midwifing or dowsing for water to make wells. They also delved in potions for healing."

"Since I grew up in Atlanta, I wasn't aware of any of that," Catcher said.

When he looked at me, I shook my head. "While I've heard of mountain folk healing, I haven't heard of the term 'Granny Witch'."

Zeke snorted. "Yeah, I should've pegged you two for city-folk."

I fought the urge to argue with him that Taylorsville was hardly a major metropolis.

"Just ask around for the Granny Witch Thornhill, and I'm sure you'll find her."

"With just that much to go on, I hope you're right," Catcher mused.

"If that's all for me, I better get back and see how Ezra's doing."

Catcher nodded. "That's it." He pulled one of his cards from his suit pocket and handed it to Zeke. "If you think of anything else, don't hesitate to call me."

"Sure thing." After putting the card in his wallet, Zeke smiled at me. "Once again, thank you for saving Ezra's life."

I returned his smile. "You're welcome."

After stuffing his hands in his pants pockets, Zeke ambled back toward the ER entrance. Catcher and I watched his retreating form until he got back inside. "I can't wait to tell the guys I'm working on a lead for a granny witch."

I tsked at him. "That would be *the* Granny Witch Thornhill."

"Isn't that what I said?"

"No. You left it way too common. Apparently this old biddy has a proper title like she's royalty or something."

Catcher snorted. "Mountain royalty I suppose."

My phone dinged in my purse. After I pulled it out and read it was from Allen, I grimaced. "Dammit."

"What's wrong?"

"I forgot it's my night to be on call for body pickups. We've had a death called in from Eastside Hospital back home." I quickly texted Allen that it would be a little while before I could get there, but I was on the way. "Sorry that I have to get back." What I really wanted to say was, "Sorry that I'm not going to be able to screw your brains out."

"No need to apologize, and no need to cut our evening short."

"What do you mean?"

"Well, why don't I come along with you to pick up the stiff? Then we can get some dinner." Catcher grinned at me. "After two dicks, a nudist resort, and snake handlers, I have yet to have the pleasure of buying you dinner."

I grinned. "Are you sure you don't mind?"

"Of course not."

"Okay. Sounds good."

Actually, it sounded a hell of a lot more than just *good*. I mean, here I was with a drop-dead sexy man who not only didn't find my profession abhorrent, but he was actually supportive. More than anything, he wanted to spend time with me. It was quite refreshing to find such a man existed. Catcher was truly turning into a man who was good for both the body and   soul.

CHAPTER 11

After we got home from the boonies, Catcher swung by the funeral home so I could pick up the hearse. As he opened the passenger side door, Catcher chuckled. "What's so funny?" I asked, as I slid across the leather seat.

"The fact I'm about to take a spin in a hearse, and I'm not dead."

"Yeah, I guess it is a little weird the first time."

"Your dad didn't drive you around in this, did he?"

I laughed. "God, no. It was bad enough being the girl with dead people in her house. The last thing I would have needed was to be the girl with dead people in her car."

Catcher snorted. "I see your point."

Eastside Hospital was a quick ten minute drive from the funeral home. Compared to the hospitals in the bigger cities like Marietta and Atlanta, Eastside was pretty small.

I pulled around back to the loading dock. "You can wait here if you want," I said, as I grabbed my identification badge out of the dash.

"And miss seeing you in action? Ha! Never."

I grinned. "It's really not that exciting."

"Anything with you is exciting, Olivia," Catcher said sincerely, which when spoken in his sinfully, sexy voice sent my heart beating erratically and caused me to feel lightheaded.

Without my normal elegance, I stumbled out of the hearse. After recovering, I went around to the back and opened the door, pulled out the gurney, got it upright, and then locked it in place. With what felt like rote movements, the wheels rattled along the pavement as I approached the backdoor. I gripped the rails on the gurney so it wouldn't go careening away as I rang the bell. The last thing I needed was to make a fool out of myself in front of Catcher.

"Yes?" a voice questioned.

"Olivia Sullivan from Sullivan's for a pickup."

The door buzzed open, and I rolled the gurney in with

Catcher on my heels. After following the maze of hallways to the elevator to the first floor, I picked up Mr. Marvin Delaney—a stroke victim who had been brought in to the ER earlier that day.

I was greeted by Marco—one of the orderlies. He had started work about six months ago, and he had always been really nice to me. He was probably what you would call nerdy cute with his thick glasses but a built body.

"Hey Liv, what's shaking?" he asked, flashing me a grin.

"Not much, Marco. What's up with you?"

"Same old, same old." At the sight of Catcher standing behind me, his smile faded. "Got a new apprentice?" he questioned, a hopeful lilt to his voice.

When I opened my mouth to introduce Catcher, he stepped in front of me. He thrust his hand out a little too forcefully. "Catcher Mains."

"Marco D'Angelo."

"And I'm not a new funeral home apprentice—I'm Olivia's boyfriend."

What. The. Fuck. I stared at Catcher in absolute shock at the fact he had referred to himself as my "boyfriend." I mean, we hadn't actually been on a real date yet. I couldn't bring myself to consider our meeting at The Rusty Ho as a date. Sure, we'd spent a lot of time together in the last two and a half days, but it was in the pursuit of a murderer.

I wasn't the only one staring at Catcher in shock. Marco wore the same deer-in-the-headlights expression as I assumed I did. Finally, he shook his head like he was shaking himself out of a stupor. "Hey man, that's great."

"I like to think so."

As the tension grew in the air, I put the brake on the gurney. "I guess I better get Mr. Delaney."

When I started to slide the sheet under Mr. Delaney to do the transfer from the bed to the gurney, Marco jumped forward like he usually did. "I'll get that, Liv."

Before he could, Catcher knocked him out of the way. "I got it."

Once again, tension crackled in the air so thickly that you could almost hear the hum. Although I didn't think Catcher had any experience with body transfers, he managed to do a great job getting Mr. Delaney on the stretcher. After buckling him and putting on the drape, I turned to look at Marco who was staring daggers at Catcher with his arms crossed over his chest. "Um, I guess that's it. Good seeing you again, Marco."

Instantly, his expression changed from sullen to smiley. "It was good seeing you too, Liv. Always a pleasure."

At the word "pleasure", Catcher stiffened next to me. I decided it was time to get the hell out of there. "Okay then. Bye," I said before promptly banging the gurney and poor Mr. Delaney into the wall. "Oops."

It then took me a few seconds of maneuvering to get myself out of the corner. "You got it?" Marco asked.

"Oh yeah. I'm fine," I quickly replied before he and Catcher had a chance to trade evil looks.

When I got out into the hallway, I exhaled the breath I had been holding. "Need me to get that?" Catcher asked when I once again banged the stretcher into the wall.

"Nope. I've got it." *Get a grip, Sullivan. You're making an ass out of yourself. You haven't done the stretcher shuffle since the first summer you worked for your dad.* After inwardly berating myself, I was able to make it down the rest of the hallway without any further incidents.

After rolling the gurney onto the elevator, I turned back to see Marco standing outside Mr. Delaney's room. He threw up his hand and smiled.

"Bye," I replied, which caused Catcher to growl.

When the elevator doors closed, I turned to glare at Catcher. "What the hell was that about?"

Catcher stared straight ahead. "What do you mean?"

"Um, the fact that for a minute, I thought you might go all Motown on me by pissing on my leg to show possession."

Catcher snorted before cutting his eyes over to me. "I was not as bad as your dog."

I cocked my brows at him. "Seriously?"

"That douchebag was totally scamming on you."

"Marco was not scamming on me."

"Get serious, Olivia. The guy is probably going to jerk one out in the bathroom over you."

Wrinkling my nose, I replied, "Ew. I seriously doubt that."

"Are you really that blind?"

I shrugged. "He was just being nice. Marco's always been very friendly and helpful."

"Yeah, so he could get in your pants."

I widened my eyes. "No. He so doesn't think of me that way."

"Oh yeah, he does." Catcher shook his head at me. "No wonder you were in such a sex drought. You can't pick up when a man is coming on to you."

"I hardly think that Marco was trying to come on to me when I was picking up dead guys."

Catcher snorted. "Babe, as long as we're not dead or our dick's not dead, we're going to pick up a woman regardless of the situation."

The elevator door dinged open. "And that's why men are pigs."

"Hey, don't shoot the messenger."

Ignoring him, I then rolled Mr. Delaney through the hallways and out to the hearse. Catcher stood by ready to lift a hand, but it was as if he sensed I wanted to do it on my own, so he didn't interfere. The fact that he got me—the real me—was very endearing. For the first time, I felt like I had a met a man who was strong enough for me. As the strains of Sheryl Crowe's *Strong Enough* played in my head, I closed the gap between Catcher and me.

I raised my hand to cup his cheek. "You know, you were kind of a Neanderthal back there, which is terribly unattractive to a feminist like me." When he started to protest, I put my finger over his lips. "But by the same token, I've never had a man who cared enough about me to be so aggressively possessive. And God help me, I liked it. I liked it a lot."

A smirk curved on Catcher's face. "You did, huh?"

"Yeah, I did."

"Well, that's just who I am, babe. An overly possessive alpha male that borders on being a caveman." With a grunt, he brought his hands to my breasts. "Mine."

I laughed as I pushed his hands away. "Stop before someone sees us."

"If you think storeroom sex is hot, you should try al-fresco-hospital-parking-lot-sex."

"No thank you. The last thing I need is to be involved in a sex scandal. That would be the final straw for my mother."

Catcher laughed as he started around the side of the hearse. "Fine. I'll be a gentleman and preserve your virtuous reputation."

"Thank you, kind sir," I replied with a grin.

When we got back to the funeral home, Catcher surprised me by following Mr. Delaney and me to the door. "What?" he asked at what must've been my shocked expression.

"Nothing. I just thought you would probably wait in your car for me."

"No way. I want to see the inside of your place."

I laughed. "My place is five minutes down the road. This is just where I work."

"You grew up here though, didn't you?"

"Yes, I did."

"Can I see your teenage bedroom?"

"Why on earth would you want to see that?"

"In a way it would be like an anthropological dig. I could see who you were back in the day."

"Trust me, you wouldn't find it interesting."

Catcher waggled his eyebrows. "The part where I fantasized about a young, curious girl discovering herself would be."

I wrinkled my nose. "Ew, that's disgusting."

"My fantasy or you getting yourself off?"

"The fantasy."

"Ah, so you're admitting that you got yourself off back then."

Ignoring him, I unlocked the back door and pushed the gurney inside. "Oh come on, Liv. Be a big girl and admit that you diddled yourself back in the day. Buttering your biscuit as a teenager is nothing to be ashamed of. I was twelve the first time I spanked the monkey."

I glared at him over my shoulder. "Would you please have some respect for the dead? I don't think it's too much to

ask for the words "diddled" and "spanked the monkey" not to be spoken around Mr. Delaney."

Catcher grinned. "Ha, that's just an excuse to avoid the question."

"Whatever," I mumbled. After easing Mr. Delaney into the first prep room, I walked into the second prep room to turn up the freezer. I would keep him on ice tonight until I could talk to his family or next of kin about their wishes for burial or cremation. Once the temperature was adjusted, I opened the freezer door and leaned in to see the fan had started cooling.

The next thing I knew Catcher grabbed me by the waist and jerked me back against his hard body…and his hard cock. He buried his head in the crook of my shoulder and licked a fiery path from my collarbone up to my ear. "What the hell are you doing?" I demanded.

"I would think it would be self-explanatory that I want to fuck you."

"H-Here? N-Now?"

"Hell yes."

One of Catcher's hands slid up my ribcage to cup my breast. My traitorous body instantly responded to his touch. "Do you have some kind of necrophilia fetish that you haven't told me about?" I asked as I tried to ignore my hardening nipple.

He chuckled. "No, babe, I don't. It's more about the fact when you leaned over just now, I not only got a fabulous view of your ass, but you're wearing those sexy-as-fuck thigh highs."

"So it's a pantyhose specific fetish you have?"

I gasped as Catcher's other hand dipped between my legs. "Yeah, it is."

Since the funeral home was empty without any visitations and Mr. Delaney was hanging out in the other room, I decided to give in and have hot, dirty sex. Catcher's sexts from earlier coupled with the way he had kissed me in my foyer had been like an extended foreplay through the evening. I reached behind me, cupping the growing erection in Catcher's pants. He groaned into my ear.

Just as I started working him over his slacks, he whirled me around. His hands came to the buttons on my blouse. After fumbling unsuccessfully for a few seconds, he jerked the fabric apart. I gasped as the buttons went flying through the air. I narrowed my eyes at him. "You ruined my shirt."

"I'll make it up to you with an extra orgasm."

I grinned. "Deal."

My bra was jerked away with the same desperation as my shirt. Catcher dipped me back as his mouth closed over one of my nipples. "Hmm," I moaned, my hands jerking through his hair. God, the man had a mouth like a Hoover. When his lips went to my other nipple, his hands slid down my ribcage and came to the hem of my skirt. He jerked it up over my waist before tearing my panties down my thighs.

When his hand cupped me between my legs, I moaned.

His fingers tapped over my clit like he was doing Morse Code before he thrust two of them deep inside me. "Oh fuck, Catcher," I groaned.

"Does that feel good, baby?" he asked, his breath scorching against my neck.

"Yes. Oh yes."

"After you come, do you want me to eat your pussy or put my hard cock where my fingers are?"

Hmm, decisions, decisions, decisions. As I bit down on my lip to keep from shrieking with pleasure, I glanced at the doorway. So much for worrying about Mr. Delaney hearing "diddled" and "spanked the monkey." Mr. Dirtytalk was putting that to shame.

I gripped Catcher's shoulders so tight I was sure I would leave marks. I panted and whimpered as my hips moved frantically to rub my clit against Catcher's hand. And then my body tensed as I came hard. "Catcher!" I screamed.

He brought my mouth to his for a lingering kiss. He didn't remove his fingers until my walls had stopped convulsing. His fingers then went to unbutton and unbuckle his pants.

I gave him a lazy smile. "I guess this means no oral satisfaction, huh?"

Catcher shook his head. "I've got to get inside you, or I'm going to explode."

I couldn't argue with that one. Catcher glanced wildly

around the room before grabbing me under my ass and hoisting me up onto the empty gurney. He bent over to retrieve his wallet from his pants that were now around his ankles. After grabbing a condom out, he tossed his wallet behind him.

He opened the condom and slid it on in record time. The next thing I knew he was filling me with his masterful dick. When he thrust into me a second time, his foot hit the lock on the brake, sending the gurney careening forward. Each time he pounded into me, the gurney went gliding further around the room. As we banged, we banged into walls and the furniture in the prep room.

Although the scenery wasn't the most romantic or seductive, it didn't take away from the sex. It was just as amazing as in the storeroom and at the Holiday Inn. There was something almost mystical that happened when Catcher and I got together. Like a seismic shift occurred when our bodies were connected. Everything around us melted away to where we were the only people in the world.

Of course in this instance, I wouldn't have wanted anyone else to see us like this. Not only we were screwing a few feet from a dead guy, but I'm sure we looked pretty ridiculous doing it. You had me flung half-way across a mortuary gurney with my skirt hitched around my waist, shirt ripped open, with my legs spread as wide as my semi-physically fit body would allow.

Then you had Mr. Alpha Male with his navy blue suit

pants bunched around his ankles with his delectable ass full mooning, his belt clanking along the floor with every awe-inspiring thrust into my pussy while at the same time attempting to reposition me and the gurney.

Pretty sure we would never make it into a movie sex scene. Instead, it probably would find a home in some weird fetish porn.

"Oh God, I'm coming again!" I moaned into Catcher's neck.

"Me too, babe. Let's do it together."

As our bodies shuddered and convulsed, we rode out the high together. When Catcher fell against me, the stretcher lurched forward one last time. That was when I felt something ice cold press against my butt cheek.

"EEEEEEEEE!" I screamed. In my pleasure haze, I didn't realize that Catcher had fucked us into the other room and bumped the gurney with Mr. Delaney on it. Somehow Mr. Delaney's arm had fallen off the table. With the beginning of rigor mortis, it had stretched out straight, instead of falling down.

And Catcher last thrust had propelled me to the back of gurney, causing Mr. Delaney's hand to brush against my bare ass.

I began flailing my arms and kicking my legs to get the gurney to move. When it didn't budge, I scrambled away, shoving Catcher off me. With my skirt pushed up over my hips, I then did a heeby-jeeby dance around the preparation room. "Ew, ew, EW!"

"Babe, what the hell? You totally just killed my post-fuck buzz." Catcher stood facing me with his pants around his ankles, and his deflated, condom-attired penis against his thigh.

I rubbed my ass cheek as if I could rub off the ickiness of having a corpse cop a feel on you. Sure, I had brushed up against the dead before and during preparation, but I had on my work apron and gloves.

After glancing back and forth between Mr. Delaney and me, Catcher finally burst out laughing. "Did you just get goosed in the ass by a dead guy?"

"It's not funny."

"Actually, it kinda is."

"Yeah, I'd like to see how much you'd like it," I grumbled while pulling my thong back on. I then shimmied my skirt back down my thighs. As I started to put Mr. Delaney's hand back on the gurney, I froze, holding it in midair

"What is it?" Catcher asked.

I glanced up from Mr. Delaney's hand to look at Catcher. "His fingernails have arsenic lines."

His eyes widened as he closed the distance between us. "Holy shit. Poisoning?"

"See the wide, white lines in his nail beds."

Catcher leaned over and examined Mr. Delaney's hands. He let out a low whistle. "I'll be damned."

I shook my head dejectedly. "I can't believe I didn't see it before."

"It wasn't like you were answering a call for a suspicious death. Hell, the hospital didn't even notice it."

"He was probably just exhibiting signs of a stroke brought on by the poisoning. If they even saw the early lines, they would've probably just thought it was a lack of oxygenation."

Jerking his chin at Mr. Delaney, Catcher asked, "What do you know about him?"

I shrugged. "Nothing really. I've never seen him before tonight. He must be new to town..." My voice trailed off as my hand flew to my mouth. "Oh my God. Mr. Delaney had something to do with Randy's murder, didn't he?"

"I'd say it was pretty fucking likely." Catcher started straightening his clothes. "I've got to call this in—get the guys figuring out what connection Delaney could possibly have to Randy."

"Of course."

He grabbed his suit jacket off the floor and dug his cell phone out of it. He started punching numbers but then stopped to look at me. "This weird ass turn of events means I'm not going to get to take you to dinner tonight."

"That's okay. I understand."

Catcher gave a frustrated shake of his head. "No, it's not. I've had you four times now and have yet to buy you dinner."

I laughed. "You bought me tequila at The Rusty Ho."

"It's not the same."

I pressed myself against him and wrapped my arms around his neck. "You truly are a gentleman for worrying about buying me dinner, did you know that?"

He grinned. "I'm glad you realize that."

"Of course banging me on a gurney in a funeral preparation room might knock your status down just a tad," I teased.

Catcher held up one of his hands. "Scout's Honor that I will only bang you in the sanctity of a bedroom from now on out."

I laughed as I played with the hair at the base of his neck. "I'm not sure that's an oath I want you to make."

His brows popped up. "Oh really?"

"We might lose some of the fire if we took out the scenery spontaneity."

"Hmm, you might have a point there." He dipped his head to kiss me. "I sure wouldn't want us to lose any of the fire."

"Me either."

"Okay then. I think I see a way to make this up to you."

"And what's that?"

"Come hell or high water, I'm taking you to dinner tomorrow night."

"Okay."

"Where's the nicest place around here to eat?"

My mind immediately thought of The Distillery, a steak and seafood place on Main Street. But close on the heels came another thought about how conspicuous it would be to eat there with Catcher. Since most of the town dined there at least once a week, they would be all about the fact I was there with a man. I could just feel the stares and hear the whispered conversations behind lobster tails, or one of the older men shouting over his prime rib, "Damn, Olivia, I thought we'd never see you with a man."

I shuddered at the thought. "Um...we really don't have a lot to choose from here. Why don't we go out of town?"

"I've got an even better idea. I'll cook you dinner."

I widened my eyes at him. "You cook?"

"Yes ma'am, I do."

I grinned up at him. "You really are a man of many talents."

Catcher chuckled. "Damn right I am. But I do have an ulterior motive in cooking for you."

"And what's that? You're secretly cheap?"

"No, Miss Sassy Pants that's not it. I really want to show you my house."

"You do?" I asked breathlessly. My poor senses were on overload after he said he wanted to cook for me. Throw in the fact he wanted me to see his house, and I was close to throwing a hand against my forehead and swooning.

"Yeah, since my brother and I built it, I'm kind of proud of it."

"So what time should I come to your house?"

"Let's really make this a date, and I'll come pick you up."

"But don't you live like forty-five minutes from here?"

"I can make it in thirty-five," he replied, with a teasing glint in his blue eyes.

"Fine. You can pick me up."

After one final kiss, Catcher started for the door. "See you tomorrow at five."

"I'm looking forward to it."

Catcher threw a wink at me over his shoulder. "And I'm looking forward to having you for dessert!"

CHAPTER 12

The next day found me slammed with work at Sullivan's. We were holding Mr. Peterson's services in the chapel, which were to be followed by the procession to the National Cemetery in Canton where as a World War II veteran, he would be afforded military rights. Since it would be an hour back to get home, I was going to be pushing it to meet up with Catcher. It was one of those times that I really lamented the fact that I was the one in charge and couldn't pawn this off on

Allen or Todd.

Since I was going to be cutting it short on time, I'd brought what I needed to the funeral home, and I would just get ready upstairs. Although I had picked out a sassy skirt and blouse combo, Jill had immediately vetoed it and promised to bring me back something else sexy. Considering I'd seen her closet before, I knew it runneth over with sexy attire.

I was on the way to Mr. Peterson's graveside service when I got a call from Todd. "Hey Liv, the crime lab just called for us to come pick up Randy."

"Oh shit. I'm too far away with Blackie and Old Blue is in the shop."

Yes, folks, we named our hearses. Blackie was an onyx colored Cadillac XTS Landau Coach I splurged on two years ago. While Old Blue was the navy Cadillac LTS hearse my father had purchased ten years ago.

"Don't worry about it. I can throw a stretcher in the back of the floral truck."

I groaned. "How classy."

Todd laughed. "Hey, it just says Sullivan's on the side. They won't know it's the floral truck."

"Okay. That's fine. If you make it back before me, just put him in the freezer. I'll have to get confirmation from Freelings Crematory before we send him." Since we were a relatively small-time operation, we didn't have an onsite crematory. We had to send bodies an hour down the road.

"I will do that. Bye."

"Bye. Todd."

Thankfully, the graveside service went pretty quickly, and I arrived back at Sullivan's with just under an hour before Catcher arrived. Coincidentally, Todd had also just arrived back with Randy and was wheeling him up the ramp.

"Glad to see you made pretty good time."

"Yeah. I never thought I'd make it through Atlanta traffic that fast."

Todd's phone started ringing. When he glanced down at it, he grimaced. "Shit."

"What's wrong?"

"It's Mary. I was supposed to be at the ballpark for Justin's game ten minutes ago."

"Answer it, and tell her you're on the way." I then shooed him away from the gurney. "Go. I can handle the rest."

"Are you sure?"

I smiled at him. "Would you just get the hell out of here?"

He grinned. "Thanks, Olivia."

"No problem."

As I wheeled Randy into the funeral prep room, Todd ran out the back door. After I got Randy into the freezer, a knock came at the door, which I assumed was Jill with my dress. When I threw open the door, I found Pease, Allen, and my mother instead. I glanced around the group. "Hey guys."

Without a hello, Pease said, "We're here to see them."

"Them?"

She rolled her eyes. "The dicks. We wanna see Randy's two dicks."

I stared at her in disbelief. "Please tell me you're joking."

"Hell no. Randy's dicks are like the 8th Wonder of the World," Pease argued.

"Um, I'm not running a peep show here."

"Oh come on, Liv. It's not like we're asking you to degrade Randy by charging admission. And I'm thinking in his case it would be more of a freak show, than peep show," Pease argued.

I crossed my arms over my chest before staring pointedly at my mother. "I would expect this out of the two of them, but really Mama, you too?"

She nervously fingered the pearls around her neck—the ones my father had given her for their thirtieth anniversary. "I just figured if they were going to take a peek, I might as well too."

Sweeping my hands to my face, I rubbed my eyes. "Unbelievable."

"What's unbelievable?" Jill asked. She appeared behind the peepshow crew with a black dress thrown over her shoulder and a pair of black stilettos in one of her hands.

"That my mother, brother, and grandmother want to stare at a dead guy's two penises."

Jill's green eyes widened. The next thing I knew, she

threw the dress onto one of the high-back chairs before pushing past me into the funeral prep room. "I gotta see this."

I bit my lip to keep from coining the famous line from *Julius Caesar*, "E tu Brute?" I should have realized that this would have been something right up Jill's alley.

Realizing I was fighting a losing battle, I threw up my hands in defeat. "Fine, fine. If you guys don't have the decency to respect the dead, then go for it." I pointed a finger at Allen. "You can get Randy out of the freezer and put him back in. I will have no part in it. Besides, I have plans this evening, and I need to get ready."

Mama's face lit up like a Christmas Tree. "Plans? Does that mean you have a date?"

Before I could answer, Jill said, "You think she's wearing one of my sexy dresses and come-fuck-me-heels to pick up a body?"

In truly overdramatic fashion, Mama swept a hand over her chest as she gave me a toothy smile. "Oh honey, do you know how thrilled this makes me?"

"Yes, Mama. I do."

Pease peered curiously at me. "And just who are you going out with?"

"Catcher Mains."

Both Pease and Mama cried, "The one-night-stand guy?"

I rolled my eyes. "Yes. That would be the one."

A pleased smile curved on Pease's lips. "Well, well, Olivia, you must've made one hell of an impression on him if came back for more." She nudged my arm with the top of her cane. "I didn't think you had it in you."

Allen groaned. "Um, could you guys please not talk about my sister's sex life in front of me?"

"Are you kidding me? I'm so excited she even *has* a sex life again that I want to yell it from the roof tops," Pease argued with a wicked grin.

Sweeping a hand to my hip, I countered, "This conversation is wrong on so many levels that it's not even funny."

Mama nodded. "Olivia is right. We shouldn't be talking about her love life. Some things should remain private."

"Thank you."

She smiled as she added, "Even if we're ridiculously happy that she's seeing someone."

Her words caused tears to prick at the back of my eyelids. She jerked her chin at me. "Now you get on upstairs and get ready. You don't want to keep Mr. Wonderful waiting."

I glanced at the clock on the wall. "Shit. He'll be here in forty minutes." I hurried past them out of the funeral prep room. After I grabbed the dress and shoes from the chair, I turned back to Allen. "Make sure you lock up after you're done."

He saluted me with a smile. "Aye, aye, Captain."

"Smartass," I mumbled as I started up the stairs.

After I got out of the shower and glanced at the time on my phone, I proceeded to do my hair and makeup in almost record speed. Once again, Jill had come through for me with a form-fitting, black tunic dress that had beading around the bodice. It was just dressy enough for a date, but at the same time, it didn't look like I was trying too hard. I slid on a pair of lacy thigh highs I knew Catcher would enjoy before putting on the stiletto heels.

Since I figured Catcher would have the top down on his convertible, I grabbed a red sweater out of the closet. It was one I had several of in different colors. Not only was the Georgia weather unpredictable, but so was the temperature in the funeral home. You learned to dress in layers.

I had just started down the stairs to wait on Catcher when Pease's voice floated up to me. "My, my, Agent Mains, aren't you one strong, strapping man?"

Fuuuuuuuuuck! I almost tripped over my heels and face-planted on the landing. Oh no. Please no. For the love of God and everything holy, why was Pease still here? It wasn't like we had any bodies for her to hold a PAM meeting. She should've got her peek at Randy's King and Kong and headed out to the Moose Lodge to play Bingo with all her other old cronies while flirting with the old codgers.

I hurried down the rest of the stairs as fast as I could. I

whirled around the bannister to find Catcher sandwiched between my mother and Pease on the front room sofa. Both Mama and Pease were staring appreciatively at Catcher.

At the sound of my heels on the hardwood floor, they all looked up. Surprisingly Catcher didn't wear an expression of horror at being subjected to the two. Well, Mama was basically harmless unless she alluded to the fact she wanted Catcher and me married. Like yesterday. It was Pease who was the loaded gun. I cringed when I thought of what might've already come out of her mouth in my absence.

Catcher stood up from the sofa and came over to kiss me. On the lips. With a little tongue. When he pulled away, he gave me a killer grin. "You look absolutely gorgeous."

My cheeks burned under his compliments. "Thank you."

"I'm sorry I was a little early."

"No, no. It's fine," I lied.

"I had planned to wait in the car until closer to five since I didn't want anyone thinking I was a prospective client who needed to be shown caskets while hearing pricing plans. But then your grandmother knocked on my window and told me to get my handsome ass inside." He glanced over his shoulder and grinned. "Those were your words, weren't they, Mrs. Sullivan?"

Pease chuckled. "Why yes. They were."

"I figured it would be rude not to comply with her wishes, and I certainly didn't want to get off on the wrong foot with your grandmother, and in turn, the rest of your family."

"How considerate of you," I mused.

Mama rose off the couch to join us. "You didn't tell us how charming your friend is, Olivia," she said with a coy grin. I stared aghast as she actually batted her eyes at Catcher.

Pease harrumphed from her place on the couch. "Forget charming. You didn't tell us how drop-dead sexy he was."

Catcher preened beside me under their compliments, causing me to roll my eyes. "It's been so busy and so crazy around here that I haven't had a chance to tell you much about him."

Mama fingered her pearls. "Yes, Holden has been telling us all about the developments in Randy's murder."

Pease poked the back of Catcher's thigh with her cane. "If you have to go back to the nudist colony, I want you to take me with you, Agent Mains. That's something I've always wanted to try."

He laughed as he glanced at her over his shoulder. "I would be happy to take you anywhere you'd like to go, Mrs. Sullivan. Even to a nudist colony."

"Resort," I corrected under my breath.

"What was that, sweetie?" Mama asked.

"Nothing. Catcher, I guess you and I should get on the road."

"Yes. We do have a drive ahead of us."

"You two headed to some fancy-schmancy place?"

Pease questioned.

"Actually, I'm taking Olivia to my house to cook for her," Catcher replied.

Pease's eyes widened behind her glasses, and I feared she might swallow her snuff from the shock. "You cook?"

"Sometimes. I'm still learning."

She shook her head before pointing her cane at me. "You might've gone through a hell of a long dry spell, but this one is sure worth the wait."

I rolled my eyes to the ceiling and silently questioned God what I had done to deserve this level of punishment. I guess I was really paying for hot storeroom sex and seeing a dick pic in a church sanctuary.

Catcher took my hand in his. "I have to say that Olivia is worth the wait, too."

As Mama went, "Aw" and Pease replied, "I'll be damned", I stared wide-eyed and open-mouthed at Catcher. Did he really mean that, or was he just saying it to look good in front of Mama and Pease? I couldn't help noticing the sincere look in his eyes.

I didn't have a lot of experience with men, but it seemed that he and I were moving at almost warped speed from hot sex to a relationship. The rational side of me questioned what I really knew about him besides he was a hot-as-hell GBI agent with a great sense of a humor and a fantastic cock? I tried pushing the voices of doubt out of my head. I wanted to enjoy what we had for as long as I could.

"You are just about the sweetest man I've met in a long, long time," Mama cooed. She patted my arm. "Isn't he just the sweetest?"

"Yes. He really is," I replied, staring directly at Catcher.

"You ladies are going to make me blush," he teased.

Pease snorted. "I doubt there's anything that would make you blush. I'm sure with your looks, you've just about seen and done it all."

With that comment, the moment's previous spell was broken. "And on that note, it's time to go." I reached out and took Catcher's hand. "See you all tomorrow."

When I started dragging Catcher to the door, Pease called, "I hope you packed a toothbrush in that purse. And some clean panties."

After chuckling, Catcher muttered, "Jesus."

Glancing over my shoulder, I said, "I'll stop for a toothbrush. And no need for panties. I'm not wearing any now."

A quiet "Fuck me," came from Agent Sexy Pants beside me. And with that, I slammed the front door. As we started for his convertible, Catcher asked, "Were you serious about not wearing any panties?"

I laughed. "I guess you'll just have to be a good boy and wait to find out."

·

CHAPTER 13

After making a quick stop at my house to pick up my overnight bag, we got on the road. Once we neared Catcher's house, he surprised me by wheeling the convertible into a Publix parking lot. Before I could question him, he turned to me with a sheepish smile. "Call me an unprepared ass, but I haven't had a chance to make it to the grocery store yet."

"That's okay. I don't mind helping you shop."

"You sure? You can wait here in the car if you want."

I laughed. "Would you roll the window down for me like I was a dog?" I teasingly questioned.

"For you, I'd leave the car running," he replied, with a wink.

I reached for my purse. "I'm more than happy to shop with you."

Catcher nodded and then got out of the car. He shocked the hell out of me when he jogged around the front so he could open my door. "You know my mother and grandmother aren't here to impress anymore," I joked.

"Har, har. I'm a gentleman even when there isn't anyone around to impress."

"Even without opening the door for me, you made a hell of an impression on my mother and Pease."

With a grin, Catcher said, "Your grandmother is really something."

"Yes. She is."

"Did you know she goosed me in the ass with her cane?"

"I'm not surprised. I kinda got the vibe that she was a little hot for you. Like some unresolved sexual tension."

Catcher's eyes bulged. "Only on her part," he protested.

I giggled. "Of course. I know you're not about to leave me for a roll in the hay with my grandmother."

He shuddered as he pulled out a cart for us. "You know, I think she might've tried to touch my junk if your mom hadn't been there."

"Probably."

"Damn," he muttered.

"Welcome to my world."

Catcher steered the cart over to the produce section. "Are there any vegetables you don't like?"

"I'm not a fan of radishes, but that's about it. I pretty much eat anything."

Catcher grinned. "Since we're in public, I'm going to be a good boy and leave that potential innuendo alone."

"That has to take some serious resolve to do that."

"It does."

"What can I get to help move things along?"

"Get me two yellow squash and two zucchini."

"Coming right up."

After rifling through the pile of squash for the best ones, I picked two and then bagged them. I was deciding between two enormous zucchini when Catcher rolled up with the cart. "Remind you of me?" he teasingly asked.

With a roll of my eyes, I countered, "I thought you were going to behave since we're in public?"

"I had a momentary lapse there. I'll try to do better."

"I'm not going to hold my breath."

"You know me too well."

Once we were finished in the produce section, Catcher steered the cart over to the bakery. He selected a long loaf of French bread before moving on to the sweets. "What should we have for dessert?"

"I'm deeply wounded you didn't bake me a cake or make a pie," I teased.

"Desserts aren't my specialty. I usually leave that to my mother."

"Aw. How sweet."

"Why is that sweet?"

"You know, that you're a Mama's Boy."

Catcher scowled. "I wouldn't say that." When I cocked my brows at him, he replied, "Fine. Maybe a little bit."

I smiled. "Does your mama spoil her baby boy?"

"Pretty much. Now she's retired, she loves cooking dinner for me. Since Jem's married, she feels she has to take care of me since I don't have a wife to do it."

"That's very sweet."

"Speaking of sweet…" Catcher held up a container of a half dozen cupcakes. "I kinda have an addiction to cupcakes."

"You do?" I asked, unable to hide my surprise.

Catcher appeared affronted. "Can't a man like a cupcake without it emasculating him?"

With a laugh, I replied, "My apologies."

He grinned. "It's not exactly classy, but what about cupcakes for dessert?"

"Are they vanilla cake with buttercream icing?"

After examining the label, Catcher answered, "Yes."

"Then I'm all in."

"I knew there was a reason I liked you," Catcher said

before a brief kiss on my lips.

I'd never in a million years imagined a grocery store could be romantic. But in that moment, I felt like I was in the middle of a sugary-sweet RomCom, and I loved every minute of it.

"What's your favorite meat?" Catcher asked. Before I could answer, he added, "Well, excluding my dick."

I rolled my eyes. "You really need help for the innuendos."

"Like an Innuendo Anonymous meeting?"

"Something like that."

"It would probably be a waste of time because whenever someone would get up to tell their story, some other ass would find something sexual in what they said."

I laughed. "Good point."

Catcher then stopped the cart in front of the seafood counter. "I was thinking about some pan-seared salmon. How does that sound?"

"Delicious. I love salmon."

"Good."

"Can I make just one request?"

"Sure."

"That you buy that kind." I pointed to the tray filled with descaled salmon.

"Why those?"

"It's silly really, but I'm not a big fan of seeing the scales or having eyeballs looking up at me."

Catcher laughed as he waved the attendant over. "No scales it is."

"Thank you."

"Anything for you, babe."

And just like that, I was back to floating along in my grocery   store   RomCom.

CHAPTER 14

We didn't take too long at the store, and before long, we were back on the road to Catcher's house. After we'd traveled for ten minutes, Catcher eased the car off the main highway onto a two-lane road. "Have you lived out here long?"

"About two years. My parents retired from teaching at Westminster Prep in Atlanta ten years ago, and they wanted to move out of the city to the country. They found this place with ten acres. They gave my brother, sister, and me each two acres. Jem built his house right away, and then he and I worked on mine for probably a year or two. Doing a little here and there when we could."

After making a right turn, we started down a small paved road. "That's my parents' house," Catcher said, pointing to a two-story colonial with a wide, wrap-around porch.

"Wow, that's beautiful," I replied, as he stopped the car to let me get a good look.

He leaned across me and pointed to a Cape Cod on the right. "And there's Jem's."

I smiled when I saw the white picket fence yard was filled with toys. "How many children does he have?"

Catcher rolled his eyes. "Four and another on the way."

I turned in my seat with surprise. "Five children?"

"Three girls and two boys—well, the third girl is on the way. Jem always wanted a houseful of kids. Thankfully, he found a chick who felt the same way. They got married at twenty and started popping kids out like clock-work after she finished her teaching degree two years later."

I peered curiously at him. "It doesn't much sound like you like kids."

He shook his head. "I love kids."

"Then why did you roll your eyes about Jem's kids?"

"Because I don't want a houseful like he has. Give me one or two, and I'll be fine."

I didn't realize I'd been holding my breath until my lungs screamed in agony for relief. I exhaled in a long whoosh.

"Thought I was a heartless bastard who didn't want kids, eh?" Catcher asked.

A nervous laugh bubbled from my lips. "No, no. I wasn't thinking that at all."

"Of course you were."

"Okay, maybe I was." I held my thumb and forefinger close together. "Maybe a little."

"I knew I was right."

"You're so cocky."

He glanced down at his crotch and then back over to me. "Don't we know it?"

"Catcher, please."

He held up one of his hands. "Fine, fine. I'll stop. I can assume that you want kids one day from the reaction you had to me potentially not wanting them."

"Yes. I do want kids. I want them very much." I stared down at my hands. "It's an unfulfilled dream to be a mother...and a wife." The moment the words left my lips, I cringed. I had just committed one of the cardinal sins of dating. I'd been emotionally slutty by revealing too much about my relationship goals. Admitting I wanted to get married would probably have Catcher shriveling in his seat.

Catcher took my hand. "Olivia, I'm thirty-three years old. I've had my wild party years. I've got a mortgage on a house with two spare bedrooms—bedrooms that when I was building the house, I envisioned putting Little Catchers in."

I couldn't help giggling at his description. "That was very practical of you to think ahead."

"Thank you. I'm a pretty practical guy." He brought my hand to his lips and kissed it. "I know what I want, and I relentlessly pursue it until I get it."

Butterflies began break dancing in my stomach at his comment and the way he was looking at me. Was it possible after all these years and all the emotional subterfuge, I had finally found the one? And had I found the one after only a few days? In the back of my mind, I couldn't help wondering if Catcher was feeling the same connection. I mean, was that the reason why he'd said he wanted to settle down too? I wasn't sure if I was jumping to conclusions or leaping. The last thing I needed after getting back in the game was to get my heart broken.

Catcher tenderly placed my hand back on my lap. "Now let me show you my house."

My reply of "Okay" came in an almost breathless whisper because I was still trying to recover from the heaviness of the conversation.

After we left his parents' and brother's house in the distance, Catcher pulled up outside of a beautiful log home that looked like it could've been on the brochure of a mountain getaway. It even had a green-tin roof.

"Wow," I murmured.

"Good wow, or bad wow?" Catcher asked.

I turned to him and smiled. "That's a very good wow."

Relief appeared on his face. "I'm glad to hear it."

"You and your brother really built this?"

"We sure did...with a little help from his crew."

"It's amazing."

After hitting the button to open the garage, Catcher eased the convertible inside. "You look around while I get the groceries."

"Are you sure?"

Catcher grinned. "Don't worry. I've hidden all the sex toys and drugs."

"Ha, ha. Very funny."

After giving me a playful kiss, Catcher got out of the car and went around to the trunk to get the bags, so I went to the door leading into the house. When I opened it, I entered the kitchen. Setting sunlight streamed in from the back wall that was filled with windows. Everything appeared new and modern from the stainless steel appliances, beige granite countertops, and sandy-colored tile floor.

When I heard Catcher behind me, I couldn't help asking, "Do you have a cleaning lady?"

He set the bags down on the deep mahogany kitchen table. The cabinets were the same rich color. "Actually, it's all me."

"You're kidding."

Catcher laughed. "No. I'm not. I'm pretty much a neat freak." He cocked his head at me. "What about you?"

"I'm kinda a cross between a neat freak and a slob."

"Is that even possible?"

"Come to my house, and you can find out," I replied with a smile.

"I've been to your house, remember?"

"You saw the foyer and part of the living room. You can't really judge based on those. It's more into my bedroom and bathroom."

He slid his arms around my waist and drew me to him. "I would love to spend time in your bedroom."

I laughed. "You might abandon any thoughts of sex because you were so grossed out by the mess."

Catcher shook his head. "The bedroom would have to be on fire for me to abandon you."

The beat of my heart felt like it was doing a trippy hopscotch. My eyelids fluttered a few times as I stared at Catcher. "I'm fighting the urge to pinch you right now."

"Can I suggest my ass?"

"I was being serious."

"So was I."

After a playful smack on the arm, I said, "I mean, I was wanting to pinch you to see if you were real. These past few days feel like a dream."

"Considering we've been involved with nudists, snake handlers, and a guy with two dicks, I'd wager that would be more of a nightmare than a dream."

I tugged the strands of hair at the base of his neck. "I'm

serious, Catcher."

"I know you are. I also know after everything you've been through with guys, it's hard for you to say what you're feeling. I was giving you an out with the jokes in case you needed one."

I shook my head. "I don't need one. Not with you."

"I'm glad to hear that."

Oh shit. He was serious. And he wanted me. Yes, *me*. The eternally single woman.

Leaning forward, I brought my lips to his. After a few breathless moments of kissing, Catcher pulled away. "We've got to stop this, or there won't be any dinner made."

I pressed myself tighter against him. "I don't mind."

He gave a frustrated grunt. "I do. I've got to get at least one dinner in you."

With a laugh, I eased back. "Okay. I can wait."

"Good." He took my hand. "Let me show you the rest of the house."

"Sure."

I let Catcher drag me into the living room. It had high, cathedral ceilings, and the walls were light-colored wood that matched the floors. There was a leather sofa and loveseat along with a giant-screen television. "I'm a little minimalist when it comes to decorating," Catcher said.

"You don't need much—a rug with some good earth tones, maybe some curtains."

"Hmm, so I need a woman's touch to my swinging bachelor pad?"

I cupped his ass through his pants. "A woman's touch is always a good idea, isn't it?"

He grinned. "You're killin' me, Smalls."

Giggling, I removed my hand. "Sorry. I'll try to be a good girl from now on out."

"Just be good until dinner is over. After that, you can be as bad as you want to be."

"I'll keep that in mind."

Catcher then gave me a tour of the rest of the house. Everything was beautiful, and if I allowed myself, I could imagine living here with him. In my fantasy of playing house with him here, I tried ignoring the nagging fact that he was forty-five minutes away from my work.

When we returned to the kitchen, Catcher patted one of the bar stools. "Up."

"Yes, sir," I replied as I hopped onto the stool.

"Would you like a glass of wine?"

"I would love one."

Catcher headed over to the fridge. "I've been saving this white for a special occasion."

I bit my tongue to keep from asking if it was for an occasion with another woman. I didn't want to think about the potential string of hussies who had sat on this barstool. Regardless of how well things were going between us, Catcher's past was just too depressing to think about.

He interrupted my thoughts by setting a glass of white wine in front of me. "Thank you," I said before taking a sip. As I let the liquid roll over my tongue, I nodded appreciatively. "This is really delicious."

"I'm glad to hear it." He poured himself a glass before taking the vegetables out to wash.

"Can I help you with that?"

He shook his head. "Nope. Dinner tonight is all on me. You are to just sit there and relax."

"Wow. How nice of you."

He winked at me before saying, "My pleasure."

"Trust me. Watching you cook for me is *my* pleasure."

"Guess that means you've never had a man cook for you?"

"If you consider one guy microwaving Ramen noodles for me in his dorm cooking, then yes, I've had a man cook for me."

Catcher shot me a look of disgust. "Microwaving that bullshit is not cooking."

"Then you can be my first," I teasingly said.

"I'll pop your cherry any day, babe."

I wrinkled my nose. "Ugh, I really hate that expression."

"Would you prefer I took your male-cooking V-card?"

"That's somewhat better."

Catcher nodded. "So tell me something."

I swallowed down a sip of wine. "Okay."

"Did you always want to be a mortician and coroner?" he asked as he began cutting the vegetables.

My fingertips traced over the rim of my wineglass. "Not exactly."

Catcher paused in his chopping. "You mean, you weren't holding Barbie funerals, or playing funeral home instead of house?"

I laughed. "Um, no, I wasn't. And if I had been doing morbid shit like that, my parents should have put me in therapy as soon as possible."

With a grin, Catcher said, "So what was it you wanted to do?"

"Growing up, I was pretty indecisive about my future. I wavered back and forth between a ton of different things. One day I wanted to be a teacher. The next a nurse. Then it was a hair stylist." I took a thoughtful sip of wine. "I guess it was my way of delaying the inevitable."

"The inevitable being you should go into the family business."

I nodded. "If I had bailed on the mortuary business, I'm not sure what would have happened to Sullivan's. I don't think my younger brother would have taken it on. Maybe Todd or Earl, the guys who work for us, would have wanted to run it. Who knows, we might've had to close the doors. That would have killed my father." An ache burned its way through my chest, and it wasn't from the wine.

"Tell me about him."

I blinked at Catcher in surprise. "Really?"

He nodded. "He obviously was someone very important to you, so in that token, he's important to me."

This time I blinked at him because I was fighting the tears that his words caused. "He was a lot like his dad—soft-spoken and reserved. He was fair and honest in all facets of his life. He was compassionate and caring, especially when it came to his family and to his job. He loved UGA football, dancing around to the oldies, and taking his old bird dog with him hunting."

Catcher smiled. "He sounds like an amazing man."

"He was," I replied. And he had been. Whenever he called me Liv Boo in public, I had wanted to hide in embarrassment. But I've missed it. I've missed him so very much. He had certainly set the bar high when it came to men considering the way he had treated my mom like a queen. Of course, growing up, I'd found it a little sickening. Now I wanted the same thing—for a man to look at me with the same love and adoration my dad had looked at my mom. Someone who respected me as he had Mama. A love that lasted a lifetime and beyond.

After clearing my throat, I asked, "What about you? Did you always want to be a GBI agent?"

"Not exactly. I think I always wanted to do something that was helpful and useful. Like being a cop or a fireman. I never really imagined going to college."

"You didn't?"

"Surprisingly not, even with parents who were teachers. Elementary school was hell for me because I had a mild case of dyslexia. I didn't get sorted out with reading and writing until middle school. I compensated for feeling like a dumbass in the classroom by being very physical. Whatever sport there was, I was going to play it and be good at it."

"I totally saw you as a jock in school."

"We don't ever shed how we're labeled, do we?"

"Sadly not. What happens to us as kids stays with us a long time."

"Yeah. It does. But thankfully for us, we've both made a success of our lives."

I smiled ruefully. "Yes, professionally I'm a success. Personally, I'm pretty sure I'm a small-town pariah for being single and unmarried. Well, there's also the whole working with dead people thing."

Catcher turned the heat on the stove. "It's totally unfair how women are made to feel like failures just for not marrying early." He added the pan and began searing the salmon. "Of course, I get tremendous pressure from my mother to settle down and procreate."

"Same here."

Turning around, he picked up his wine glass before throwing a grin at me. "Here's to our pain-in-the-ass mothers whom we love dearly."

With a laugh, I picked my glass up too. "To our

mothers."

I tossed back the rest of the wine and then waved the glass at Catcher. "This is so good that I think I'm going to need *a lot* more. Like the bottle more."

A mischievous look twinkled in Catcher's eyes. "It would be my pleasure to ply with you alcohol, so I can take advantage of you later."

Well, it was official. Catcher was as good in the kitchen as he was the bedroom. I practically gorged myself on the delicious salmon and vegetables, not to mention buttery French bread. When we finished dinner, my dress even felt tighter.

As I reached for my sweater on the back of the chair, Catcher asked, "Are you cold?"

"Just a little."

"Here. I'll make us a fire."

"That would be nice," I murmured. Catcher had no idea that a secret fantasy of mine had always been to make love in front of a roaring fire. Of course the way my luck ran in the sex department, someone's ass would end up getting burned, and it would totally ruin the moment.

Feeling domestic, I cleared the table while Catcher worked on the fire. Once the dishes were loaded into the dish washer, I joined Catcher in the living room where he had the aforementioned fire roaring in the stone fireplace.

I held my hands out to the flames, warming my chilly skin. "God, that feels good.

"Jem tried to get me to do gas logs because they're easier and cleaner and blah, blah. But I wouldn't hear of it. I love a real fire—the way it smells and sounds."

"Me too. But since I'm not much of a lumberjack, I got gas logs at my house."

Catcher smiled at me. "If you want real logs, I can take care of getting your firewood."

Tilting my head at him, I replied, "Are you sure about that? You seem more metrosexual than lumbersexual."

"Trust me, babe, I can chop wood with the best of them. And I have a few flannel shirts in my closet."

"Mmm, you do?"

"Don't tell me you have a lumberjack fantasy where you help a man with his wood?"

With a laugh, I said, "Um, no, I don't. It's more about liking a woodsy man in flannel."

He waggled his eyebrows. "Want me to go get that flannel shirt?"

The two glasses of wine I'd had fueled my response. "For right now, I'd rather you just be naked."

Catcher's eyes flared. "You would?"

I bobbed my head. "I want to see your fabulous body illuminated by just the firelight." What the hell? Had I actually just said that? Damn, what was the alcohol content in that wine?

"Well, then. Your wish is my command."

When Catcher's hands went to his tie, my breath came wheezing out like a deflated accordion. As he loosened it, his eyes never left mine, and for the life of me, I couldn't bring myself to look away. When he started unbuttoning his shirt and exposing his fantastic chest, I licked my lips, causing Catcher to groan. "Fuck me, you're sexy when you do that."

"I can't help it. You're making my mouth run dry." Catcher's burst of laughter took me by surprise. "What?" I demanded.

He tore off his shirt and dropped it to the ground before replying. "You should have seen the expression on your face. You looked horrified by what you just said. Like you were suffering from a split personality."

Warmth flooded my cheeks. "You and the wine bring out the naughty in me."

"I'll be sure to restock that brand," he said with a teasing twinkle in his eyes. He then loosened his belt and dropped it to the floor. After unbuttoning and unzipping his pants, he whisked them away.

Seeing him standing before me in all his naked glory caused an ache of longing between my legs. Just as I was about to say something that would have embarrassed me, I bit down on my lip to keep it safely inside.

Catcher closed the gap between us. He tilted my chin up to look at him. "What were you about to say?"

"Nothing," I lied.

He reached around behind me to smack my ass. "Don't be bad and lie to me."

Normally I would have told him to shove his hand up his ass before hitting mine again, but gaaaaah, it was so sexy the way he did it. "I was going to say just looking at you makes me wet."

Catcher swept his thumb over my bottom lip. "God, I love that mouth of yours."

I reached between us to take his growing erection in my hand. "Would you like it wrapped around your cock?"

"Hell yes, I would."

With my hand firmly around his erection, I sank down to my knees. To me, there was something so sexy about looking up at a man when you had his pride and joy in your mouth. During my college years, I'd become a connoisseur of giving blowjobs. Of course, I was all about being in control, and if some douchebag ever tried the ol' "I'll hold your head down so I can fuck your mouth' bit" I was off my knees and out the door.

I flicked my tongue out and swirled it around the head of Catcher's dick. I planted kisses down his shaft and then onto his balls. "Liv, please," he begged.

Smiling to myself, I then slid him achingly slow into my mouth. When he finally bumped against the back of my throat, Catcher groaned. Fighting my gag reflex, I pushed him back out before starting to glide him in and out of my mouth. When I

gripped him harder, Catcher threw his head back. "Oh fuck, Olivia."

My free hand went to caress his balls, alternating between gently squeezing them and rolling them between my fingers. Over and over, I bobbed up and down on him, alternating between increasing and decreasing the pressure.

"Fuck, I'm going to come."

I popped his dick out of my mouth and glanced up at Catcher. "Then come."

He stared down at me with eyes hooded with lust. *That look.* Damn, did I love that look of lust. And I loved having Catcher at my mercy, loving everything I was doing to him.

"You sure?" he questioned in a strained voice.

I answered him by taking him deep into my mouth. He grunted and began flexing his hips. It was an incredible ego trip when he called out my name as he came. Although it wasn't my favorite thing in the world, I swallowed quickly.

Catcher helped me up off my knees. He swept my hair out of my face and gave me a lingering kiss. When he broke away, he gave me a lazy smile. "I think I'm in the mood for some dessert."

I blinked at his retreating form. "Um...okay." I mean, I guess a cupcake would be nice to get the cum taste out of my mouth. I had just thought maybe I would get a little oral reciprocation or something along those lines.

When Catcher returned with the container of cupcakes,

I started for the couch, but he stopped me. "Strip."

"Excuse me?"

"I said to strip."

I bunched my eyebrows in confusion. "But I thought you said you wanted dessert?"

A wicked look flashed in Catcher's baby blues. "I do. I plan to eat this cupcake off your naked body."

Well now. That wasn't something I was expecting. "All righty then," I replied.

My hands went around my neck to find the zipper on my dress. Once I let it down, I brought my arms through the holes and then pushed the dress off my waist to the floor. "Nice lingerie," Catcher mused.

I glanced down at the almost transparent black bra and panty set I had found in the back of my underwear drawer. Since I'd wanted to match the dress that Jill brought, I'd resorted to my old stash in my chest of drawers that I'd found after moving back home. The last time I'd worn the set was in college. I was surprised I hadn't found them moth-eaten when I pulled them out.

"I'm glad you like them."

"I'd like it better if you hurried up and took them off."

Obeying his wishes, I whisked away the bra and panties, and they joined my dress on the floor. I stood before him in only my heels. When I bent over to take them off, Catcher stopped me. "Keep them on. And lie down on the floor."

"Bossy, bossy," I murmured as I got down on the floor. The fire had heated the wood, and it quickly warmed my bare ass.

Catcher eased down on the floor to lie beside me. He dipped a finger into the icing of one of the cupcakes. He then brought the icing-caked finger to my mouth and traced my lips. I fought to the urge to lick some of it off.

He dipped his head, and his tongue darted out to brush the icing off my lips. "Damn, that's good," he said.

When he began to suck the leftover icing off my top and bottom lips, I rubbed my thighs together. I never could have imagined an icing-encrusted kiss being erotic, but damn, if it wasn't. I couldn't help wondering what it might feel like for him to be doing the icing licking on a different set of my lips.

After swiping the icing off another cupcake, he placed a large dollop on each of my nipples. The feel of the cool confection against them had my nipples already puckering before Catcher even brought his mouth to suction off the icing.

"Mmm," I murmured as I ran my fingers through his hair. When I tugged on the strands, his mouth tugged harder on my nipples. My legs were now scissoring back and forth to get much-needed friction to my pussy.

I peered curiously up at him when he took the icing-less cupcakes and crumbled them over my breasts and abdomen. "You look good enough to eat," he teased while wagging his eyebrows. He then dipped his head and began eating the cupcakes off me. His tongue and teeth grazing my skin caused me to moan. "Does that feel good, babe?"

"Oh yeah."

"Fuck me, Liv. You tasted sweet as hell before, but I don't think I'll ever get enough of tasting you now."

The feeling was mutual. I didn't think I could ever grow tired of the feel of his lips and teeth on my skin as he nipped and sucked every morsel of cupcake off my body.

As if he had read my mind earlier, Catcher took his next bunch of icing straight between my legs. He slathered it over my pussy, covering my clit and labia. I had a momentary panic that like Jesse and the latex condom, I had some undiscovered vaginal allergy to baked goods, and my hoo-hah was going to swell up.

After flashing me a wicked grin, Catcher buried his mouth in me. "Oh God, Catcher!" I cried. One of my hands smacked down on the floor while the other went to his hair. My nails raked across his scalp as his teeth grazed my clit. His tongue seemed to be everywhere as he licked and sucked the icing. My eyes rolled back in my head.

Holy Shiiiiiiiiit! Never. Felt. This. Good. His tongue. The pressure. His tongue. Damn, it was too much.

An orgasm came charging through like a freight train. I convulsed and cursed as I rode it down. How the man had managed to deliver such an orgasm without even laying a finger on me, or more specifically *in* me, was beyond my comprehension. He had serious talent.

Of course, I was probably going to be combing cupcake crumbs from my vag for at least a week, not to mention probably getting an icing-induced yeast infection. But damn, it was worth it.

Catcher raised his head up from between my legs and swiped his mouth with the back of his hand. "Best. Fucking. Cupcakes. Ever."

And even though I hadn't had a single bite of one, I had to agree with him. But now I needed him inside me. Reaching up, I pulled his face to mine and kissed him, hoping he got the message. Boy, did he ever.

After that night, I would never be able to look at another cupcake without getting slightly aroused.

CHAPTER 15

The second time I spent the night with Catcher it was the sunlight streaming through the curtains, and not a rooster, that woke me up. A pleased sigh escaped my lips at the feel of his warm body pressed against mine, his arm wrapped protectively around me. Everything about last night had been wonderful. Getting to have a real date with him was everything I hoped it would be and then some. I'd never in my wildest dreams ever imagined turning a one-night stand into a relationship, but with the way things were going, that's where we seemed to be headed.

A relationship.

Two words I'd given up ever hearing my name associated with again. But here I was.

Although I hated to leave the comfort of Catcher's bed and embrace, my bladder was screaming in agony to be relieved. So I took his dead-weight arm and put it behind me. Then I slid across the mattress and got out of bed. I tip-toed across the hardwood floors to the bathroom so as not to wake Catcher.

"Wow," I whispered when I walked into the master bathroom. It was seriously gorgeous with dark brown tile and brown and white granite countertops. As I took in the jetted tub and double glass doors of the shower, I couldn't help being impressed that Catcher and his brother had done the work themselves.

An idea popped into my head. I wanted to do something to show Catcher how much I cared about him. What better way to do that than by cooking him breakfast and then serving it to him in bed. I wasn't holding out a lot of hope for that since we'd had to get the ingredients for dinner last night at the store. At the very least, I could bring him coffee in bed.

Once I flushed the toilet and washed my hands, I borrowed Catcher's comb and smoothed down my out-of-control bed hair. Since frying anything naked was not only not hygienic, but potentially painful, I grabbed Catcher's robe off and slid it on. My eyes closed in bliss as Catcher's scent enveloped me. Just his smell sent an electrifying tingle between my legs. While I wanted nothing more than to run out of the bathroom and tackle him for a quick morning delight, I stayed strong in my resolve to surprise him with breakfast.

After stepping back into the bedroom, I found Catcher on his back, his arm draped over his eyes as he snored softly. Inwardly, I did a little happy dance that I hadn't woken him up. I eased the bedroom door closed before padding down the hallway.

When I walked into the kitchen, I did a double take at the sight of a tall, willowy, twenty-something blonde lounging on one of the bar stools. She glanced up from the magazine she was reading.

At the sight of me, her blue eyes lit up. "Good morning."

"Um, good morning."

She gave me a sheepish grin. "Sorry. If I'd known Catcher had company, I wouldn't have stopped by."

Since the odds of Catcher having a platonic relationship with Coed Barbie were pretty slim, I tried everything within me not to lose my shit. A tempest of anger and hurt swirled within me, and if I didn't get out of the kitchen, I was either going to punch Barbie in her perfect face or puke.

I started backing up. "No. That's okay. I mean, you obviously have a key, so you two must be serious."

She held her hand up. "Wait, don't go. I like meeting Catcher's girls."

Girls? Catcher had *girls?* It was bad enough seeing Coed Barbie in Catcher's kitchen, but now she was saying there were more women in his life? Oh, hell no! "Um, I appreciate you being friendly and all, but I'm really a fan of monogamy."

Barbie frowned. "Excuse me?"

"Just can it, okay? As soon as I can get dressed, I'm out of here, and he's all yours. Or I guess I should say he's yours and all the other Barbie bimbos he's stringing along." I whirled around and stomped out of the kitchen and down the hall.

I threw open the bedroom door, sending it flying back into the wall. Before Barbie, I would have been horrified I had damaged the paint, but now I didn't give two shits if I had mowed down the entire wall.

Catcher was reclining back against the pillows with his hands behind his head. "Morning, Liv-Bug," he said with a sexy smile.

I just stood there, staring incredulously at him, as my heart began to crumble in my chest.

He flung the sheet back, showing me his straining cock. "We were both sad when we woke up to find you gone."

Well, I'm sure Barbie would be happy to tend to your needs. Without a second thought, I barged over to the bed. I couldn't contain my overwrought emotions, so I reached over

and grabbed one of the pillows. I then promptly whacked the hell out of Catcher with it.

Catcher pushed the pillow out of the way. "Olivia, what the fuck was that for?"

"Oh, I don't know. Maybe the fact there's a blonde bombshell out in the kitchen."

Catcher's smile faded a little. "You met Molly."

"Although we didn't exchange names, yes, I did meet her." I motioned to his crotch. "And as far as he goes, you can get the Bimbo Barbie to take care of you because I'm leaving."

"Oh fuck, Liv," Catcher grunted.

I went over to chair where I'd put my clothes after our fireplace sexing. Catcher took me by surprise by hopping out of bed and grabbing me in a bear hug.

"Let me go," I demanded as I fought against him.

"Not until you let me explain."

"What is there possibly to explain? It was all just made perfectly clear to me. I'm just one of many in your harem."

Catcher chuckled. "That's not what it is at all." When I started thrashing against him again, he pressed his face into my neck. His warm breath tickling the tender skin of my earlobe momentarily paralyzed me. "Molly is my baby sister."

At the word "sister", I went limp in his arms. "She's your sister," I repeated lamely. Sweet baby Jesus, I'd just completely made an ass out of myself over nothing.

"Yes. My very spoiled sister who likes to raid my fridge

and mooch off my cable when my parents have cut her off."

"Oh God," I moaned as extreme waves of mortification rolled over me.

"It's okay, Olivia."

"No, it's not. I not only made a fool out of myself in front of you, but I was a total bitch to your sister."

"That's okay. She usually deserves it." When my response came as another moan, Catcher squeezed me tight. "Come on. Let's get dressed, and I'll properly introduce you to Molly."

After swallowing down my continued embarrassment, I nodded at Catcher. "Okay."

He surprised me by bestowing a tender kiss on my lips. When he pulled back, he smiled at me. "I gotta admit that what you just did, acting all crazy jealous, I liked it. *A lot.*"

I rolled my eyes. "You would, Mr. Egomaniac."

Catcher snickered as he dropped his arms from around me. "I was just trying to get you to stop beating yourself up."

"I suppose you get a B for effort."

"At least it's not an F," he mused, as he threw a shirt over his head.

Although I was glad to have the opportunity to make things right with Molly, I was going to feel like an ass doing it in my sexy dress from last night. Once we were clothed, Catcher and I headed out of the bedroom. Instead of being on the bar stool, Molly stood at the top of the hallway, peering at us. As I took her in, I realized that I had been pretty blind not to notice how much she and Catcher resembled each other. They had a lot of the same facial features, including their shared blue eyes.

When I met Molly's gaze, she held her hands up. "I'm so, so sorry. I thought you knew who I was."

"No. I didn't. But I'm the one who is sorry. I totally went off on you like a bitch from Hell."

Molly laughed. "You had every reason to. I'm sure I would have done the same if I came out of the bedroom to see some other chick at my guy's place."

"What do you say we start over?"

"That would be great."

With a smile, I extended my hand. "I'm Olivia Sullivan."

Molly returned my smile as she shook my hand. "Molly Mains."

"Nice to meet you."

"Nice to meet you, too."

When I looked at Catcher, he was grinning. "I'm glad that's sorted out."

"Me too," Molly and I both replied.

"Now how about some breakfast?" Catcher asked.

"I'd love some. I actually came into the kitchen to fix you something when I ran into Molly."

Catcher's eyes flared as a pleased expression lit up his face. "You were going to fix me breakfast in bed?"

"I was going to try. I was pretty sure it hinged on what

you had in the pantry and fridge."

Catcher chuckled. "I'm not sure how well you would have come out. I try to keep the freezer stocked, but when I'm involved on a case, a lot of fresh stuff goes bad."

"You've got some eggs and bacon," Molly piped in.

"Are you keeping tabs on my food supply?" Catcher asked.

She grinned. "Not really. I just saw those when I was getting out the milk for my cereal."

Catcher rolled his eyes. "Of course you've already eaten, you little mooch."

She playfully smacked his arm. "Can I help it I'm a growing girl with an appetite?"

"An appetite that you never seem to appease on your own budget."

"I'm a sophomore in college on a meal plan. I don't have a budget."

After crossing his arms over his chest, he suggested, "You could get a job."

Molly wrinkled her nose. "It's too hard going to school and doing sorority stuff plus a job."

Catcher glanced from Molly to me. "Can you tell she's the spoiled only girl of the family?"

I laughed. "Maybe."

"My parents were total hard asses on Jem and me. Then Little Miss Surprise comes along when we're ten and twelve, and they absolutely lose their minds."

"So what literary character are you named for?" I asked Molly.

"Mine is actually a combo of Moll from *Moll Flanders* and Molly Bloom from *Ulysses*."

"Ah, I've never read those."

Molly rolled her eyes. "I've never read them either. I don't share my parents' passion for the classics. I would have much rather been named Hermione or Bella."

Catcher snorted. "Hey Ace, those books weren't out when you were born."

She waved her hand at her brother. "Whatever."

"How about that breakfast you were going to make?" Catcher prompted.

"You point me in the direction of the ingredients, and I'll whip something up."

After taking out some eggs, bacon, and frozen biscuits, I made breakfast while Catcher and Molly sat on the bar stools and chatted with me. I loved the teasing that the two gave each other. It reminded me a lot of Allen and me. I was also grateful Catcher had such a good relationship with his family. That was something I really looked for in a man.

Just as we were finishing eating, Catcher's phone started ringing back in the bedroom, and he went to answer it, leaving Molly and me alone. Since she had piqued my curiosity about her brother's love life, I stop myself from questioning her. "I hope it wasn't too shocking see me in your brother's robe."

Molly laughed. "No. It wasn't. Trust me, I've seen way worse in the dorms."

"Where do you go to college?"

"North Georgia."

"Oh, that's a good school. Beautiful campus."

"And being a military college, there's lots of hot guys around," she said, with a wicked grin.

I laughed. "That too."

Tilting her blonde mane at me, she asked, "Are you and Catcher serious?"

"Um, well, we've only known each other a few days."

Her brows shot up in surprise. "Really? I would've thought you guys had been dating longer."

"Why do you say that?"

"By the way he looks at you." She waggled her eyebrows. "He's got it bad for you."

Warmth flooded my cheeks. "Oh," I murmured. Hope rose within me with at her remark. Although it was still so soon, I wanted Catcher to have it bad for me. He was such a keeper considering the way he had forgiven me for my psycho misunderstanding.

"Listen, when I said I liked to meet Catcher's girls, I didn't mean it like he was some giant manwhore."

Once again, all I could say was, "Oh."

"I mean, don't get me wrong. He can be a pig when it comes to women, but for the most part, he's a decent guy who

wants to settle down with someone. He just hasn't met her yet."

Just when I was about to eloquently respond with "oh" again, Catcher came out of the bedroom. "That was the field office. I've got a lead on the Granny Witch Thornhill."

Molly's gaze flickered between the two of us. "You're an agent, too?"

I shook my head. "No. I'm a mortician along with being the coroner for Taylorsville."

Her eyes widened. "That has to be the coolest job ever."

I couldn't hide my surprise. "You really think so?"

"Yes. I've watched every single *CSI* out there. And *Bones*. I'm a Forensic Science major."

"Get out of here. That was one of my majors at The University of Georgia."

"Would you be willing to let me shadow you for one of my upcoming courses?" she asked with a hopeful expression.

"Of course you can. My town is pretty boring, but I'd be happy to go over the basics with you."

Molly gave me a beaming smile. "Awesome."

Catcher cleared his throat. "Um, if you two are finished bonding, Olivia and I need to get on the road."

"*We* do?" I asked.

Catcher grinned. "You've been along for everything else. You might as well come along for this one."

I smiled. "Okay. Where are we going?"

"About an hour from here to Ellijay."

After glancing down at my dress, I frowned. "I'm going to need to go get my change of clothes first."

"You go hop in the shower, and I'll get your bag out of the car."

"What about your shower?"

Catcher flashed me a wicked grin. "I'll join you when I get back."

"Um, ew. On that note, I'm out of here," Molly said.

"Good riddance," Catcher said. But then he pulled Molly to him and hugged her tight. "Take care of yourself."

"I will." After she pulled away, she kissed his cheek. "You be careful, too. Especially since you're investigating dark shit like witches."

Catcher laughed. "She's not a real witch, so there won't be any alleged 'dark shit.'"

"I hope not." She pulled out of Catcher's embrace to come and hug me.

Although I was a little taken aback, it felt good that at least one member of Catcher's family liked me. "It was nice meeting you, Olivia."

"Same to you. And I look forward to having you come out to shadow me next semester."

Molly smiled. "Me too."

"I'll walk you out," Catcher said. He then pointed at me. "Shower."

After giving him a salute, I said, "Yes, sir."

CHAPTER 16

After one shower quickie, Catcher and I got on the road a little after ten. We stopped for a quick lunch along the way. It was a gorgeous late February afternoon in Georgia where the weather gave a hint that springtime was just around the corner. I sat shotgun next to Catcher in his convertible. In spite of drawing my hair back into a twist, tiny strands whipped around my face from the top being down.

Although we were on official GBI business, Catcher

chose to drive his convertible since it was such a pretty day. When I'd questioned if he would get in trouble, he'd merely shrugged and said, "I've got one of the best records in over half the Georgia field offices. Let them try to give me shit."

So we zoomed along the interstate farther into the mountains to work on the Granny Witch lead which Zeke had given us. After Catcher and his fellow agents had done some investigating, he traced the woman to a New Age store called *The Crow's Caw* on the outskirts of downtown Ellijay.

Catcher eased the convertible off the main road and into the store's parking lot. The store was actually in an old house that looked like it had been built in the 1920's. It had three cement stairs leading up to a wide front porch. We got out and made our way up the stairs. When Catcher opened the door for me, a bell tinkled over our heads, announcing our arrival.

From the moment I stepped inside, I was jolted into sensory overload with the different sights and sounds. An exotic drumbeat played overhead through the stereo system, and if I closed my eyes, I could also imagine being in the Caribbean. The smell of incense filled my nostrils as my gaze bounced around all the multicolored crystals.

A woman, who appeared to be in her sixties, poked her head out of a door made of beads. "Hello. Can I help you?"

"I'm not sure. We're looking for someone called the Granny Witch," Catcher said.

A cat-like smile filled the woman's face. "I haven't heard

that term in a while."

"I apologize if there is any negative connotation. You certainly don't look like a granny or a witch to me," Catcher said.

"That's because I'm not."

"Oh," he murmured.

"I'm Jewell. The woman you wish to see is my mother."

"Does she live close by?" Catcher asked.

Jewell nodded. "Yes. About five miles up the mountain. Just what business do you have with her?" Before Catcher could answer, she tilted her head at us and said, "Hmm, I would imagine an attractive couple like you who appear to be so in love wouldn't need one of her love spells. Maybe something for fertility? She can get you pregnant just like this." Jewell snapped her fingers.

I waved my hands furiously back and forth. "No, no. We don't need anything like that."

With a mischievous twinkle in his eyes, Catcher said, "I haven't tried to knock her up yet, but I'll keep that in mind should my swimmers be slow starters."

When I turned openmouthed to him, he winked at me before reaching in his suit for his badge. "I'm Holden Mains with the GBI."

Jewell's smile slid from her face as her brown eyes widened. "Is my mother in some kind of trouble?"

Catcher shook his head. "No. We believe she might

have some information regarding a homicide we're investigating. You don't happen to know anyone by the name of Randy Dickinson do you?"

"No. I don't. But my mother has had so many clients over the years that it's hard to keep up." Jewell crossed her arms over her chest. "It's probably best if you go up there and talk to her yourself."

"Thank you. We will," I said.

Taking out his notepad, Catcher asked, "Do you have an address for her?"

Jewell laughed. "Where you're going isn't going to be on a GPS. The best way I can tell you is go five miles past Turniptown church. Then turn right by a mailbox with a peacock on it. Her house is up the hill."

Catcher furiously scribbled on his pad. "Five miles, mailbox with a peacock."

"That's right."

"Once again, thank you for the help."

"You're welcome."

We started for the door when Jewell said, "Be careful. Mama likes to answer the door with a shotgun."

While I gasped in alarm, Catcher merely chuckled. "I'll keep that in mind."

Ten minutes and twenty expletives from Catcher about how his car was getting banged to hell by the gravel roads later, we made a turn by a faded peacock mailbox that read THORNHILL. "How the hell does anyone live up here, least of all an old lady?" I questioned as the convertible bumped and hopped along the gravel drive up a massive embankment to the Granny Witch's house.

"Your guess is as good as mine," Catcher replied, as he had to put the convertible in low gear to make it up the hill.

We finally pulled up in front of an ancient-looking log cabin. It was the kind that you imagined Abe Lincoln living in back in the day or something like off *Little House on the Prairie*.

When we got out of the car, two, long-eared hound dogs came barreling out from under the porch. They started bellowing at us in unison. Since I really didn't want my life to end by being mauled by two hound dogs, I reached back into the car for the leftovers from lunch.

"Not my ribs!" Catcher hissed. Ignoring him, I tossed ribs and fries at the dogs. They dove at them and immediately began to devour them. With the dogs occupied, we started across the yard to the porch.

"I can't believe you just gave twenty dollar's worth of ribs to two backwoods hound dogs," Catcher grumbled.

"It was either the barbecue ribs or our ribs. Besides, you can stop by for more on the way home."

"Fine."

The front of the cabin was lined with flowerbeds and

rose bushes that would be beautiful in the springtime. After climbing the steps, we walked tentatively across the incredibly worn floorboards.

As I rapped my knuckles on the gnarled wooden door, Catcher palmed his gun in his holster. After all, we didn't know what might be lurking behind the door. A few moments passed, so I knocked again.

"What do you want?" a creaky, somewhat muffled voice questioned.

"Excuse the interruption, ma'am, but we need to speak to the Granny Witch."

There was a flurry of locks being turned, and then the door swung open. A diminutive woman with a face lined like a road map stood before us in a faded calico housedress. Just like her daughter had said, she had a shotgun in the crook of her arm. With her size, I couldn't help wondering how she possibly had the strength to lift it.

She narrowed her eyes at us. "I assumed you was looking for the Granny Witch. I sure as hell knowed you wasn't a bunch of Jehovah's Witnesses comin' out chere to see if I knew God. I don't believe Avon has ever called on me either." She tilted her head at us. "The question is what do you want with me?"

Once again, Catcher took out his badge. But before he could explain what we were doing there, the little woman shook her head. "Randy's dead."

Catcher and I both stared at her open-mouthed. "How

did you—" Catcher started to question.

She waved a weathered hand dismissively. "Saw it in the tea leaves this mornin'."

My brows furrowed in confusion. "The tea leaves?"

The Granny Witch pursed her lips at me. "Yeah, girlie, ain't ya never heared of readin' tea leaves?"

Since my only reference of the reading of tea leaves was in *Harry Potter and the Prince of Azkaban*, I decided it was best just to say no. With a grunt, the Granny Witch grabbed the sleeve of Catcher's shirt and dragged him inside. "Yer lettin' out all the heat."

"My apologies, ma'am. I didn't want to be rude since we hadn't been invited in," Catcher explained as I followed the two of them in. I quickly shut the door behind me before the Granny Witch could yell at me…or put the evil eye on me.

The Granny Witch led us across the worn hardwood floor and motioned for us to have a seat on a lumpy looking couch with a seventies design. I couldn't help stopping to wonder how the hell furniture was delivered out here.

"My name's Holden Mains. What's yours?"

"Olive Thornhill."

I smiled. "What a small world. My name is Olivia."

Olive didn't seem to appreciate the similarities of our names quite like I had. She eased down into a creaky rocking chair next to the fire. "When did Randy die?"

"He was found three days ago."

After nodding, Olive asked, "So what happened to him?"

"He was poisoned," Catcher answered. I tried to hide my surprise at his response. I figured he must be playing some kind of mind game with her to see what kind of information he could get.

"Why you lie to me boy?"

"Excuse me?"

"You and I both know Randy wasn't pizened. He was shot." Of course, it took me a minute to decode *pizened* in her dialect to mean *poisoned*.

Catcher shot straight up off the couch. "How could you have possibly known that?"

Olive narrowed her eyes at him. "I done tole ya I seen it in the tea leaves."

As the hair on my arms tweaked up, I started to feel like Catcher and I had stumbled into an episode of the Twilight Zone. I mean, it wasn't like we hadn't already experienced weird with Randy and two dicks, not to mention crazy snake handlers.

After swiping his hand across his face, Catcher eased back down on the sofa. "Do excuse my doubt, Mrs. Thornhill. I've been a GBI agent for eight years, and I have yet to ever come across anyone who read tea leaves."

A pleased smile crept on Olive's face. "That's 'cause it's a dyin' art. Not everyone has the gift, and if you do, you has to be acceptin' of it."

"The tea leaves actually showed you Randy?" I asked curiously.

"It showed me an 'R' with a dagger. The dagger in tea leaves means harm, so I figured harm was a comin' to Randy."

"Fascinating," I murmured.

Olive cocked her brows at me. "You two want a reading?"

Catcher and I exchanged a glance. Call me a pansy, but I was scared to death of what the bottom of Olive's tea cup might reveal. Thankfully, Catcher let us both off the hook when he said, "We better stick to the facts involving Randy's murder."

"Whatever," Olive replied as she shifted in her rocking chair. "But before I answer anymore questions, I wanna know how you knew about me."

"One of Randy's clients said he once referenced getting some of his knowledge from the Granny Witch."

Olive shook her head. "Randy shoulda knowed better than to be runnin' his mouth about me. I tole him what we did was to be a secret. Our knowledge in the wrong hands is dangerous. You'd a thought with him drinkin' an antidote for poison on a daily basis fer twenty-five years he woulda knowd that better than anyone."

"Why would he have the need to take a poison preventative?" Catcher asked.

"Because he was afraid of being pizened," Olive answered matter-of-factly like Catcher was the biggest dumbass in the world not to know that.

Catcher leaned forward on the couch. "Excuse me for it not being obvious, Mrs. Thornhill, but why would anyone need to take an antidote every day?"

"Randy needed it cuz he feared the man who was a lookin' for him might try to pizen him."

"Randy had someone after him?"

Olive nodded. "Fir over twenty-five years." She shifted in the rocking chair, causing the wood to groan. "I guess I better start at the beginnin'."

"That would be good," Catcher said.

"Randy grew up down the mountain in town. His daddy was the president of the bank, and his mama owned the dress shop. They done way better than most families after Dubya Dubya Two. When he was seventeen, his daddy done fell over dead at his desk from a heart attack. Five years later, Randy's mama got the cancer. That's when Randy come to see me."

"He wanted you to cast a spell to cure his mother?" I asked.

Olive scowled at me. "Girlie, Imma God fearin' woman. I ain't never cast no spells."

I held up my hands. "I'm sorry. It's just since they call you Granny Witch, I assumed you did some kind of witchcraft."

She gave a disappointed shake of her head. "You sure got yur idies messed up 'bout what a Granny Witch is. We

practice hillfolk hoodoo, not voodoo. Ain't no spells cast."

"Forgive my ignorance, but just what is hoodoo?" Catcher asked.

"Fir starters, it ain't no dark magic or tied to a religion. It's about usin' the gifts of the earth that God give us. It's been passed down from generation to generation, and it come over with our ancestors from Ireland and Scotland. Then it got mixed in a little when we were a intermarryin' with the Tsalgi's."

"The who?" I asked.

"The Cherokees."

I nodded. "Ah. I see. So it's a cross-cultural thing."

"I guess you could say that. Anyways, when Randy come to see me, I's able to make a yarb for his mama that give her another year. But I ain't the good Lord, so I couldn't save her."

"A yarb?" Catcher questioned.

Olive waved her hand dismissively. "You city-folk would call them herbs."

"Ah, I see."

"Anyways, I didn't see much of Randy after his mama died. Then one day outta the clear blue sky he come to see me. Said he wanted to learn my ways so he could mix it with the ways he'd learned at school."

"And you agreed to teach him?"

Olive nodded. "'Cause I seen the gift in him. I hadn't

seen it in anyone since my Jewell. Randy was an honest boy, so he promised me half of all the profits he made on his side ventures. I ain't never had no need for money, so onced I took care of a headstone for my dead husband, I give it to my children and grandchildren."

"That was awfully kind of you," I said.

"Randy was a fast learner. Whatever I made, he's able to improve on it and make it just a tad better. He was particularly interested in the man boosting yarb I made."

"Did this yarb give a man extra energy or something?" Catcher asked.

Olive smirked at him. "You might call it a resurrection yarb. It made dead peckers rise again."

Catcher and I exchanged a glance. "You mean you made an herbal Viagra?" I asked.

"Sho did."

"I'll be damned," Catcher mused.

"Men up chere in the mountains been needin' and usin' my man-booster long before any of them companies made stuff."

"I see."

Olive winked at Catcher. "Curious about it, ain't ya?"

Catcher grinned. "I would be lying if I said no. At the same time, I don't need any help in that area if you catch my drift."

"It ain't just fir dead peckers. It's fir the whole experience."

Catcher licked his lips and leaned forward. "Just exactly what does it do?"

Since the conversation was getting way off course and way too weird, I cleared my throat. "So what exactly does this man-enhancing yarb have to do with Randy being in hiding?"

"Like I said, Randy had been enhancin' my mixtures. He made the mistake of getting' a little greedy, and even though he hadn't perfected the mixture, he went ahead and sold a batch to the wrong man." She glanced around before continuing. "A man in the Dixie Mafia."

Catcher sucked in a breath. "Wait, the real Dixie Mafia?"

"Is there another one?" Olive huffed.

"No. It's just I've been in the area investigating them."

"You ever hear of Ronald Krump?"

Catcher's forehead creased. "No ma'am. I don't believe I have."

"Well, he's the one who had a beef with Randy over the man enhancing."

"Because he sold him the bad batch of man yarb?" Catcher questioned.

"That's right."

A question had been forming in my mind. "What made the batch bad? Did it not work or something??"

"Oh, it worked all right. Too well." Olive shook her head. "He's a terrible man, but I wouldn't wish that on my worst enemy."

"What happened to Ronald?" I asked.

Olive exhaled a deep breath. "His pecker blew off."

Silence permeated the room as Catcher and I sat there staring at Olive. I think we were both waiting on her to say, "Just kidding." But she never did. So we just kept sitting there trying to process the possibility of what she had just said.

Finally, after what felt like a brief eternity, Catcher said, "I'm afraid I didn't hear you correctly."

"I said his pecker done blew off."

Just when I thought things couldn't get any crazier..."Are you trying to say that Ronald's penis exploded?" I questioned in disbelief.

"It sho did."

Catcher turned to me with an incredulous expression. "How is that even possible?" he muttered.

Olive harrumphed. "Well, I dunno know how it's possible. I just knowed it happened."

"I would assume the medicine caused his penis to swell so quickly and intensely that the blood flow had nowhere else to go," I suggested.

"Except kaboom."

I rolled my eyes at Catcher. "It would be more of a forceful hemorrhage."

Catcher peered curiously at Olive. "Do you know what

happened to his penis?"

"Apparently he had to undergo several reconstructive surgeries, but it was never the same." A wicked look flashed in her eyes. "And it sho wasn't operational after that either."

"Damn. That blows," Catcher said before snickering at his pun.

Ignoring him, I asked, "What happened with Ronald and Randy after that?"

"Well, onced Ronald got out of the hospital, he started lookin' for Randy. But a few months into his search, he got arrested fir drugs and attemptin' to murder the man his wife was foolin' around with. I mean, Ronald shouldn't been surprised his wife was cattin' around when he had no dick." She stared us both straight in the eyes. "A woman has needs."

Oh. My. God. The last thing I needed at that moment was Olive talking about her needs.

"So what happened to Randy after Krump went to jail?" I inquired.

"He finally decided on Taylorsville as the place he could restart his life. Thankfully, Ronald was so hell-bent on taking revenge on Randy himself that he never put a hit on Randy. He was also so embarrassed by what happened that he didn't tell too many people how he lost his pecker. He led a lot of people to believe he got it shot off in combat during the first Gulf War."

"Ugh, what a slime-ball to pretend to be a wounded

veteran," I remarked.

Olive sighed sadly. "Although he was supposed to be in for life, I guess ol' Ronald musta got out of the big house and finally found poor Randy."

Catcher and I both sat in a stupefied silence, overwhelmed by what all we had just heard. The main question in any murder investigation was motive. You needed a reason to kill. In many cases, it's revenge. Sometimes it's revenge for an affair or revenge for ruining a person's business.

And now we knew that revenge was the motive in Randy's case. Revenge for a man's penis being blown up after taking a homemade male enhancement drug. Although I didn't have all the facts and statistics, I was pretty sure that in the annals of legal history, there had not been another case prosecuted over an exploding penis. Yet here we were.

After everything we had been through, I shouldn't have been surprised. Yet, I was completely bamboozled. I really don't know who I thought would be Randy's killer, but a penis-less member of the Dixie Mafia hadn't even been on my radar.

Olive rose out of her chair. "You two look like you could use a drink. I've got a little White Lightning up at my work shed."

I held up a hand. "That's awfully kind, but I wouldn't care for any."

When Olive turned to Catcher, he shook his head. "I appreciate it, Mrs. Thornhill, but I'm not permitted when I'm on the clock." He stood up. "I would love to take a look at your work shed though."

With a flick of her wrist, she motioned us to follow her. I wasn't too keen on seeing inside her work shed, but I didn't think I had much of a choice. So, I got up off the couch and followed her and Catcher out the back door of the cabin. Olive grabbed a cane that was leaning against the porch railing before hobbling down the stairs.

Once again I was amazed that someone her age and in her physical condition could make it up the steep embankment behind her cabin. But she did. The work shed was actually a one-room cabin that I'm surprised hadn't been condemned.

The inside wasn't much better than the outside. The sawdust-covered floor didn't look like it had been swept in years. At least one corner of the room was well kept. It had floor-to-ceiling wooden shelves that overflowed with small bottles and fruit jars.

"You two got any stomach ailments? Don't sleep? Need energy?" Olive asked.

I could have used something to sleep better, but I decided to keep my mouth shut. I wasn't quite sure if I believed in the validity of Olive's powers. More than anything, I wasn't convinced her yarbs weren't toxic.

As Catcher was eyeing the concoctions on the shelves, Olive picked up a small, blue bottle with a corked lid and handed it to me. "But I—"

"You don't get enough sleep."

"How did you know that?" Catcher asked.

"Probably from the bags under my eyes," I suggested.

Olive harrumphed at me. "I know from what you were thinking."

The hairs at the back of my neck rose at her words. "You can read my mind?"

Shaking her head, Olive replied, "I can feel your thoughts."

Aaaand, things had officially gotten too weird for me. It was time to get the hell out of there. I waved the bottle at her. "How much do I owe you?"

"Nothing."

"I can't just take this."

"Yes. You can." She jutted her chin out. "My payment will come when you realize the power of hoodoo."

Yep. Definitely time to go. "Well, thank you." I turned to Catcher. "Agent Mains, I need to make a phone call. I'll be in the car."

His forehead lined with confusion, but I didn't stop to explain anything. I just powerwalked right out of that hellhole before sprinting to the car. When I got inside, I locked the door. With one fleeting glance at Olive's yarb, I tossed it into my purse. Although I wanted to chuck it out the window the first chance we got, the curious part of me wanted to give it a try.

Thankfully, Catcher wasn't far behind me. He had his

phone in his hand, and I could hear the conversation inside the car. "Yeah, it's Mains. I need you guys to run a check on a man named Ronald Krump. He had been doing time, so you might want to start with the prison records. Thanks."

After Catcher hung up, he opened the car door and slid inside. "Now it's time to hunt down our suspect."

"At least finding out a name was one good thing to come out of this trip," I grumbled.

"Miss Olive spooked you a little, didn't she?" Catcher asked as we started down the hill.

I turned in my seat to pin him with a stare. "You mean you weren't freaked out with all the hoodoo craziness?"

Catcher chuckled. "I'll admit it was a little freaky, but whatever power she has, Olive uses for good."

Wanting a subject change, I asked, "Now the cat is out of the bag, so to speak, can you tell me why you were investigating the Dixie Mafia?"

"We've been looking for one of their members who is a drug kingpin. He came under our radar a few months ago. He's been running drugs across Georgia into Alabama and Tennessee."

"Who is he?"

"We really don't know."

I arched my brows in surprise. "You don't *know*?"

Catcher nodded. "He's called The Shadow. No one can adequately identify him. Most of the men under him have

295

never seen him—his orders come over a go phone or an email. He's been known to alter his appearance with minor plastic surgery, hair and eye color changes, and weight that yo-yos fifty pounds. We're not sure if the weight is something he actually does to alter himself, or if it has to do with him being on drugs."

"Do you think this Shadow guy and Ronald might know each other?"

"It's possible. Hell, with this case, anything is possible. I'm trying to pin down something that has The Shadow, Delaney, and Ronald all together."

"Could Delaney be The Shadow?"

"While we haven't completely ruled that out yet, I don't think he is."

"It's too ironic your case with The Shadow and Randy's murder ran together. It was like our paths were destined to cross." Oh jeez. Had I really said one of the worst cliché's out loud?

Catcher's response came in the form of a grunt. When I glanced over at him, his expression was pained. "What's wrong?"

He grimaced. "Nothing."

"Are you sure? You look like you're hurting."

"I'm fine."

The next thing I knew he'd whipped the car off the main road and driven into a heavy thicket of trees. "Catcher, what in the world are you doing?"

He slammed on the brakes and threw the car into park before turning to me with a wild expression and crazed eyes. "We have to fuck. *Now.*"

Before I could ask him if he had lost his mind, my gaze dropped to his crotch. "Holy shit!" The bulge straining against the zipper of his pants was bigger than it had ever been. It was huge. Like *colossally* huge. "What happened to you?"

"After you ran out of the work shed, Olive snuck me some man yarb to try," he explained as his hips bucked up. His head fell back against the headrest, and he groaned as his pelvis swiveled. Beads of sweat began to line his forehead.

"Are you insane? After Ronald's dick blew up, you actually thought it was a good idea to take that shit?"

Catcher gritted his teeth. "Olive doesn't make the stuff that blew up Ronald's dick. Hers is safe."

I rolled my eyes. "Like she has FDA approval."

He didn't respond. Instead, he bit down on his lip as his hand went to shift the bulge. "Fuuuck," he groaned.

"Okay, regardless of whether or not it was safe, why in the world would you take it now?"

"I thought it would be a while for it to take effect. Like we would get home, and I'd be ready." After his hips punched forward again, he lunged at me. He took my face between his hands. "Baby, please. I've got to get inside you."

I knew I couldn't leave him high and dry in his hour of desperation. There was also something very erotic about a man pleading with you for sex. It was a hell of a power trip. "Backseat?"

Relief momentarily flickered on his face. After throwing a glance over his shoulder, he shook his head. "Too small."

After swallowing hard, I suggested, "Outside."

Catcher nodded. "The hood."

While I was glad he didn't plan to nail me up against a tree, I hadn't exactly planned to become a hood ornament. "Okay. Let's do this."

We scrambled out of the doors and around the front of the car. Catcher crashed into me, his mouth frantically meeting my own. He kissed like a man on death row—desperate, intense, and consuming.

His hands slid up under my dress and ripped my flimsy thong from my body. "You're going to owe me a fortune in underwear, Mr. Neanderthal," I teased breathlessly.

Catcher grunted in response as he worked his pants down over his hips. My mouth ran dry at the sight of his erection. Below the waist, moisture pooled between my legs. Olive's potion didn't hold back any punches. I decided then it was just best to go with the flow and let Catcher do what he needed to do to find relief. "Take me," I instructed.

He didn't need to be told twice. He whirled me around and placed my hands on the hood of the car. Using one of his knees, he knocked my legs wide apart. His fingers dug into my hips as he slammed into me, causing me to shriek.

Catcher immediately froze. "Oh fuck, did I hurt you?"

Turning my head, I glanced back to see his apologetic expression. "No, no. It's good."

"Thank God," he murmured. He slid slowly out of me only to slam back again. His dick then began a relentless pounding of my pussy. My fingers curled on top of the hood, and I knew my nails were going to leave scratch marks on the paint. I'd never had it so hard or so rough. There wasn't a doubt in my mind I was going to be deliciously sore for days. My first order of business after returning home would be to write Olive a thank you letter and ask her for a six-month supply of man-enhancing yarb. That and to put an ice pack on my pulverized vag.

One of Catcher's hands came to intertwine in my hair. When he gave the strands a harsh tug, the feeling, coupled with the pounding, sent me into a screaming orgasm. After I came back to myself, I realized Catcher was still going.

And like the Energizer Bunny, he kept going and going. He flipped me over to lie on top of the hood before continuing to drill me. It was when I came the second time that Catcher tensed and came flooding in me. And just like the pounding, his orgasm went on and on.

When he finally finished, he collapsed onto me and let out a long, agonized groan. "You okay?" I questioned.

He raised his sweat-soaked head to look at me. "Holy fucking shit."

I giggled. "I guess that's a yes."

"Some pharmaceutical company should invest in Olive's man enhancer. It's worth a fortune."

"That good, huh?"

Catcher whistled. "Not that every time with you isn't good."

"Nice save."

He laughed. "But this was out-of-this-world good. I didn't think I was ever going to stop coming." He cocked his brows at me. "Was it good for you, too?"

"Uh, I'm pretty sure *good* isn't the right word. Phenomenal. Overwhelming. Life-altering. Those seem more accurate."

Catcher grinned. "Damn. What a high." He frowned slightly. "Overall, I'd have to say that the mood was slightly dampened by my original fear that my dick was going to explode like Ronald's."

"So does that mean you won't become an addict?"

"No. I think it's best to leave it alone. It's not like I'm hurting in that area."

I grinned as I craned my neck to kiss him. "You're magnificent. "

"Stop. You'll make me blush," he teased.

At the faraway sound of a car, I pushed Catcher off me. "We better get out of here before someone sees us."

He snorted. "I can see the headlines now. GBI Agent and Coroner arrested for public indecency and lewd behavior." When he reached for his pants, he groaned. "Shit."

"What?" I asked as I slid off the hood. I was momentarily distracted from Catcher's question by the fact I had spunkiness going on between my legs. I sure as hell hoped Catcher had some napkins in his dash so that I could clean up.

When I looked at him, his expression was ashen. "I forgot a condom."

"It's okay. I'm on the pill."

"You are?"

I rolled my eyes. "Yes, Even though it seems like a ludicrous idea for a woman not having sex to be on birth control, trust me, I am."

Catcher exhaled a relieved breath that came out more as a wheeze. "Not quite ready to make little Catchers yet, are you?" I teasingly asked.

"Not yet." He jerked his pants up before smiling at me. "Not until I put a ring on your finger."

I stared wide-eyed at him before shaking my head. "For you to say that aloud, I think all the blood in your head went to your dick."

He chuckled. "Not today, babe. But someday."

Even though he was still tripping in an amazing sex haze, I knew he was serious. It should have alarmed me considering we barely knew each other, but it didn't. Instead, it made me feel all warm and gooey on the inside like I was thirteen again and getting asked out to the movies by my crush. It felt hella surreal to be wanted and desired by a strong, handsome, amazing man.

I was pretty blown away that despite the short amount of time we'd spent together, Catcher still saw a future for us. And I felt the same way. I was just hoping and praying that the other shoe wouldn't drop because Agent Sexy-Ass Mains had gotten under my skin.

CHAPTER 17

The next few days passed without any crazy incidents or further information on Randy's murder. Catcher was asked to consult on a different drug case while he was waiting on leads for both Randy and The Shadow. As for me, it was pretty slow at Sullivan's with only one service to preside over.

Although Catcher was busy and lived forty-five minutes away, it didn't stop him from burning up the phone lines and roads to see me. And whenever we were together, our sex life set fire to whatever surface we could find be it the bed, the floor, the bathtubs at our houses, the backseat of his convertible. Thankfully, we were pretty creative when it came to places to have sex....and flexible. Of course, after my pounding on the car hood, it took me a couple of days for my vag to feel like its old self and be fully operational again.

But our physical connection was becoming rivaled by the emotional connection we had. Even though it had only been a week, I was starting to envision a future with Catcher. The rational side of me reasoned that it was ridiculous and "insta-love" wouldn't last. But the teenage girl in me sent me doodling *Mrs. Olivia Mains* or *I Love Catcher* on my notepad while taking down funeral information. Oh yes, it was just that sickening.

On the fateful day that led to me being bound and gagged outside of a sexual scenario, I was in my office catching up on paperwork when the phone rang. I couldn't hide my goofy grin when I saw it was Catcher. "Hey you."

"Hey, babe, I've got some news." He sounded out of breath.

I leaned forward in my chair. "What's up?"

"You're never going to believe this."

"Considering what we've seen in the last week, try me."

"You know how I told you we've had a secret informant giving us information on The Shadow."

"Yeah."

"Turns out, Mr. Delaney was the informant."

I gasped. "You're joking."

"It's crazy, but I'm not."

"How did you guys find out?"

"Our IT department started decoding Delaney's laptop, and then all the emails from him to us showed up."

"So that means that Krump killed Delaney too?"

"Yup. Apparently Krump worked as a hitman for the Dixie Mafia back in the day."

"And he's definitely out of prison?"

"Yeah, somehow the fucker got released six months ago. Allegedly for good behavior."

"I'm guessing the twenty-five years in prison didn't change him since he's been on a killing spree since he got out."

"It's looking that way. Listen, I gotta run up to Ellijay to have Olive sign a deposition. You wanna come with me. We could have lunch at that barbecue joint we liked. I know you said you wanted to go downtown and look in all the shops."

"I really need to stay here and do paperwork."

Catcher grunted. "You can do paperwork anytime. It's a beautiful day, and I've got the top down."

Damn him. He was such a bad influence on me. As I nibbled my lip, I glanced down at Motown who was snoozing at my feet. "Can I bring Motown along? He loves car rides."

At the mere mention of "car", Motown's furry head jerked up, and he stared pleadingly at me.

"Sure you can bring him along. The more the merrier."

I grinned into the phone. "Okay. Where can we meet you?"

"Come down to Jasper. We'll meet at the shopping center off Hwy 515."

"Okay. See you in thirty minutes."

"Bye, Liv-bug."

My heart flip-flopped. "Bye, Catcher."

After meeting up, Catcher, Motown, and I headed north to Ellijay. We bypassed the barbecue place, so we could eat outside at one of the cafés downtown that was dog friendly. We did a little window-shopping, and then Catcher babysat Motown while I went inside a few places.

Once we were finished, we headed up the mountain to Olive's. When we passed the turnoff where we'd had our hood hookup, I couldn't help giggling.

"What is it?"

"I was just thinking about our sexcapade out in those woods."

Catcher waggled his brows. "Oh yeah."

"Just make sure while you're signing the deposition you don't let Olive slip you any more male-enhancer."

"Are you sure? That was some pretty epic fucking."

"Yes, it was. But I'm not sure my vagina can withstand another pounding like that."

Catcher chuckled. "Okay, okay. No more man yarb for me."

We pulled into Olive's driveway. Since she didn't own a phone, we hadn't been able to call ahead to see if she was home. I guess we could have tried Jewell at *The Crow's Caw.*

I had just reached for the door handle when my phone rang. After seeing it was Allen, I turned to Catcher. "Go on in. I need to take this."

"Sure thing.

"Hey. What's up?" I asked as I answered the phone.

"I've got a real cunt-bag on the phone who is demanding to talk to you."

"Take a message, and I'll call her back."

"Uh, yeah, Ace, thanks for the tip. I've already done that. She keeps calling back."

"Who is it?"

"Felicia Brown."

I groaned. The unfeeling widow whose sons' antics had led to all the craziness last week. "You have got to be joking."

"She's saying we're charging her for things she didn't agree to."

"Patch her through," I muttered. When the phone beeped, I said, "Hello, Mrs. Brown. What seems to be the problem?"

I spent the next ten minutes arguing with Mrs. Brown and defending my business tactics. Finally, I'd had enough.

"Look, I'm not going to discuss this with you anymore. Either you pay the bill, or I'll see you in small claims court." When she started arguing with me again, I shouted, "Bye, Felicia!" into the phone before hanging up.

"What a bitch," I grumbled as I tossed my phone into my purse. I threw a glance in the backseat to see Motown snoring away. "Figures. You sleep through everything, including me yelling at a cunt-bag," I mused.

When I opened the car door to go join Catcher, Motown raised his head. "Stay, boy. I'll be right back." He yawned and then lay back down.

As I made my way across the yard, I was surprised I didn't see or hear Olive's hound dogs like I had the other day. They were probably off chasing squirrels in the woods. I climbed the steps and made my way across the porch. When I knocked on the front door, it creaked open. "Catcher? Olive?"

After pushing the door wide, I saw the living room and kitchen were empty. I stepped inside. "Helllooooo?"

"Well hello."

The sound of a strange and incredibly creepy voice had me whirling around. A heavyset man in a red and white checked flannel shirt stood blocking the front door. I swallowed the rising panic down in my throat at the sight of Creepy Voice.

Oh shit. Oh shitty-shit-SHIT! This was so bad. My gaze bounced around the room, desperately searching for any sign of Catcher. Although I should've been concerned about Olive's

whereabouts too, Catcher was the one with a gun and hand-to-hand combat training.

Slowly, I started inching toward the back door. If I could just get outside, I might have a chance to get away. I'd been a half-way decent runner back in the day when I ran track in high school. But then I bumped into something warm and fleshy. When I spun around, an overweight man in a John Deere hat grunted at me. The next thing I knew he pointed a shotgun at me. "Let's go."

John Deere grabbed my arm and dragged me down the porch steps. My heart was beating so frantically that I was afraid it was going to explode right out of my chest. Fear had me almost paralyzed. I would've been frozen in place if I hadn't been forced along by the burly redneck.

When he shoved me toward the hillside, I momentarily faltered. Nothing good could come from going up there. John Deere and Creepy Voice were either going to take me into the woods and rape and kill me, or they were going to take me into the work shed and rape and kill me.

I didn't want to die. Not now. Not after I'd finally found a man to love and have hot sex with. That would just be entirely too cruel.

John Deere jabbed the shotgun into my back. "Move it."

Tears welled in my eyes. "Please don't kill me," I whimpered.

"That ain't up to us. Ronald will make the decision on

that one," Creepy Voice said.

Oh God. There could only be one Ronald he was talking about. The one who had shot Randy and poisoned Mr. Delaney. Swallowing hard, I pushed my trembling legs forward. Somehow I found the strength to make it up the hillside. John Deere escorted me into the work shed. What I saw before me brought fresh tears to my eyes.

It was Catcher, and thankfully, he was alive. Of course, it was an epic bummer that his wrists were bound by rope, and his arms were tied over his head to one of the wooden beams in the middle of the room. His eyes widened at the sight of me. "I'm sorry, Liv," he lamented.

"It's not your fault."

"I should have never asked you to come along today."

I shook my head. "You couldn't have possibly known a simple trip to Olive's would be dangerous."

"Are you okay? They didn't hurt you, did they?"

Creepy Voice crossed the room and smacked Catcher across the face. "Shut yer yappin'!"

Catcher gritted his teeth while venom burned in his eyes. John Deere dragged me over to the beam. He shoved me down on the floor. Creepy Voice tossed him some rope, which he used to tie my wrists and ankles together. Unlike Catcher, he didn't tie me to be beam. Of course, considering how I was trussed up, it wasn't like I was going to be able to run anywhere.

Once I was tied up, the Redneck Twins wrapped a gag

around both of our mouths before leaving us alone. An eternity seemed to pass. It felt like hours, but it might've only been a few minutes. It was in those moments that my love life flashed before my eyes, and I relived my past.

I was jolted from my thoughts by the work shed door opening. A tall, lanky man stepped inside the room. He wore a white button-down shirt with no tie, and a pair of black dress pants. A pungent smelling cigar was in his mouth. On top of his head was the worst toupee I'd ever seen, and that was saying a lot since I'd worked on a lot of bald men in my funeral days.

I knew without a shadow of a doubt that it was Ronald Krump. Of course, my gaze couldn't help zeroing in on his crotch. Even in what could have been my final moments, I couldn't help wondering what a reconstructed penis looked like. Did it feel like a dildo or smooth like real skin? And where did the extra parts come from to rebuild it? I mean, it wasn't like men were lining up to donate their penises. It certainly wasn't on the checklist for organ donations. I wondered if he would grant me a last request by dropping his pants and showing it off.

"Well, well. I have to say you two are a surprise. I had my men come up here to detain the bitch who helped take away my manhood, and instead of her, we get you two."

A relieved breath whooshed out of my nose. They hadn't killed Olive. Thankfully, she hadn't been home and was safe somewhere.

Krump crossed the room to stand in front of us. He jerked Catcher's gag away. "Agent Mains, it's so nice to finally meet the man who has been putting so much heat on my ass these last few months."

"*You're* The Shadow?" Catcher questioned incredulously. I was just as surprised as he was.

"Yes. I am."

"But how the hell is that possible? The Shadow has a drug operation that's been underway for over a year. You didn't get out of prison until six months ago."

"There's a simple explanation for that. While I ran the operation from inside the big house, my two associates, that you just had the privilege of meeting, did all the leg work on the inside."

"That's why your appearance kept changing with people's descriptions."

Ronald grinned. "Pretty ingenious, isn't it?"

"How did you even get started on the drug trade when you were inside?" Catcher inquired.

"When it looked like I would get paroled, I knew I needed to start working on building a new life when I got outside. Through a few contacts on the inside, I hooked up with Larry and Daryl, and the business was launched. Things were rolling along until my old enemy in the mafia, Delaney, got wind of what I was doing and decided to pull a snitch." Ronald shook his head. "A little bit of cyanide took care of

312

him."

"What about Randy?" I questioned behind my gag.

Ronald left Catcher's side to come stand before me. He cocked his brows before snatching away my gag. "And just what is it you wanted to know?" He ran his fingers across my face, causing me to shudder in revulsion. He licked his lips. "You sure are a pretty thing, aren't you?"

"I asked about Randy."

A sour look came over Ronald's expression. "Oh yes, how could I forget about Randy Dickinson? The man who ruined my life."

"It was your choice to take a non-FDA approved male-enhancement drug," I countered.

Ronald's nostrils flared in anger. "You shut your damn mouth!" he snarled. He raised his hand to hit me, but then he lowered it. He began pacing in front of me. "Do you have any idea what it is like to lose your penis? To have the one part of you that makes you a man violently taken away from you."

When he paused for me to reply, I quickly said, "Um, no. I don't." I knew better than to argue that as a woman, I didn't have a penis, so I just couldn't relate to having my manhood taken. He was already so mentally unhinged I didn't want to do anything else to set him off.

"I was just looking for a good time—something to make sex interesting again. When it came to fucking, I'd done just about everything there was out there. Except for doing a dude.

313

I needed something to take me to the next level. Then I hear about this guy who made a drug that could make sex out of this world."

He narrowed his eyes at me. "Randy was a pharmacist, for fuck's sake. He worked with drugs every day. Why shouldn't I have trusted him? How was I to know he was working with some backwoods hoodoo psycho to make some of his drugs?"

He exhaled a trail of foul-smelling smoke in my face. "He had to pay for what he did to me. It didn't take me too long to find him. But I took my time about killing him—I had to get the logistics just right. Through my drug connections, I was able to bribe someone in the security company that handled Randy's account to deactivate his security system. Fucker was fast asleep in dreamland. Of course, I made sure to wake him up, so I knew the last thing he saw was my face."

"You sure aren't worried about running your mouth off to us, are you?" Catcher asked.

Ronald sneered at him. "What does it matter if I confess to you two? You're going to be dead in ten minutes."

His words sent an icy chill down my spine, and I shuddered. Glancing over my shoulder at Catcher, I desperately hoped he had some kind of plan to get us out of this mess. But the ashen expression on his face caused my hope to shrivel.

The Redneck Twins appeared in the doorway. "You ready, boss?" John Deere asked.

"Yeah. I am. Go ahead and untie them." Ronald tossed his cigar onto the floor and stomped out the embers. Then he glanced at Catcher and me. "You two are going to take a little walk into the woods with my associates." He flashed us a maniacal smile. "It's nothing personal. I just can't have you on my ass anymore, Agent Mains." He took a step toward me. "And as for you, well, I'm sorry, but you know too much to keep you around." After motioning for the twins, he started for the door. "Now if you'll excuse me, I'm going back to the shithole that witch calls a house to wait on her to come home."

With a flick of his wrist in farewell, he headed out the door. John Deere got busy untying my ankles. He then yanked me up off the floor before he untied my hands. After having my legs tied, they were wobbly, and I stumbled several times on the way to the door.

As I started out of Olive's shack, I fought the tears threatening to overrun my eyes. I couldn't believe it had really come to this—being murdered in the backwoods by a member of the Dixie Mafia who had once had his penis blown off. My worst fear of dying unmarried had come to fruition. After years of judging people's lives as I wrote their obituaries, I couldn't help judging my own.

Olivia Sullivan, 30, Beloved daughter and sister. Co-owner and proprietor of Sullivan's Funeral Home. Coroner for Taylorsville County. Spinster.

Because I was the county coroner, I would get a decent

write-up in the local newspaper. I hoped Allen would remember where I had left the instructions for my funeral. Being dead would suck, but it would suck even worse with my mother making all the decisions. Or worse, if Pease was doing it.

Peering over my shoulder, I threw a final glance at Catcher. Although I might be dying unmarried, I had at least found love in the eleventh hour. It would have been nice to have a future with him. To fill the house he had built with our children. To grow old and gray together. I couldn't hold in my emotions any longer, and I began to quietly weep.

When we started into the woods, a low growl echoed around us. I whirled around just as a white ball of fur came hurtling at us. At first, I thought it might be a mountain lion or a coyote. But then my heart surged when I realized it was Motown.

He lunged at John Deere, knocking him to the ground. As Motown started using John Deere as a chew toy, Catcher swung into action. He started throwing punches at Creepy Voice.

John Deere writhed on the ground as Motown snarled and snapped like a mad dog. I'd never seen him act like that. When Catcher got Creepy Voice down on the ground, I yelled his name. As soon as he glanced up, I tossed the shotgun that John Deere had abandoned over to him.

Catcher picked it up just as Creepy Voice lunged at him. The shotgun's blast took me off guard. It also caused

Motown to momentarily quit mauling John Deere. It was then that Catcher sank to the ground, blood pouring down his leg. My mouth gaped open wide to scream, but nothing came out.

At that moment, the woods became alive with a flurry of activity. Men came running out of nowhere outfitted in black jackets with the words *GBI* emblazoned on the back. There were a few Gilmer County Sheriff deputies as well. The agents I'd met at Randy's, Solano and Capshaw, knelt down beside Catcher.

A GBI Agent jogged up to me. "Ma'am, are you okay?"

I started to brush past him. "Ma'am?" he asked again.

"I'm fine. I swear." I didn't have time for this bullshit. I needed to get to Catcher to make sure he was all right. From what I could see over the agent's shoulder, Catcher's eyes were closed, and he wasn't moving.

Once the agent let me go, I raced over to him. "Catcher?" I cried as I sank to the ground beside him.

His eyes popped open. "Hey, Liv-Bug."

"Oh, my God, are you okay?"

"Just peachy."

Fearing he was going into shock, I countered, "You were shot."

"Tis but a scratch," he teased with the line from *Monty Python and The Holy Grail*.

I glanced over to where Solano had ripped open Catcher's pants leg to examine the bullet wound. Over the years, I'd seen enough shotgun wounds. I feared at close range it might be a pretty extensive wound. But at first glance, it didn't look that bad.

Agent Solano snorted. "He's right about the scratch thing. The bullet grazed him more than anything. He's practically a miracle. A couple more inches, and it would have nicked his femoral artery."

"And you would have bled out," I said to Catcher.

When Catcher nodded almost nonchalantly, I fought the urge to smack him. Just hearing how close he had come to death sent the shakes rolling through me. I didn't know how he was taking things so calmly.

Catcher flashed me a wicked grin. "It's even more miraculous that a few more inches to the right, and I might've lost my dick."

Clenching my fists at my side, I had to hold myself back from strangling him. "How can you think about your dick at a time like this?!"

He frowned. "I'm sorry. I was just trying to make the situation a little lighter."

My emotional dam broke at that moment, sending tears streaming down my cheeks. "You could have died." I sniffled. "I could have lost you."

"But you didn't. I'm going to be fine. A few stitches and I'll be good as new."

I swiped my runny nose with the back of my hand. Since I was used to dealing with dead people, I wasn't sure how to gage the wounds of the living. "Really?"

"Well, Solano isn't a paramedic or doctor, but I value his opinion."

When I glanced over at Agent Solano, he grinned at me. "Yeah, he's going to be fine."

Those simple words had me losing it again. I buried my head in Catcher's chest and wept unabashedly. "Babe, it's okay. *I'm* okay," Catcher murmured in my ear.

"I know. I just can't bear to think about how I almost lost you." I rose up to stare him in the eye. "I love you, Catcher Mains. I know we barely know each other, and it's incredibly fast, but I know that I love you. It's been coming on for a while, but when the Redneck Twins took us out on our death march, I knew then how much I loved you."

With Agent Solano hanging on to my every word, I wasn't sure what kind of reaction Catcher might have. I imagined him going all macho Han Solo and saying, "I know," to my "I love you." But instead, he leaned forward and brought his lips to mine. "I love you, too."

"Awwww," Solano said.

"Bite me," Catcher grumbled against my lips.

The paramedics arrived then, and one began working on Catcher's leg. I held his hand as the paramedic began to clean the wound. "Glad I got you. I'm sure my partner is having a hell of a time taking care of those dog lacerations."

It was then that I remembered poor Motown. I rose to

my feet and whistled for him. He came charging up and began to lick me. Ordinarily I was okay with that, but at the moment, he was covered in John Deere's blood. The paramedic passed me an extra towel from his bag, and I began to wipe Motown down.

"You are such a good dog," I cooed as I scratched his ears.

"That's a pretty heroic pooch there to take on the bad guys," the paramedic replied.

"Yes, he is. After he has a bath, I'm going to make sure he has a nice, juicy steak." I glanced at Catcher and grinned. "I'll be giving both my men some TLC tonight."

"Lucky us," Catcher mused.

I momentarily paused in wiping Motown down. "There's one thing I'm wondering about."

"Like what does Krump's reconstructed dick look like? I'm sure we could pull his pants down before they take him away."

I rolled my eyes at Catcher. "No. That's not it. I was wondering how your fellow agents knew to come here."

"When I got to the front door, I noticed it was slightly ajar—something Olive would never do considering the way she felt about leaving the door open the day we were here. I went ahead and took out my phone, so that I could press the panic button to the agency if I needed to. Once I got inside, the Redneck Twins, as you call them, ambushed me. Thankfully, I got to press the button before they had me drop my phone. Then I just tried to play it cool like there wasn't anyone on the way." Catcher shot Solano a look. "Of course, these fuckers took their own sweet-ass time getting here."

"I would second that," I said.

Solano held up his hands. "My apologies. But do keep in mind how you guys were in the Boonies. It's not so easy to get out here."

"Speaking of Krump, did you guys get him?" I asked Solano.

"Sure did. We nabbed him just as he was starting back into Ms. Thornhill's cabin."

Inwardly, I did a fist pump at the news. It was nice knowing that he would be going back to prison. Of course with Randy and Mr. Delaney's murders on his hands, he would be going for life.

"Okay. We're ready to transfer you to the ambulance now," the paramedic said.

"Can you walk?" Solano asked Catcher.

"Yeah. As long as I don't put any weight on this leg."

"I'll help you."

Solano and the paramedic lifted Catcher up before each one put Catcher's arms on their shoulders. Catcher winced and sucked in a harsh breath, but he hobbled along down the hillside before collapsing onto stretcher. "Motherfucker," he hissed.

"Ma'am, you want to ride with us?" the paramedic

321

asked.

"Yes. But my dog has to come along with us."

"I guess we can make some allowances for a hero dog."

I grinned. "Thank you."

Motown and I walked along the side of Catcher's stretcher. "I'm probably going to get a plaque for this," Catcher remarked.

"Really?"

He nodded. "Yeah. Considering I was wounded in the line of fire taking down a notorious drug dealer and his thugs."

"If you get honored by the bureau, I will be sitting in the front row, taking pictures and cheering you on."

Catcher beamed. "So it's a date, huh?"

"Yep. It's a date."

I had a feeling it was going to be one of many dates I would have with Catcher. Our future seemed bright.

# EPILOGUE
SIX MONTHS LATER

As the organ music struck up the familiar chords of *Here Comes the Bride*, I sucked in a deep breath and tried to once again still my out-of-control nerves. The last thing I needed was to face-plant while walking up the aisle. Today was my big day—the one I'd waited what felt like a lifetime for.

My *wedding* day.

Allen offered me his arm. "Ready, sis?"

"Ready as I'll ever be."

He gave me a warm smile. "You've been ready for this for years. You've been through hell to get here, and you deserve all the happiness in the world. This is your time to shine."

I blinked a few times at him in disbelief. When had my baby brother become so wise and supportive of both matrimony and me? "Oh Allen," I murmured.

"Now quit bitching and get your ass down the aisle," he commanded.

Laughter bubbled from my lips. "That sounds more like you."

Since I couldn't have my father walk me down the aisle, I had asked Allen. He had seemed touched in the moment, but then when it came to tuxedo fittings and other wedding oriented events, he had pissed and moaned.

The wedding coordinator waved her hand furiously at us like, "Let's get the show on the road."

After sliding my arm through Allen's, I took one last calming breath before taking a step forward. The double doors to the First Baptist's sanctuary swung open while every head in the house whirled around to catch a glimpse of me in my strapless ivory gown with the beaded, satin bodice and fluffy toile bottom. A glittering tiara held my long, flowing veil in place. It cascaded over my shoulders to lie against my long train.

Although I could feel every eye on me, there was only one particular pair I was interested in. A set of ocean-blue, bedroom eyes. The ones that belonged to my future husband.

When I saw him, I momentarily faltered in my march down the aisle. God, he looked so gorgeous in his tux. Like James Bond. Instead of his signature drop-dead-sexy smile, he wore an expression of absolute awe. It was the look every bride hopes and prays she sees on her groom's face. The one that makes you fall in love with him all over again.

I pushed myself forward, wanting nothing more than to get to Catcher—my future husband. It was still hard for me to think I had finally found the one. The one who completed me and all that jazz. The truth was Catcher did more than complete me. He brought out the best in me. He challenged me to be the best person I possibly could. He didn't want me to conform to what society's ideas were about what a woman should be personally and professionally.

But better than that was the fact he embraced all the worst in me—my insecurities, my sometimes klutzy moments, my embarrassing sex past, my years of datelessness. For some reason, he was attracted to every part of me—the good, the bad, and the ugly. When I hoped and prayed for someone to love, I couldn't have imagined the good fortune I would be getting.

As I made my trek down the aisle, I took in the faces of those standing in the pews. The church was packed with our friends and family. There were those I'd known since childhood, those from my career like Ralph and Todd and Earl, and those I had met with Catcher like Patricia Crandall, who thankfully had on a beautiful pink suit, rather than her birthday suit, and Olive and Jewell. Of course, Jill was absent from the pews because she was my matron of honor—yes, I had finally received that call that she and Chase were getting remarried in Vegas. Since I had a matron of honor, I had made Molly my maid of honor.

Of course, my mother's beaming face could have lit up the entire church. She sat on the first pew with her now husband, Harry. Tears of happiness streamed down her face. I could tell she was barely able to contain her happiness that I was finally getting married. I couldn't hide my surprise that even Pease had happy tears sparkling in her eyes.

On the other front pew was Catcher's parents along with Jem and his wife and kids. Martin and Sarah Mains were going to be the best in-laws. I already loved spending time with them. Considering they were both English teachers, I had expected them to be stuffy and pretentious. Thankfully, I'd found them to be the complete opposite. Martin possessed the same irreverent humor that Catcher had, and dinners around their large, mahogany table had me in stitches with Catcher and Martin's antics. Molly was fast becoming the little sister I never had, and I adored spending time with Catcher's three nieces and two nephews. Of course, whenever I did, my biological clock went into overdrive.

Although the commute was going to be hell, I was moving into Catcher's house. On nights when we had a late visitation, I'd merely sleep upstairs in my old bedroom. Of course, Catcher's grand vision was for me to open a second Sullivan's closer to home. It was something I was considering, but for the time being, I was happy without having to preside over a chain of funeral homes.

When I reached the altar, Catcher gave me a beaming smile. "You look so beautiful."

Tears filled my eyes at his words and the sincerity with which he spoke them. "Thank you. You do, too."

Catcher merely grinned at me alluding to him being beautiful, rather than handsome. He was beautiful both inside and out. Just like the vows we were reciting, I loved him for better or worse. Sure, he was a neat freak who got all huffy when I left my clothes and wet towels on the bathroom floor. He also tended to reek up the bedroom with gas after we had Mexican or Indian food. He could be bull-headed and stubborn and run as hot and cold as a woman on a hormone kick. But I loved every facet that made Catcher who he was. And now, he was going to be all mine.

Reverend Patterson, who I was on good terms with both personally and professionally, smiled at Catcher and me. "Dearly beloved, we're gathered here today to join Holden Caulfield Mains and Olivia Rose Sullivan in the bonds of holy matrimony."

After those initial words, the rest of the service seemed to fly by at warped speed. One second we exchanged vows, the next Catcher slipped a platinum band on my finger, and the next we were lip-locked to thunderous applause from the crowd.

"Get ya some!" Pease shouted from the first bench.

I jerked away and shot her a murderous look. After turning back to Catcher, I shook my head and whispered, "Can we just start the honeymoon now?"

He grinned as he leaned forward to speak into my ear. "We gotta get through the reception first. You don't want to miss me smearing cake down the front of your dress and eating it off like I did those cupcakes."

The image that flashed in my mind of his illicit cupcake feasting had me flushing head to toe. This man was the devil to make me think some impure thoughts on the altar of a church. Just as we were about to start down the aisle, Catcher said, "And by the way. Olive brought me a bottle of man-enhancer as a wedding gift." He waggled his eyebrows. "So it's going to be on like Donkey Kong."

My once male-neglected vagina cheered with happiness. We were both very, very lucky to have Catcher Mains. It had been a rough road to this moment, but all the great love stories have a few twists and turns and a dick...or maybe even two.

ACKNOWLEDGEMENTS

Thanks to Todd Sanders for the mortuary knowledge and tour of the funeral home back room!

Thanks also goes to Earl Darby for sitting down with me to answer my coroner related questions. Whatever poetic license I took for the story is in no reflection of what you or Todd taught me!

Thanks to JB McGee at IndiePixel Studio for formatting. Especially since it's always last minute!

Thanks to photographer, Scott Hoover, and model, Colby Lefebvre, for an amazing cover shot.

Thanks also to Letitia Hasser at RBA Designs for an amazing cover.

Eternal gratitude to Marion Archer and Kim Bias for helping to make my books the best they can be through editing and beta reading. You guys are the wind beneath my wings, and I couldn't put a book out without you. Thanks also to Kim for your daily writing check-ins and talking me down from the ledge!

Thanks to my beta readers Jen Gerchick, Jen Oreto, and Cara Gadero for helping to make Drop Dead Sexy the best it could be.

Thanks to Kiki Chatfield at Next Step PR for all her help on release promotion. Thanks to Jessica Alderette for the amazing graphics!

Thanks to every blogger who took a chance on me being funny and agreed to read and review Drop Dead Sexy. I couldn't do it without you!

# ABOUT THE AUTHOR

Katie Ashley is a New York Times, USA Today, and Amazon Best-Selling author. She lives outside of Atlanta, Georgia with her baby Olivia. She has a slight obsession with Pinterest, The Golden Girls, Shakespeare, Harry Potter, Star Wars, Designing Women, and Scooby-Doo.

With a BA in English, a BS in Secondary English Education, and a Masters in Adolescent English Education, she spent eleven years teaching both middle and high school English, as well as a few adjunct college English classes. As of January 2013, she became a full-time writer.

Made in the USA
Charleston, SC
10 May 2016